THE BOOK OF WAR

THE LAST ORACLE, BOOK 8

MELISSA MCSHANE

Night Harbor Publishing

Dedicated to the Arcadian Bookstore, French Quarter, New Orleans, which was the inspiration for Abernathy's miles of irregular shelving. This extraordinary store must be seen to be believed.

1

Rain spattered the plate glass window with ABERNATHY'S painted on it, from my perspective in reverse. The faint sound of cars passing on the very wet streets was an occasional *whoosh* rising above the sound of raindrops striking glass. I leaned with both elbows propped on the cold glass countertop and let my mind wander far from the store, which today smelled like strawberries. It was a scent of spring, though this was late March and winter hadn't yet loosed its grip on Portland. Three more hours, and I could go home for the weekend—an Abernathy's weekend, which meant Sunday only. I loved my job as custodian of the world's only living oracle well enough that I didn't resent the long hours.

The sound of metal scraping across linoleum with a skin-tingling *skree* brought me out of a daydream about what Malcolm might be cooking for dinner. I sat up and called out, "Judy?"

Another shrill scrape followed by a muffled curse drew me

out of the front of the store and down the short hallway to the break room. The Formica-topped table that normally stood beside the door of the tiny room was folded away to lean against the wall, and Judy had shoved the two metal chairs to sit beside it. It made the room feel bigger to have the furniture out of the way. "Finally got sick of the freezing cold chairs?" I asked.

Judy pushed her short black hair out of her face where it had fallen and glared at the tableau. "Yes. I did. I'm going to get someone to haul them away tonight and bring in replace-ments tomorrow."

Her dress had a skirt short enough that I sympathized with her desire not to freeze her butt off. "You don't have to do that. Abernathy's should pay for it."

"It's no big deal. Besides, I didn't feel like waiting." She prodded one of the chairs with her toe, clad in a black patent leather pump that probably had a designer name.

I wanted to remind Judy that the store's debit card was available for use for things like this, but her closed-off expres-sion made me wary. She'd been edgy lately, irritable in a way I wasn't used to—had been ever since my wedding more than two months ago. The two probably weren't related, but I couldn't help wondering if something that had happened that night had changed her.

I'd caught her making out with Malcolm's teammate Mike Conti, someone she'd been at odds with until that night, and I'd have passed it off as one of those things that happens at weddings if she hadn't acted weird around him ever since—unwilling to meet his eyes when he came into the store, hesi-tating when she said his name as if it were in a foreign language. I had a feeling they were, if not dating, at least still seeing each other, but she'd never said anything to me or Viv. Why Judy felt she needed to keep her love life a secret from her two best friends was a mystery to me, but in the face of her brusqueness I felt awkward about bringing it up. So mostly I just pretended not to notice.

"Okay," I said. "Maybe next we could get rid of the furniture in the front. That chair by the door is a lawsuit waiting to happen."

"No, the next thing I'm going to do is move that desk in the office around. I don't like how its back is to the outside door. It gives me an itch between my shoulder blades."

"That outside door only leads to your apartment. It's not like anything will come through it to attack you."

Judy shrugged. "It's still uncomfortable. But I'll leave it for Monday, or maybe—" She shut her mouth abruptly and her cheeks turned pink. "Yeah. Monday."

Once again, I didn't know what to say. Her embarrassment made no sense. "I'll help you with it then."

Judy nodded and left the break room. I contemplated the furniture, helped myself to a Diet Coke from the small refrigerator, and headed back to the front of the store. The weather was just nasty enough that even the Ambrosite "rush" at two o'clock hadn't lasted longer than half an hour. I settled onto the stool and took a long swig of caffeinated goodness. Two hours and forty-five minutes. I tried not to count down the time, because that made the hours pass more slowly, but on days like this it was hard to keep my eyes off my watch.

My phone rang. I dug it out of my stupid girl pocket that was way too shallow for comfort and saw an unfamiliar number. Probably a telemarketer, but it was local, so... "Hello?"

"Mrs. Campbell?"

"Yes?" It still felt strange being addressed by my new name, let alone being a Mrs. Most people used Ms.

"This is Darius Wallach at the Gunther Node. Do you remember me?"

"Of course I do, Mr. Wallach. Can I help you with something?"

"Actually, I was hoping I could help *you*."

"Really? With what?"

"It's too complicated to explain over the phone. Can you come to the node this evening, around eight o'clock?"

"I guess so, but—"

"Perfect. Just tell them you're there to meet me and someone will direct you to my department. Oh, and bring a piece of clothing. Underwear, by preference. Something you've worn close to the skin and haven't washed yet. Thanks." He hung up abruptly.

I stared dumbfounded at my phone. Underwear? What kind of "help" did Wallach have in mind? He'd created the aegis that had made Malcolm a magus again, and I'd seen him build an ansible out of glowing glass, so I was willing to trust him, but…underwear? *He's a genius; everything he does looks crazy to ordinary people.*

"Should I be worried that Darius Wallach wants to help me with something?" I asked Judy, who'd just come through the stacks holding the wide-headed push broom.

"He wasn't specific?" Judy said.

"Just that he wanted me to bring something I've worn but not washed."

"That could mean anything. I'd be worried if I were you. Crazy Wallach's 'help' sometimes creates more problems than it solves."

"Maybe it's something to do with the oracle," I said. "What if he's thought of a way to automate the production of the catalog? That would be worth something!"

"I doubt it could be that practical," Judy said. "Don't you think we're getting faster at it? It only took a week this time."

"A week is six days longer than I want to think about the catalogue." Abernathy's catalogue wasn't a list of books for sale, but a minor divination tool for questions too unimportant to pay for a full augury. It wore out every couple of months, requiring us to produce a new one three times a year, and if I were going to be resentful of anything to do with my job, that would be it. "Isn't it a little early to start cleaning?"

"All the mail-in auguries have been processed and the database is up to date. Cleaning is all that's left."

"This is one of those days where closing up early has its appeal." Though I wouldn't close early no matter how attractive the idea was. I still had another month of my probation for violating the Accords to go, and even though my new liaison with the Board of Neutralities, Ariadne Duwelt, was much less nasty than her predecessor, I didn't kid myself that that meant she'd be lenient on me. I hopped off the stool and headed for the basement and the bottle of glass cleaner. Cleaning calmed me.

I texted Malcolm the news of Darius Wallach's request as I walked, and received his response as I was climbing the stairs: SHOULD I COME ALONG?

I thought about it. WOULD RATHER YOU DROVE, HONESTLY. I hated driving at night in the winter, particularly when it was raining, even though I could finally find my way to the Gunther Node by myself.

AFTER DINNER, THEN, Malcolm replied.

I heard the bells over the door jingle distantly and shoved

my phone back into my pocket. When I emerged from the stacks into the front of the store, I found three people waiting, all of them with the athletic, powerful appearance that characterized front-line fighters in the Long War. I didn't know any of them, but I'd only been a Warden for about two and a half years and there were a lot of hunters I didn't know. "Welcome to Abernathy's," I said. "Can I help you?"

"Augury," the woman in front said. She had narrow, Asian features, but the delicacy of her face was at odds with her heavy build. She towered over average-sized me, and her male companions, one fair-skinned with bright red hair, the other with the copper skin of a Pacific Islander, towered over her. I suppressed feelings of nervousness and accepted the slip of paper she handed me.

"One minute," I said, and took three steps into the timeless silence of the oracle.

Things had changed so much since that day in November, years before, when I had performed my first augury. Some of that was me growing used to my custodian's role, but some of it, I was sure, was an alteration in the oracle itself. "It's been one of those days," I told it conversationally, though I didn't expect a response. "The weather is keeping even the invaders indoors, I think. I wonder if you're aware of weather? As something that affects you, I mean. You would have seen it when you were transported from England to Portland all those years ago. I'm so glad that's never going to happen again."

I could feel the oracle's attention on me, but idly, as if it were listening to two conversations at once. It didn't bother me; the oracle's consciousness was something I barely comprehended. "I don't even feel anxious about it," I continued. "I feel I should, maybe. The Mercy have been quiet since that thing with the second oracle, but that might just mean now is the time they'll attack again. Maybe the Wardens need to go on the offensive. I don't know anything about fighting, but it can't be good to just react all the time."

I unfolded the augury slip. I was fairly certain, at this point, that the oracle didn't need me to read the augury in order to produce an answer, but not reading it felt weird. *Where should we hunt tonight?* A simple, straightforward request. I hoped the oracle would give them a straightforward answer.

I tucked the slip into my pocket and wandered the narrow aisles, barely wide enough to fit the head of Judy's broom, looking for the blue glow of an augury. After a few turns, I saw it—a light like a tiny blue sun radiating from the top of one of the shorter bookcases. I still had to stretch to reach it, but it fell into my hand, weightless as a feather. *The House of Mirth,* by Edith Wharton. I'd never read it, but it looked like something a college professor might assign in some American literature course. I tucked the small paperback under my arm and turned to leave.

Ahead, another blue glow beckoned.

I dropped the augury, which hit the linoleum with a soft thud. My hands and face felt numb enough that even if I'd dared look away from the blue light, I couldn't have picked up the fallen book. "*No,*" I whispered. "No. It can't be happening again."

I left *The House of Mirth* on the floor and stepped forward, feeling my way along the shelves like a blind person because I was afraid the light would disappear if I looked away from it. The last time this had happened, the oracle had been under attack by the Mercy's secret operatives, who'd used illusions to try to destroy Abernathy's. It had nearly worked. But surely the Mercy wouldn't try the same trick twice?

I rounded a corner and found a fat, palm-sized book

blazing with light that gave me a sharp-edged shadow. Gingerly, I reached out and brushed my fingers against the spine. Nothing unexpected happened; I felt the same tingling of a live augury I always felt. Gripping more tightly, I pulled the book from between its neighbors. The blue glow faded, as did the tingle. I ran my fingers over the embossed title on the cover. *The Art of War.* When I flipped it open, I read, in silver ink, the words *Lucia Pontarelli, No Charge.*

I stared at the letters. That was definitely not the same behavior I'd seen before. Back then, the Mercy's illusions had caused the oracle to produce multiple auguries for the same person all at once, or one augury for the wrong person. This was…different.

I flipped through the pages, not reading, just making sure they weren't blurry or vanished or anything, then walked back to where I'd left the Ambrosite hunters' augury. The slim paperback had fallen on its face, and the cover was creased back, putting a line right through the face of the elegantly dressed woman lounging across it. Well, they didn't need to know this wasn't the original condition. I'd retrieved auguries missing their covers entirely. I checked the title page: *Midori Watanabe, $1250.* I'd forgotten to ask the woman's name. Surely the oracle had gotten that one right.

Clutching both books in front of me like a shield, I made my way out of the oracle, still feeling like a sleepwalker. The rules were clear and simple: one question, one augury. And yet…I'd seen the oracle do things that verged on the miraculous, and I knew it was a living creature, if one whose existence was stranger than I could imagine. Maybe I was wrong about the rules. I hoped I was wrong about the rules. The alternative was too terrible for me to contemplate.

When I emerged from the stacks, I got another shock. "Lucia!" I exclaimed. "What are you doing here?"

Lucia arched a dark eyebrow at me. "Waiting," she said. Her short, dark hair was damp with rain, making me wonder why the hood of her jacket wasn't up. Knowing Lucia, she probably felt that was a sign of weakness. The Ambrosite hunters had drawn closer together and were eyeing Lucia warily, like a flock of sheep who aren't sure whether the four-legged newcomer is a dog or a wolf.

"But——" I shut my mouth and held out *The House of Mirth* to the female Ambrosite. "That's $1250," I said, feeling as if the words were rattling out of me on autopilot. "Judy will take payment." I left Judy to accept their vials of *sanguinis sapiens* and turned to Lucia. "I think the oracle knew you were coming," I said, and extended *The Art of War* to her. "It's no charge."

Lucia exchanged glances with Dave Henry, who stood next to her carrying a familiar briefcase I knew was full of cash. "Take a look at this anyway," she said, handing me the augury slip. I unfolded it and read *What is the Mercy's weak spot?*

"Maybe I should see if there's another augury," I said.

"You do that," Lucia said, "but I'm betting there isn't. This book might be valuable even if it's not the answer to an augury question."

I had a feeling Lucia was right, but I took the request into the oracle anyway. This time, I could feel its attention on me, impatient and a little cranky, clearly saying *I gave you an answer already, stop wasting my time.* "All right," I murmured, "sorry," and hurried back to where Lucia and Dave waited. The Ambrosites were gone. Judy perched on the wobbly stood behind the counter and toyed with the keys on our antique cash register.

"It's never done that before, anticipated someone's request," I said. "I think it cares about your question."

"Doesn't it care about all of them?" Dave asked. He set the briefcase on the counter and flexed his fingers like it was heavy.

"I don't think so. That is, it's always interested enough to provide an answer, or not, but some questions…it feels like it gets more involved. Especially the ones it doesn't charge for." I leaned against the counter and crossed my arms over my chest. "And I think it cares about winning the Long War. Ken Gibbons told me the Mercy had sent many augury requests in secretly, and every one of them came back 'no augury.'" That was before the Mercy's attempt at a second oracle had turned Ken's mind into tapioca.

"Good to know it's on our side," Lucia said. "Thanks."

"Wait!" I exclaimed as she and Dave turned to go. "What's the augury for?"

"You know I don't tell you my plans, Davies," Lucia said. She didn't seem to care that I'd taken Malcolm's last name when we married—or maybe she thought two Campbells were too much work to keep track of.

"Yes, but—" I felt uncharacteristically pushy, but the memory of that second blue glow had me on edge. "The oracle took a proactive step in giving you that augury. If it's going to start handing out auguries to people before they even ask for them, I'd like to know why."

Lucia regarded me with a narrow-eyed stare that a year before would have made me back down. "I guess you'll know soon enough," she finally said. "But don't spread this around, anyway." She turned her glare on Judy. "That goes for you too, Rasmussen."

Judy just returned her stare. I said, "Of course. But what about—"

"Tell Campbell if you want. He'll get his marching orders soon enough." Lucia let out a long, slow breath. "We're taking the fight to the Mercy. In a few days, the Wardens are going to war."

2

"It felt like…doom was coming," I told Malcolm as his cherry-red Mustang swept along the freeway north toward the Gunther Node. "Like Lucia planned to take a step the Wardens couldn't come back from."

"It's past time for it," Malcolm replied. "So far, we have been reacting to the Mercy's attacks—the murders of the steel magi, the devastation of South America, even their attempt to create a second oracle. That is not the way to win a war."

"That's what I was thinking. So what does it mean?"

"I can only speculate. It's unlikely Lucia is acting alone, but the Board of Neutralities has traditionally been a policing force, not military. It's more likely that Lucia proposed a course of action the Board is willing to support." He frowned. "I wish I knew what she was thinking."

"She said you'd know soon enough."

He glanced at me briefly before returning his attention to the wet road. "Only a combined effort by Nicollien and

Ambrosite forces can possibly be effective against the Mercy. You know how unlikely that is."

I scowled. "I know it's stupid. If a common enemy isn't enough to make the factions see sense, what is? More magi deaths?"

"Possibly," Malcolm said. "And as horrifying as this is, I have to say…maybe it would be worth it."

My mouth fell open. "Malcolm!"

"Better a few lives lost now than thousands later. We have to defeat the Mercy if we are to win the Long War. But that's the cynical, heartless approach. I hope Lucia has found some way to convince the factions to set aside their differences."

"So do I," I said, but I couldn't help wondering if Malcolm was right, and more death was the only thing that would turn Nicollien and Ambrosite thinking around.

We traveled the rest of the way in silence until we drove up to the airplane hangar that was the entrance to the Gunther Node. At this time of night, there were several of the node's signature small white vans parked on the gravel surrounding the structure, but no people around.

Malcolm parked at the end of the row, and we got out and crunched through the gravel to the smooth concrete floor. It wasn't really an airplane hangar, since there were no runways out this way, but it was the right size and it smelled of engine oil and exhaust the way I imagined an airplane hangar would smell. I had never seen a vehicle of any kind inside it. Its only distinguishing features were a plain metal box the size of a shoebox hanging on the back wall and a patterned white circle painted on the floor. It looked like a flower circlet a girl would wear when dancing around a maypole and, I knew from experience, was big enough to fit twenty people standing close together.

Malcolm opened the box to reveal an old-fashioned telephone handset. He picked it up and said into the mouthpiece, "Helena and Malcolm Campbell." He hung it up without waiting for a response and came to join me in the circle, taking my hand. It was a gesture I never got tired of.

The world blinked. Suddenly, we were elsewhere—a vast concrete chamber with a ceiling a couple of stories tall, filled with people pushing carts laden with glowing purple-blue ore or walking rapidly along one of the many colored lines that made a spaghetti tangle in the middle of the floor. The familiar scent of gardenias came to my nose, an incongruous smell in this hard-edged place. No one seemed to notice our arrival. I hadn't expected a welcoming committee, but it occurred to me that I didn't know where I was supposed to go. "He said to ask someone," I began.

"Mr. Wallach's department is this way," Malcolm said, shepherding me along the yellow line. I remembered the first time I'd been to the Gunther Node, how overwhelmed I'd been and how strange it had all seemed. Though that first time, I'd been injured and bleeding and Malcolm had been in handcuffs, so being overwhelmed had probably had little to do with the node itself. Even so, it felt strange to remember that time and compare it to how familiar it all was now.

I nodded and smiled at the few people I recognized, who waved in return. We passed through the yellow door, which was actually a really big opening outlined in yellow, and immediately entered a hallway with a much lower ceiling. The lights seemed to come from inside the walls, which weren't concrete, but some white spongy-looking substance. Doors set into the walls were recessed and had no knobs or handles. They looked as if they would slide open like patio doors. The whole thing looked so much like a set for a low-budget *Star Trek* knock-off I half expected to see cameras wheeling down the corridor following us.

Malcolm stopped at a door that looked just like all the others. A plaque with the number 34 embossed on it was set into a recess above the door. Malcolm pressed a button beside the door and waited.

Eventually, a voice said, "*Who is it?*" It sounded raspy and far away.

"Um. Helena Campbell? Mr. Wallach is expecting me?" I hadn't meant to sound uncertain, but I couldn't tell where the voice was coming from, couldn't see a speaker grille or anything, and it was unsettling.

"*Oh. Hang on.*" The voice went silent. After about ten seconds that felt like ten hours, the door whooshed open with a pneumatic hiss. Hesitantly, I stepped inside.

The room looked like the one where they held the Damerel rites for making someone a magus, something I remembered clearly from having witnessed Malcolm go through it last year, except it didn't have an operating table in the middle. Glass-fronted cabinets lined the walls, each containing things I couldn't make out because the glass was smoky instead of clear. The white vinyl floor squares were scuffed from much use, and wheel marks showed where heavy carts had passed.

Across the room, another of the sliding doors stood, this one with a small glass window in its upper half. "Are you sure this is the right place?" I asked Malcolm, but before he could answer, the second door slid open, and Darius Wallach stepped through, gathering his snowy hair back from his face into a pouf at the back of his head. He wore black scrubs with tiny skulls printed on them, not a look that inspired confidence, and extended a hand to me.

"Thank you for coming, Mrs. Campbell," he said. "Mr. Campbell." Wallach checked the giant watch he wore on his left wrist. "Mrs. Campbell, if you'd come this way? I'll have to ask Mr. Campbell to wait here."

I glanced at Malcolm, who didn't seem perturbed by this. "Sure," I said, following Wallach into the next room.

It was, if anything, barer and more sterile than the first room. It was perfectly round, with no furnishings or cabinets, and the walls curved inward, making it feel like I was inside a ceramic pot. Softly glowing lights circled the ceiling, filling the room with white light. Wallach touched the wall next to the door, and the door swished shut. Malcolm's face appeared in the little window. I smiled at him, then turned my attention to Wallach, who'd crossed the room to another door. This one was low to the ground and had a handle. Wallach squatted and took hold of the handle. "Don't be afraid," he said. He pulled the door open, releasing a whiff of paint thinner.

Something big and black and chitinous leapt from the opening. I screamed as the invader flung itself toward me, all its hundreds of clawed legs scrabbling to attack me.

Behind me, I heard Malcolm shouting and pounding on the door, but his words were muffled by the glass. I turned and sped for the door, mashing the unseen button as hard as I could. Nothing happened. I spun around just in time to see the thing launch itself at my eyes, and screamed again, pressing myself into the door like I could pass through it by will alone.

The invader didn't touch me. It rebounded off what seemed like an invisible wall, doing a backflip in the air and landing hard on its back several feet away. It got to its hundreds of feet and shook itself for all the world like a dog coming out of deep water, then ran at me again. This time, I was ready for it, and kicked it across the room with a perfect punt my Pee Wee soccer coach would have been proud of. "Get it away from me!" I shrieked.

Wallach stood and held up a black fob, pressing its single button. Instantly the invader drew in on itself, its legs all quivering with pent-up energy. Now I could see a silver harness constraining its torso. A bound familiar, not a free invader. The smell should have given it away.

Wallach walked over to it and picked it up. It was only the size of a cat, after all. "Excellent," he said.

"What the *hell* was that?" I shouted. Malcolm was still pounding on the door, which shook under his blows. "Why did you sic a familiar on me? Don't you know how custodians attract them?"

"Of course I do," Wallach said. He put the familiar back in the wall cubby and closed the door. "That was the point, establishing a baseline."

Something cracked behind me, and the door wheezed open with a pained cry. "What the hell were you thinking?" Malcolm said, putting his arms around me and holding me tight.

Wallach blinked at us. "Don't be ridiculous," he said. "Mrs. Campbell was in no danger. While it's true invaders, both wild and captive, are drawn to custodians, the binding on a familiar prevents it from hurting a human unless ordered to do so. Even a custodian. You both should know this."

"It sure didn't feel safe," I said, trying to control my breathing.

"You had no right to involve Helena in that experiment, if you can call it that," Malcolm said, his voice low and furious.

"That wasn't the experiment, that was the baseline," Wallach said. "The experiment is to determine why invaders are drawn to custodians and to see if we can turn that into a weapon against the Mercy."

I stopped shaking. "You can do that?"

"Probably," Wallach said. "Did you bring your underwear?"

The abrupt change of subject made me want to laugh. "A T-shirt. It hasn't been washed." I handed him a bulging manila envelope.

"That should work. Go ahead and—" Wallach noticed the door for the first time. "What did you do to my door?"

Malcolm didn't budge. "I'm not leaving Helena alone again."

"I don't need her for this part. You can wait in the antechamber, if you can get the door to shut."

It took Malcolm and me pushing together to get the damaged door to close. We watched through the little window as Wallach shook my T-shirt out of the envelope without touching it to make a puddle of cloth on the floor. He opened the small door and let the familiar out. "What does it look like to you?" I asked, whispering, though I didn't know why.

"A mastiff," Malcolm said. "I've never seen a familiar go after a human before. That was terrifying."

"You have no idea," I said.

This time, the familiar crept on all its horrible little legs, as if uncertain of what it faced. It paced the confines of the room, ignoring Wallach and my T-shirt, sniffing once or twice at the seam where the door met the wall but not appearing to notice me peering through the glass. After about ten minutes, Wallach used the fob again and returned the familiar to its cage. "You can come back in," he said.

Malcolm manhandled the door open as Wallach looked

on, grimacing. "That's going to be a bitch to get repaired," he muttered. "Maintenance is always busy this time of year."

"I feel no urge to apologize," Malcolm said. "Did you learn anything?"

"That it's not your scent it responds to, Mrs. Campbell," Wallach said. "That's excellent news. Altering a familiar's scent receptors would be virtually impossible and certainly an impractical solution."

"Did you really need me here for that?" I asked.

Wallach made an impatient noise. "This room is equipped with recording devices both magical and mundane," he said. "It took down every possible measurement when the familiar attacked you, including the ambient temperature and your body mass. I'll use that in the rest of the experiments. Don't worry, you won't be exposed to the familiar again, but I'll need to meet with you occasionally to test my theories."

"Mr. Wallach," Malcolm growled.

"I assure you Mrs. Campbell will be in no danger." Wallach had his attention on me despite Malcolm's palpable menace. "It may all mean nothing, but I'm convinced learning why invaders react to custodians the way they do is key to understanding more about them. And if I'm right, it will lead to turning them against the Mercy."

"You could ask Lucia," I said weakly. I really didn't want to go near that familiar again, no matter what Wallach said.

Wallach scowled. "Lucia is busy," he said. "And she used some very foul language when I proposed the plan. It's you or no one, Mrs. Campbell."

I let out a deep breath. "All right. But no more familiars, all right? And I'd better have plenty of warning before you pull a stunt like that again."

"That's fair. Now, just a few questions." He dropped the

fob into the pocket of his scrubs and retrieved a small voice recorder of a kind I'd thought went out of style ten years ago. "Do all invaders, captive and free, react to you the same way?"

"Yes."

"Have you ever been bitten by one?"

"Yes." I suppressed a shudder, and Malcolm's arms tightened on me.

"And your reaction was idiosyncratic?"

"Yes, it leaves me euphoric, but I don't think it was because I'm a custodian, because I saw another custodian killed by a familiar and it looked agonizing."

"That's all right, I have a theory about that." He didn't elaborate. "You can see through illusions?"

"Yes." His questions seemed to have nothing to do with familiars, and I grew impatient. "Does that matter?"

"I don't know yet. How long have you been a custodian?"

"Um…twenty-eight months almost exactly."

"But your ability to see through illusions predates that."

I nodded. "It seems so."

"Hmm." Wallach clicked off the recorder. "I'd like to perform one more test—don't worry, it's non-invasive. No familiars involved."

I eyed him warily. Malcolm said, "What test?"

Wallach put the recorder away and beckoned to me to follow him. With Malcolm's hand in mine, I passed through the broken door and the antechamber and went out into the hallway behind Wallach. The elderly Warden led us down the hall following the three stripes painted on the center of the floor, yellow, magenta, and black. After about half a minute, the magenta line branched off to the right, and Wallach turned that way. The new hall had a higher ceiling, but the same spongy white walls and recessed doors. I saw no other people, and couldn't help imagining a post-apocalyptic world in which we three were the only survivors, exploring a deserted scientific compound.

Wallach stopped outside a door numbered 5 and pressed his thumb to a spot beside it that didn't look any different from the rest of the wall. The door swooshed open, and a second later, lights bloomed within. Wallach said, "In here, Mrs. Campbell, Mr. Campbell."

I stepped inside and halted abruptly enough that Malcolm bumped into me. Silver metal crates ranging in size from filing box to refrigerator lined the walls, stacked so haphazardly I couldn't imagine they were easy to access. They made the room look like a miser's storage locker, though an unexpectedly space-age miser.

But what had made me stop was the chair in the middle of the room. The chair itself looked just like the one in my dentist's office, beige and bland and possibly older than me. But spidery arms holding a multitude of terrifying tools sprang from the base, some pointed, others like narrow silver spatulas, a few with serrated edges like tiny saws. There were three magnifying glasses of different sizes, arranged for easy access by whatever maniac was torturing the poor victim in the chair. A yard-wide black glass disc hung facedown over the contraption, blurrily reflecting the chair and the implements of torture.

"Oh, no," I said. "No way."

Wallach was already standing next to the chair, bending the long, flexible arms to point away from it. "We don't need any of this," he said impatiently. "Just the disc."

To my surprise, Malcolm put his arm around me reassuringly. "But Helena can't be a magus," he said to Wallach. "What is the point of this?"

"Maybe nothing," Wallach said. "Mrs. Campbell, have a seat, and relax. This doesn't hurt."

"It really doesn't," Malcolm said. "This is a scanning device that is part of the preparation for the Damerel rites. It looks for hidden weaknesses that might make the rites fail. Though I've never seen these...things." He prodded one of the arms, which bobbed up and down in response.

"You don't want to know," Wallach said. "Mrs. Campbell?"

I gingerly climbed into the seat and tried to relax. Malcolm pulled one of the larger boxes over beside the chair and settled in next to me. The box was either empty or not very full, because it sagged slightly under his weight.

Wallach shoved another couple of boxes to one side, revealing a control panel set into the wall opposite the chair. It looked even older than the chair, with rows of toggles below pairs of colored light bulbs, blue and gold. "Just a minute," he said, with an abstracted air as if his attention was more on the panel than on me. I waited. Nothing happened. The arms didn't suddenly spring to life and attack me. I looked up at the glass disc and gasped. It reflected the chair, but not me. I raised a hand and waved at the disc—still nothing.

Malcolm followed my gaze and said, "I don't know why it does that, but as far as I know it reflects nothing organic at all."

"It's unsettling," I said. "As if I'd been erased." I looked at my hands for reassurance.

Malcolm chuckled. "I think everyone feels that way."

A loud thump drew my attention to Wallach, who'd pounded the control panel with his fist. He beat on it again, harder, and the panel lit up like an old-fashioned switchboard, the blue and gold lights making an interesting pattern against the white wall. "Hah," he said with satisfaction. "Nothing like percussive maintenance to show these things who's boss."

The room wasn't cold, but my face suddenly felt warm. The glass disc now glowed with a soft golden light, similar to how the oracle glowed when I performed an augury in the dark. The warmth soothed me, and I relaxed—not much, because the torture implements still had me on edge, but enough that I could unclench my fists and wipe my sweaty palms on my jeans.

Wallach flicked a couple of toggles, changing their light from blue to gold, glanced over his shoulder at me—no, at the disc—and flicked a few more. The disc's glow increased, though it didn't get any warmer. Wallach pressed a spot below the panel, and a flap popped open, revealing a dark space I was too far away to see clearly. He pulled a coiled cable, skinny like earbud wires, from a hidden pocket and plugged one end into the wall, then plugged the other end into a battered smartphone with a cracked screen. Why he hadn't used that to record my answers, I didn't know, but I hoped he had a reason.

"Two minutes," Wallach said. "You don't have to hold perfectly still, but don't get off the chair or it will interrupt the readings."

That made me want to freeze in place. Malcolm said, "What readings?"

"It wouldn't mean anything to you. No offense," Wallach said. His attention was on the phone screen, which flickered with a blue glow like an old television set playing a black and white movie.

Malcolm grimaced, but said nothing more. I wanted to hold his hand, for reassurance if nothing else, but I was afraid it might mess up Wallach's reading. So instead I watched Wallach, how the bluish light turned his dark skin purple in places, and wondered how two minutes could feel like an eternity just because I had nothing to do.

"I invited Mike for dinner tomorrow night," Malcolm said. "I hope you don't mind."

"Of course not." I wished I dared bring up my suspicions about Judy and Mike, but that felt weird, like I would be invading Judy's privacy. And it wasn't as if I knew anything for sure. "He's settled in all right, hasn't he?"

Malcolm shifted his weight, making the box creak. "I think so. He's not as carefree as I remember him being, but he's been through a lot, so maybe that's not so unusual. I wish he weren't so isolated. I don't think he's dated anyone since moving to Portland."

I *really* wanted to speak now. "It's only been two months. Maybe he's seeing someone and just hasn't made a big deal about it."

"Mike?" Malcolm chuckled. "He's the woman in every port type. If he were seeing someone, I'd know about it."

That went a long way toward dispelling my suspicions, except I knew Judy too well to be completely convinced. Though, suppose Judy's relationship with Mike, whatever it was, mattered more to her than to him? I suddenly felt angry on Judy's behalf. "Well, I hope he's happy," I managed. "Do you want to do anything special tomorrow? Other than dinner, I mean?"

"That's it," Wallach said abruptly, and Malcolm and I both looked at him. He unplugged the phone and the cable and flipped several more switches. The disc stopped glowing. "You can get up now," Wallach said, walking toward me. I stood and stretched.

"I don't suppose you are willing to explain yourself now?" Malcolm said, a little sarcastically. Wallach didn't react.

"Just one...ah, there it is," Wallach said. His head was down over the phone's cracked screen again, but he was smiling broadly. "I shouldn't be so pleased, because this is going to mean paperwork, and I hate paperwork."

"What is?" I exclaimed.

Wallach looked at me, still smiling. "You're a genetic sport, Mrs. Campbell."

I gaped. I knew what a sport was—an individual that was dramatically different in some way on a genetic level. It was a polite term for "mutant." But I still said, "What are you talking about?"

"Well, a sport is—"

"I know what a sport is," I interrupted him, "but what kind of mutation is it? Not something harmful, right?"

Wallach shook his head. "I'll have to analyze the data," he said, tapping the smartphone screen, "but my initial assessment is that you're capable of tapping into your own magic the way someone with an aegis does. In a very limited fashion, of course. In your case, it manifests as your ability to see through illusions."

"I've...heard about sports in the magical world." Mike Conti had told me about it a few months ago. "I assumed that's what I was. Mike made it sound like it was...not well-known, but not a secret."

"And nobody bothered to mention it to me," Wallach said irritably. "Wonderful. The important thing is not that you are a sport. It's that your reaction to being bitten by an invader is certainly related to being one. I'd guess, based on the data, that the reaction is a side effect of you being immune to having your magic drained by an invader."

"I'm—what?" I exclaimed. I felt pummeled by all the revelations.

"Hah. So you don't know everything," Wallach said. "I don't know the mechanism, but you could think of it as being insulated." He was as calm as if we were discussing the weather. "Though I wouldn't suggest testing it. Invaders have more weapons than just their ability to drain magic."

I realized Malcolm had his arm around me, supporting me, and I needed it. "But I've been drained before," I said. "Not a lot, but an invader's bite—"

"Whatever you felt when you were bitten, it wasn't being drained. The readings are conclusive," Wallach said. He held the phone face-out toward me. I stared at the squiggly lines, blue and gold and white, that crossed the screen in every direction, shivering with pent-up energy. They meant nothing to me. Wallach seemed to realize this after a few seconds. "You'll have to take my word for it. Basically, you have an underlying genetic difference that makes you immune to an invader's bite, and its side effects are that idiosyncratic reaction to being bitten and the ability to see through illusions. It would likely also make the Damerel rites lethal to you, but that's not really an issue, since you're a custodian."

I looked up at Malcolm. I had no idea what expression was on my face, but his jaw tightened and his eyes narrowed as if he were concerned. "This is all a lot to take in at once," he said. "I think Helena should go home."

"Of course. There's no more I can tell you now, anyway," Wallach said. He put the phone in one of his pockets—the scrubs seemed to have an unlimited supply—and added, "Don't be distressed, Mrs. Campbell. This doesn't change anything for you any more than heterochromia or freckles would. Less, because it's not a visible effect. Think of it as having an interesting difference."

I was afraid to ask what heterochromia was. "It's true my

being able to see through illusions isn't some kind of super power," I said. "And I avoid invaders and familiars."

"That's the spirit. I'll call you soon to schedule another session. I don't anticipate this taking very long." Wallach opened the door and gestured for us to exit, then walked away down the hall without saying goodbye.

Malcolm put his arms around me and hugged me. "You're shivering," he said.

"I feel so strange. Like there's something living beneath my skin, waiting to erupt."

He laughed. "I can understand that, but Mr. Wallach is right. You're not suddenly an invader-fighting machine. You just have naturally what I had to get from my aegis."

"That's true, I guess. And it's not like I'm the only one. Mangesh can see through illusions, too, and there are all those other people I found in my research—don't you think they're likely to be sports, too?" Mangesh Kapoor was the only other Warden I knew of who shared my ability. Mangesh—I gasped. "But Mangesh is a stone magus, and Mr. Wallach said he thought someone with my abilities would die if they went through the Damerel rites!" I detached myself from Malcolm's embrace and started to follow Wallach, but Malcolm grabbed my arm and brought me to a halt.

"Later," he said. "You need to rest. You've had a shock, and I don't like how pale you are. Let's go home, and you can make a list of questions to ask Mr. Wallach." He put his arm across my shoulders and steered me back the way we'd come. "He'll need to know that you've identified others like you, even if they're not Wardens."

We emerged from the *Star Trek* hallway into the vast central chamber and walked rapidly in what to me was a random direction. Malcolm waved down a black-clad tech. "Two to return," he told her.

We followed the woman to a smaller version of the airplane hangar transportation circle and in an instant were outside, breathing in the cold, damp air that smelled of oil and exhaust. The car waited patiently for us at the end of the gravel drive, gray in the dim light. Malcolm started the car, sending a blast of welcome warm air my way.

I drew my legs up and tried to forget the sight of a terrifying creature doing its best to claw my eyes out. My hands, clasping my knees, looked just the same as always. If I had never applied for the job at Abernathy's, would I have gone through life never knowing I was different? I'd been sincere when I'd said it wasn't a super power. I'd lived almost twenty-two years before discovering I could see through illusions, and that had only happened because I'd been gathered into the magical world.

I glanced at Malcolm, who had his eyes on the road, and some of my tension disappeared. If I was special at all, it wasn't because of some genetic mutation, it was because I'd become Abernathy's custodian. That mattered far more than any weird abilities I was born with. And I'd met Malcolm, which had changed my life even more. "Life is so strange," I murmured.

Malcolm looked my way and smiled. "Strange and wonderful," he said.

"Definitely that." I looked out the window at the rain sheeting past and the spray thrown up by the car's wheels. It made a hissing noise just audible over the sound of the engine. Comforted by the twin sounds, I rested my head against the window and relaxed into sleep.

3

I let myself into the store by the back door Monday morning and discovered the office desk no longer faced the same direction. Judy must have been more impatient than I'd thought not to leave it until today. I dropped my purse on the desk and picked up the stack of augury requests that had come by mail, neatly slit open and ready for me to tackle. The only thing missing from a typical Monday morning was Judy. She was usually downstairs before I arrived, updating our customer database. She'd been down once already, to open the mail, but I didn't know why she was gone now.

I thought about going upstairs to knock on her door. Would that seem too pushy? Like I had the right to demand her presence? All right, in a sense I did have that right, but we were friends first, and I'd never invoke it. I slapped the envelopes against my palm and headed for the store front. Judy would be back down soon. I tried not to examine my uncertainty too closely.

I set the envelopes on the counter and extracted a folded

sheet of paper from the topmost one. *How should I divide my fortune?* That was a common request for the mail-ins, right up there with *What job should I take?* and *Is my boyfriend/girl-friend/spouse cheating on me?* I could never tell if the oracle got tired of being asked the same questions repeatedly. It rarely got..."excited" was probably the wrong word, but I couldn't think of a better way to describe its occasional alert helpfulness about auguries. I folded the paper again and walked into the oracle.

Bright light shone directly into my face, making me cry out and fling up my free hand to cover my eyes. Blinking away tears, I turned my head and looked at the augury out of the corner of my eye. There was no reason an augury couldn't be right there when I entered, but it had never happened before, and after Saturday's unexpected augury, everything odd felt suspicious. I used the folded paper to block the light and swiftly removed the book from the shelf. The light faded, to my relief, and I examined the book, a nearly pristine hardcover titled *The Westing Game.* I tucked it under my arm and turned to go—

—and another blue light winked into being, far to my left.

I drew in a calming breath and let it out slowly. "More mysteries," I said. "Why now? It's almost as if you're impatient, but that can't be true. You've been around for a couple hundred years, you've given out tens of thousands of auguries, and if that's not patience, I don't know what is."

I sidled through the narrow aisles until I found the new augury and pulled it off the shelf. It was a big, floppy paperback called *It's Obvious You Won't Survive By Your Wits Alone.* Dilbert comics. I flipped open the cover. *Robert Handel, No Charge.* "I wish I understood," I said, "but I'm just your hands, and I guess—"

Another blue light flared, this one just around the corner. I sighed. "Maybe if you do enough of these, I'll figure out the pattern."

I collected a total of four unasked-for auguries. All of them were free. By the time I was sure no more lights would appear, I was feeling uneasy and a little spooked. The oracle's presence never wavered; it paid me no more attention than it ever did. I laid all four books out on the countertop, side by side, and stared at them. Two paperbacks, the Dilbert comic collection, and a hardcover, not counting the augury I'd actually gone in for, which I set to one side with the augury request tucked between its pages. The four were in varying conditions. Two were for men, one for a woman, one for someone with a gender-neutral name. I could see nothing any of them had in common.

"You're moving fast today," Judy said, emerging from the stacks. She was dressed down for her in black twill pants and a red and white checked blouse. "That must be most of the mail-in auguries."

"It's not. These four just…happened. No question, no nothing. The oracle just produced them. And all of them are free."

Judy came forward, her eyes narrowed, and flipped open the hardcover book. The glimmering silver writing that declared the name of the recipient would be invisible to her, but she turned pages as if hoping something would leap out. "No requests?"

"None." I chewed my lower lip in thought. "I didn't recognize any of the names, either, so I don't even know if they're real people."

"That doesn't worry me. Even when the oracle was under attack by those illusions, all the auguries it produced were for actual people." Judy let the cover fall shut. "What do you want to do about it?"

"Wait and see if these people come in for auguries today? I just don't understand it. If it's like with Lucia's augury, why would the oracle be so impatient? It's not as if it saves time, producing them in advance." Or...was I wrong about that?

"I think we should see what questions those people have," Judy said, "and maybe a pattern will emerge."

"Good idea." I checked my watch. 9:24. Plenty of time for more mail-in auguries. "And maybe there won't be any more of the weird ones."

I PUT my hands on my hips and surveyed the stacks of books laid out on the counter, all open to their title pages. "Twenty-two unasked for auguries," I said. "I'm seriously creeped out now."

"That is a hell of a lot of books," Judy said. She nodded in the direction of the front window at the line of Nicollien Wardens waiting for the store to open in five minutes. "What next?"

"I've organized them alphabetically by the last name of the recipient. I'll just ask each person's name and see if one of these belongs to them." I prodded the final stack of books. "Except these five, which belong to people I know."

"You're remarkably calm. I don't think I could hold it together that well if I were you."

"Oh, I'm screaming on the inside." I actually felt calm, though it was the kind of calm that hides a desire to run in circles like a crazy person. "It's just...the oracle doesn't feel agitated at all, so it's hard for me not to believe this is all going to work out."

Judy shrugged. "Let's see what happens," she said, and unlocked the door.

The Nicolliens entered, still in their orderly line. There seemed to be more front-line fighters today than usual, but nobody looked particularly grim. The man at the front of the line handed me a slip of paper. I didn't look at it. "Your name, sir?"

"Jeffrey Keane," he said. "Is that important?"

That had been the name on one of the last auguries I'd retrieved. "One moment," I said. I shuffled through the stacks until I found *Bridget Jones's Diary*. "No charge," I said. "Next?"

"Wait a minute," Keane said. "You knew I was coming?"

"The oracle did." I unfolded the scrap of paper and read *How can my team best prepare to fight the Mercy?* Huh. I shouldn't jump to conclusions based only on this and Lucia's augury, but if both were about fighting the Mercy…

I took the next augury slip and read *What is the Mercy's greatest weakness?* "What's your name?" I asked the short, compact woman who looked to be solid muscle.

"Tabitha Reyes." The woman eyed me, then glanced at Keane, who'd stepped aside and was leafing through his augury.

"Reyes…hang on." That was another familiar name. I found Reyes's book in the stack and handed it over. "No charge."

The next woman in line said, "Are you saying Abernathy's is giving out auguries for free?"

"I don't know," I said, pitching my voice to be heard over the clamor this question raised. "It seems eager to take the fight to the Mercy, and I think it's trying to help the Wardens do that. But I can't guarantee all auguries will be free, so please don't get your hopes up." It occurred to me that I wouldn't be making my usual one percent bonus of the price of the auguries I delivered. Well, it wasn't like I needed the money.

It took only half an hour to pass out all the unsolicited auguries the oracle had given me that morning. I checked every question. All of them had to do with fighting the Mercy. By 10:45, the store front was empty except for one skinny teenager in artfully torn jeans and a Five Finger Death Punch T-shirt. His question had to do with choosing a university to attend. That one, the oracle charged him $500 for. He looked disgruntled, but paid without complaint.

When he was gone, I leaned against the counter and said, "That was just weird."

"And it was faster," Judy pointed out. "That many Wardens, it should have taken you at least an hour and a half to do all those auguries."

"So the oracle…what? Wanted everyone out of the store quickly? But why?"

"I don't know. Maybe it has something else it wants you to be free to do." Judy's eyes widened briefly. "I forgot. I found something while we were moving the desk."

"The desk? We?"

Judy went red. "I had some help."

Tiredness, and the lingering remnants of my unease, loosened my tongue. "Help, as in…who?"

"Just someone." Now she wasn't meeting my eyes.

I blew out an exasperated breath. "Judy, if it's Mike Conti, why are you keeping it a secret?"

"I—" Judy began, then closed her eyes and sighed as I had done. "I don't know. I was embarrassed."

"I don't understand why you'd be embarrassed."

Judy threw up her hands. "I don't know. It's not like there's anything but sex between us. I keep telling myself to break it off, but...it's stupid, I'm stupid, and I didn't want anyone to know."

A thousand responses whirled round my head. "You know what Viv would say—"

"Viv's got a lasting relationship. I don't even know what this is. And my father would blow a gasket if he knew I was seeing an Ambrosite hunter. It's just—" Judy shook her head. "It's not serious. We both agreed we didn't want anything more than the occasional fling."

I took up a more comfortable position against the counter. "That sounds like there's a 'but' in there somewhere."

"But...Mike's a good guy, and I...like him. Yesterday he came over and helped me move the desk, and then we hung out and watched a movie. Like any couple."

"So tell him that!"

Judy shook her head violently enough to send her short black hair flying. "No. No way. He's only interested in a no-commitment relationship, and I am *not* going to be That Girl who gets all needy and demanding over someone who doesn't feel the same."

"Judy, that makes no sense."

"Maybe. But that's the way it is." She straightened and ran her fingers through her hair. "Anyway, I found something, and you're going to want to see it." She marched away through the stacks. After a confused moment, I hurried after her. I knew Judy well enough to recognize when she was done talking about a subject and there was no point pushing the issue. I wished Viv were here, because Viv understood relationships better than I did and would have known what to say. Maybe I could tell Viv Judy's secret. Better yet, if I could get Judy to tell Viv herself… Something to work up to later.

Judy went into the office and opened the top drawer. She pulled out a fat book about four inches on a side, bound in light brown leather with a strap holding it closed. The page edges were gilded, but scraped and dim from age. Judy twisted the strap, and the lock popped open. "It was a crappy lock, and I don't feel bad about breaking it," she said. She opened the front cover and handed the book to me. "Take a look."

I looked at the first page. Written across the top were the words DIARY OF NATHANIEL BRIGGS, 2014- and, in smaller letters, *Private—not for inclusion in the Athenaeum.*

I gasped. Nathaniel Briggs had been the custodian who'd hired me, murdered by his friend for refusing to falsify an augury. "This is…"

"I know," Judy said. "It had fallen down between the desk and the wall. I read some of it last night. Mostly it's boring. He doesn't write very often, and most of what he does write doesn't have anything to do with the oracle. But…I don't know what I thought. That maybe there was something in there that explains why he hired you."

"Or something more about his blackmail," I said. "What if he knew about the Mercy, and was blackmailing some of its members?"

"Lucia would have figured that out," Judy said, but she didn't sound certain.

I offered the book back to her. "Do you want to read the rest of it?"

"Only if you don't. I thought it was something that mattered more to you."

The bells over the door rang. "We can talk about it later," I said. "I'm interested, sure, but if you've already started—"

"I don't mind," Judy said.

When we returned to the store front, Viv was perched on the stool behind the counter, a multicolored scarf wrapped twice around her neck and dangling nearly to the floor. Her boyfriend Jeremiah, a powerful wood magus who looked like a stereotypical computer geek, leaned against the counter so his T-shirt was visible past his unbuttoned jacket. This one had a picture of an old-fashioned man holding a bell and a cat washing itself, with a banner reading LITTLE-KNOWN FAILURE: PAVLOV'S CAT.

"Hi!" I exclaimed. "Friendly visit, or augury?"

"I'm the friendly visit. Jeremiah wants an augury," Viv said. She'd colored her hair bright green for St. Patrick's Day last week, as usual, and looked like a slender leprechaun.

I snuck a glance at Judy, who didn't look irritated or self-conscious, and wished Jeremiah would leave so I could tackle Judy about her relationship with Mike Conti and get Viv involved. Instead, I held out my hand for Jeremiah's augury slip, which he handed over with his usual brilliant smile. *What is the pattern to the invader attacks on the west side?* was the question. "You're unusual," I said. "Most people have been in here today looking for auguries about the Mercy."

Jeremiah's smile disappeared. "That's foolhardy," he said. "It's past time we Wardens took the fight to them, but as someone who used to be part of their organization, I know exactly how skilled and deadly they are. There's no way I'd go up against them by myself."

"Which means Ambrosites and Nicolliens fighting as one, doesn't it?"

"I know. That seems impossible." Jeremiah grimaced. "There aren't many advantages to being a reformed traitor, but I have to say the differences between the factions seem completely irrelevant to me now. It's stupid that they can't make common cause."

"Nicolliens won't give up their familiars until something forces them to," Judy said, "and Ambrosites won't stop seeing that as recklessness."

"Do you really think it's only about the familiars now?" I asked. "The Nicollien leader in Great Britain ordered all their familiars destroyed after what happened with the bindings two Christmases ago, but factional strife there hasn't diminished."

"Maybe," Jeremiah said. "You're probably right, and losing the familiars wouldn't matter. But having a common enemy hasn't worked either." He smiled again, not quite as cheerfully. "If Lucia has her way, the factions will have to work together."

I wanted to ask for more details on that, but remembered the augury slip. "I'll be right back."

I only saw one blue light this time, which relieved my mind. "I wish I understood what you meant," I said as I walked toward it. "If there's something you want me to do—I mean, why else would you deliver all those auguries so quickly? Unless you just wanted all those hunters interpreting their auguries without wasting time. I guess it could be that."

I rounded a corner and walked a little faster at seeing the augury at the end of the row. "I guess I just feel helpless," I went on, "so I'm looking for things I can do. Judy would say doing my job is help enough, but Malcolm's right that I have an overdeveloped sense of justice, and this...I know it's important, what we do, but I wish I could take *action*."

I pulled the battered paperback copy of *Rebecca*, by Daphne du Maurier, off the shelf and checked inside the front cover. Jeremiah's name and $1225 gleamed back at me in silver ink. I put the augury slip between its pages and tucked the book under my arm. "I think—"

As I turned, another light caught my eye. I suppressed a sigh and trudged toward it. "I wonder who's coming to the store now," I said. "Someone who's in for a surprise."

The new augury lay on its face in a stack of other books I vaguely remembered receiving from a Nicollien last week in trade. I slid it out, balancing the stack, and turned it over. *Mind-Call*, read the title, and below that was a group of young faces with a dark man towering head and shoulders above them. I flipped it open. *Helena Davies, No Charge.*

"I didn't mean I wanted an augury!" I exclaimed, then felt bad about my reaction. "I mean—not that I'm not grateful. But I don't want you to put yourself out just because I'm impatient."

I felt the attention of the oracle focus on me immediately, a sensation like having a thousand people watching me attempt to juggle chainsaws. **Action,** I thought, and realized it was the oracle thinking through me as it had done before. I tried not to shudder; the oracle using my mind to communicate had never hurt me, but it was unsettling.

"Do you mean...you want me to take action?" I asked. "Or are you just agreeing with me?"

What I want. Action. I am different, I thought. Was that "I" me, or the oracle? It was hard to tell sometimes. I'd thought, after our last interaction, that it understood the difference between us, because it knew my name, but maybe there was something about its method of communication that was limiting.

"You mean I, Helena, am different?" I said.

Different. I speak to me. I see clear.

"That's true. I see through illusions and I can speak to

you…all that makes me different. And I can't be drained by an invader. But I don't know what that has to do with this augury."

A pulse of energy flashed through my hand holding *Mind-Call*, and I shivered. "All right," I said, "I'll study it. Thank you."

When I exited the oracle, Judy was gone. Frustration swept over me. It couldn't be healthy for Judy to bottle up her emotions like that, but I couldn't do anything about it if she kept disappearing. I put my augury on the counter and handed *Rebecca* to Jeremiah. "$1225. I guess I'll take your payment."

"What's up with Judy?" Viv asked, brushing the end of her scarf across the glass countertop. "She was practically surly."

I glanced at Jeremiah, who was digging his wallet out of his back pocket, in a way I hoped Viv would interpret. "It's just one of those days," I said.

Viv's eyebrows went up, but she said only, "I get that," and nodded to me as if to say *We'll talk later.*

Jeremiah handed me a wad of cash and waited for me to fill out a receipt. "I have to say I'm relieved to get this," he said, picking up the book and tapping it against the counter. "I can stay in and study instead of going on the hunt in this miserable weather."

"I'm in favor of that," Viv said with a grin. She looped her scarf around Jeremiah's neck and pulled him close for a kiss. Jeremiah blushed, and I looked away. He and Viv had a solid relationship, but he'd never become totally comfortable with Viv's easy manners.

"I'll see you later, then," I said. "Want to go out tomorrow night, Viv? Girls' night out?"

"Sounds good. Text me," Viv said.

When they were gone, I flipped open the cover of *Mind-*

Call again and read the description off the inside flap. It was a young adult book about a disaster, except...I read the final paragraph again. All the characters had psychic powers of some kind, and all had followed a psychic call that brought them together where they could defeat the bad guy. I closed the cover and stared at it. It couldn't be that simple, could it? I should probably study the book anyway. But after what I'd learned from Wallach, the answer seemed obvious.

I pulled out my phone and scrolled through my contacts, then tapped on a number. "Mangesh?" I said when he answered. "Can you drop by this afternoon? There's something we need to discuss."

4

Mangesh Kapoor showed up around 3:30, when the rush of Ambrosite augury seekers had dwindled to nothing. He was dressed casually for weather much warmer than this, in worn jeans and a T-shirt with no logo, and the faint lines across his forehead and at the corners of his eyes were more pronounced than usual. "I have been in India," he said, answering the question I hadn't asked. "It is a busy time, renewing wards during the rainy season."

"I guess you could call this our rainy season, too."

"But much colder. I admit I prefer India's heat." He inclined his head to me, as formal as ever. "I fear I do not have much time to spare."

"Oh! Sorry." I thought about using the break room, but it wasn't likely anyone was going to come in, and anyway there wasn't anything secret about what I intended to tell Mangesh. "The oracle gave me an augury about—I was talking to it, about wanting to do something more active to fight the Mercy, and it gave me this." I handed him the book.

Mangesh examined the cover, front and back. "I thought the custodian was not allowed an augury on her behalf."

"I can't request an augury, sure, but the oracle can choose to give me one."

He put the book down. "And you have interpreted it?"

"I haven't studied it thoroughly yet, but the cover flap says it's about psychic kids working together to defeat someone evil."

"Psychic?" Mangesh raised his eyebrows. "I think I see what you have deduced."

"It seems obvious, right? I think the oracle is saying we need to…I don't know. That the sports might be important to fighting the Mercy, or the invaders…" I propped my chin in my hand and sighed. "It sounds stupid when I say it out loud."

"Not stupid, just impractical," Mangesh said. "Unless you have found a solution to our problem."

"No." I hooked the stool with my ankle and dragged it toward me so I could sit on its cold metal seat. "Is it really a problem? We've identified a bunch of people who are genetic sports like us, and we know of at least four who know they have magical talents—"

"We assume."

"It's an informed guess I feel confident about. Anyway—so what? Even the ones who know about magic have no idea about invaders, or the Mercy, and there's no reason to tell them about any of that. My wanting to get to know them doesn't feel like adequate grounds for giving away those kinds of secrets."

Mangesh tapped the augury's cover. "Unless this gives us a reason. If they are of value to the fight, they will need to know the truth. But this is premature. You should analyze the augury and confirm your suspicions. Then we will make a plan."

"You're right. I just…it's hard to believe our small magics might matter, when the Wardens have all those magi who can do so much more. Unless it's our immunity to being drained that matters."

"Immunity?"

I realized I hadn't mentioned my visit to the Gunther Node to Mangesh. "Oh! Darius Wallach told me that's the actual mutation, being immune to invader attack, and seeing through illusions is a side effect."

"He is certain that applies to all of us, and not just you?" Mangesh's eyes narrowed.

"He was pretty certain. But maybe you should ask him for yourself."

"I would prefer not to be an experimental animal," Mangesh said with a grimace. "Being unable to have one's magic drained…that is the province of a steel or wood magus."

"Only we don't need an aegis for that to happen."

"It is miraculous indeed." Mangesh checked his watch. "I must go. But, Helena—" He tapped the augury again. "I think your initial assessment is correct. Study the book, and I will consider how to bring at least those four who are aware magic exists into the secret of the Wardens. Then we can act when you are certain."

"All right," I said. "Thanks."

When Mangesh was gone, I picked up *Mind-Call* and flipped it open randomly to the middle, but didn't read the page revealed. I did feel fairly confident about my guess, but my reluctance to forge ahead was rooted in my feeling that I was looking for an excuse to do something I wanted to do anyway. The idea of getting to know people like me was compelling, if selfish, given that there really was no reason to bring them in on the secret of the Long War. But I didn't like being so…unique, maybe, not a magus and not an ordinary Warden, but someone with a magical difference that mattered under only limited circumstances. It would be fun not to be the only one—all right, there was Mangesh, but he was gone most of the time and was too formal to be a close friend.

The bells over the door jingled, and I set the book down and sat upright. "Welcome to—oh, Malcolm!"

Malcolm smiled as I hopped down and went to put my arms around him. "My day is looking up," he said after a long, sweet, breathless kiss. "I've been thinking of you ever since I left for work this morning."

"I love it when you come into the store." It hadn't been all that long ago that we couldn't have kissed like this in public, let alone be married, and I still felt a rush of pleasure whenever I saw him walk through the door. "I'm not even going to ask you why you're here, because it's probably for an augury, and that would require me to let go of you."

He smiled. "I'm in no hurry, and there's no one waiting on your time, so…"

His lips met mine, and I slid my arms up from his waist to around his neck, twirling the short hairs at the base of his neck around my fingers. I was the luckiest woman in the world, married to the most wonderful guy who was also built like an action hero—

Someone cleared their throat behind me, a deliberate sound that was the audial equivalent of an elbow to the ribs. I broke away from Malcolm's embrace just enough to turn and see Judy there, smirking. "Don't you two have a house to go to?"

I thought about saying something about wondering where

she and Mike did *their* making out, decided that was pushing it, and said, "Yes, but I like seizing the moment."

Malcolm released me and took a step back. "And much as I enjoy being seized, I do have business." He withdrew a slip of paper from the inner pocket of his suit coat and handed it to me.

I unfolded it and read *What weapons should we use against the Mercy?* "That's odd," I said. "Every other augury request I've had about the Mercy today, the oracle answered in advance and for free."

"That just means the oracle is still mysterious," Judy said.

I shrugged and walked into the oracle—and into half a dozen bright blue lights like tiny stars. "You can't mean all of these for Malcolm, can you?" I said, reaching up to retrieve the nearest one, titled *Poisoned Blade*. Malcolm's name was inside the cover, along with *No Charge*. "Well, that's generous, at any rate. Thanks."

The second and third, however, were for Lucia, also at no charge. I added them to my stack and moved on. The next, to my surprise, was for Malcolm again—a slim paperback with a drawing of a bunch of guys in soldiers' fatigues on the cover titled *Stand Down*. "That doesn't sound good," I said. "I wonder if it matters to you that I care what happens to Malcolm? Or are you impartial in your treatment of the people who ask for auguries? I just want him to be safe—though he's not in a line of work where that's likely."

Another light winked on as I spoke, causing me to stop where I was. I realized my mouth was hanging open and shut it. "Did you just…answer my question?" I whispered.

The oracle's attention shifted to me briefly, then away again. "Um…thank you, I think," I said, and walked around the corner to take the new augury off the shelf. "*Dark Moon*

Defender. I wish I could draw conclusions about your meaning as easily all the time as with that *Mind-Call* book. But... defender, defense, maybe protecting someone?" The name inside it wasn't mine, but Malcolm's, which surprised me a little; I'd thought the oracle was giving it to me.

I retrieved the last two auguries, one more for Malcolm titled *More Guns, Less Crime*, and just as I'd stopped expecting it, one for me. This one was titled *A Gift of Magic*, and the blurb on the back of the little paperback said it was about a girl who could see a short distance into the future. I stared off into the distance, thinking. "Some of the genetic sports are precognitive," I said. "Is that what you mean?"

See. Learn. Watch, the oracle thought through me. I suppressed a shudder. At least this contact didn't make my ears bleed.

"I'll study it," I said, waving the book in the general direction of the oracle's heart. Two auguries to study meant twice as much work, but it also meant having two things to...well, you couldn't call it triangulation, with just two, but I could compare the books and get a better idea of what they had in common.

Not alone, Helena, I thought, and then the oracle's presence faded. I let out a sigh, shifted the weight of the books in the crook of my elbow, and found my way out of the oracle.

Malcolm's eyebrows went up when he saw me and my hoard. "Those are all for me?" he asked.

"Some of them are for you. Some are for Lucia. And one is for me." I spread the books out on the counter, putting *A Gift of Magic* atop *Mind-Call* and handing Malcolm his four auguries. He glanced at each, his face expressionless. "Do they help at all?"

"Auguries always help," he said, still studying the topmost

book, "and I am tempted to take this one—" He patted *More Guns, Less Crime*— "at face value. At least, I have never regretted taking more guns than I believed I needed into battle against invaders. Mike's new illusion technique makes it easy to conceal their nature, even when we are fully in public."

I happened to be looking at Judy as Malcolm said this, so I saw the slow ruddy flush spread across her cheeks, but she said, "That makes sense that he'd care about that, after Chicago."

"You aren't still holding that against him?" Malcolm said sharply.

Judy blushed harder. "Of course not," she said irritably. "I'm just saying if it were me, I'd want not to make the same mistake twice."

I agreed. Mike had been responsible for the deaths of his teammates when the illusions he'd been maintaining on their weapons collapsed, years ago, and while I didn't think he was still beating himself up about it, I was sure it was something he was determined never to let happen again.

"He won't," Malcolm said flatly. "Helena, do I owe you anything for these?"

"They were all free. Will you be ready for dinner at seven?"

He smiled, and a little of the tension introduced by Judy's mention of Mike fell away. "Always," he said, and kissed me, the kind of kiss that had a world of promises in it. I kissed him back, not caring that Judy was watching. "I'll see you tonight," he finally said, nodded at Judy, and left the store.

Judy snorted. "Newlyweds," she said.

"I think we're sweet," I protested.

"Whatever. Do you—"

The door swung open, setting the bells jingling. "Hi,

Dave," I said to Dave Henry. "And...Mr. Wallach! I didn't expect to see you so soon."

"I had something I wanted to try, and it made more sense to come to you," Wallach said. He had a plain shoebox with Manolo Blahnik printed on the lid under one arm—*not*, thank heaven, a box pierced by air holes—and wore a shiny purple raincoat beaded with droplets. Dave was, as usual, bareheaded and wearing his familiar denim jacket with the fleece collar that made him look like the cowboy hero of a romance novel, though one with a military-short blond haircut.

"You look like you were expecting me," Dave said. "Did Lucia call?"

I shook my head and extended the auguries to him. "Here you are. Tell Lucia the oracle anticipated her again."

"That's unsettling," Dave said. He set his briefcase on the counter, opened it, and rearranged the stacks of money to make room for the books. "No charge?"

"No charge. This must be something big."

Dave gave me a secretive little half-smile. "Lucia would use my head for a volleyball if I told you her plans, you know that."

"I can't help wondering."

I eyed Wallach, who was ignoring the rest of us. He'd set the shoebox on the counter next to Dave's briefcase and stood looking into it as if it contained the secrets of the universe. "Mr. Wallach, can I help you with something?"

"Nothing yet," Wallach said, not raising his eyes from the box. "It needs time to acclimate."

Despite the lack of air holes, that made me nervous. "Um..."

"Don't worry, Mrs. Campbell, this is perfectly safe." He

reached into the box and prodded something that made a soft white light come on.

The bells jingled again. We were certainly popular today. But my cheerful greeting faded when I saw who my new customers were. "Detective Acosta, and Detective Green," I said. "Augury, or business?" I hoped it wasn't business. Acosta and Green had started out as my enemies, had become uncomfortable allies, and now they were, if not friends, at least not people I had to be afraid of. But that didn't mean their presence in the store made me happy. There was always a chance it had to do with some illegal dealings rather than the perfectly innocent need for an augury.

"Augury," Green said. I relaxed. An augury, I could handle. He handed me a slip of paper on which was written, in his familiar blocky printing, *Where is the property stolen from the Hamell Bank?*

"I haven't heard about this one," I said.

"They kept it quiet because they suspect it was an inside job," Acosta said. He glanced over at Wallach and his glowing box, looked as if he wanted to ask something, then just as clearly decided not to get involved.

"Oh. Well…just a minute."

It took longer than I'd expected to find the augury, which turned out to be a North American atlas crammed into one of the top shelves. By the time I returned, Wallach's box was glowing purple rather than white, and all of them, even Judy, were staring at it, mesmerized. "What's going on?" I asked.

"Nothing, yet," Wallach said, as if glowing purple lights in shoeboxes happened to him all the time. "This is to see how your body reacts to processed *sanguinis sapiens*. It will tell me… oh, several things, like what the biological mechanism is that keeps you from being drained, and may allow me to predict what kind of magical side effect might result in any given individual."

"Interesting." I handed the augury to Acosta. "Five hundred."

Acosta pulled out his wallet and counted twenties into my hand while Judy wrote up a receipt. "So you confirmed you're a mutant?" Judy said. "When were you planning to tell me this?"

"It sort of slipped my mind when the oracle started acting strangely," I said, "and I like 'genetic sport' better. I hope you have good luck with that," I added to Acosta. I set the little stack of money on the counter. The purple glow had grown enough that its radiance reflected off my skin.

"Perfect," Wallach said. He took my hand and raised it to the level of his face, then to my astonishment sniffed the back of my hand. "Peppermint. Exactly as anticipated."

I retrieved my hand from his and sniffed the skin tentatively. Sure enough, I smelled peppermint, like those puffy fat candies stores sell at Christmastime in big buckets. "Is that— I'm glowing!" Even though my hand wasn't close to the box anymore, the purple radiance persisted; it was even a little brighter and more obvious away from the box.

"Yes, of course," Wallach said. He sounded impatient, like he'd explained it all already. "You're reacting to the *sanguinis sapiens*—that just shows what I told you before, that you're a genetic sport."

"What the *hell* are you talking about?" Acosta growled. "Is this some kind of Warden joke?"

I turned to face him, and gasped. "Detective Acosta," I said, and then words failed me. He was standing several steps away from the box, well out of range of its glow.

His hands and face radiated soft purple light.

5

"Another one," Wallach said, sounding as pleased as if Acosta had offered him a gift. "And you are…"

Acosta's olive complexion was darker in the purple radiance. He looked ready to explode. "This is Detective Acosta," I said, hoping to head off the eruption. "Detective, this is Mr. Wallach. He's a scientist at the Gunther Node."

"Why," Acosta said in a low, furious voice, "am I *purple?* What the hell did you do to me?"

"Nothing," Wallach said irritably. "I told you. You're reacting to the *sanguinis sapiens* because you're genetically different from the average person. Have you ever been bitten by an invader?"

Acosta examined his hands, which I saw now were shaking just a little. "Are you saying I'm a mutant?"

"We say genetic sport rather than mutant," I said. "Mutant sounds so X-Men."

Acosta's fierce gaze turned on me, and I managed not to

take a nervous step backward. "A mutant," he said. "Mutant how?"

"You and Mrs. Campbell are genetically immune to having your personal magic drained by an invader," Wallach said. He'd gone back to staring into the shoebox and now poked a finger at whatever was inside. The glow gradually darkened to blue. Acosta and I continued to glow purple, but after a few seconds, the glow faded. "In a few days I should know the mechanism by which that works."

"Can you reverse it?"

Wallach laughed. "Oh. You were serious. No, detective, I only dabble in genetic alteration, and never in human subjects. Too potentially messy." He glanced at Acosta. "There's really nothing to worry about."

"It's why I can see through illusions," I volunteered. "One of the side effects is a minor magical ability."

Acosta lowered his hands. "I can't see through illusions."

His inability to see through illusions had been key to Acosta's introduction to the magical world. "No, but you could…" I looked at Wallach. "It could be anything."

"I…think I know what it is," Detective Green said.

Acosta stared at him. "You don't seriously think I have some kind of superpower."

Green shrugged. "Not a superpower. But you do have an unsettling instinct for when someone's not telling the truth."

"I'm just…" Acosta's voice trailed off. "Harris, that's ridiculous."

"Is it? We've seen some damn strange things in the past year, Greg. I'm finding it a lot less difficult to believe in the impossible than I used to."

"He's right," Wallach said, looking up from the box.

"Detective Acosta, you have a sensitivity to the physiological discontinuity created when someone attempts a deception."

We all stared at him. "People's bodies react when they lie," Wallach said, rolling his eyes. "You can sense that."

"Remember when we first met, back when Mr. Briggs was murdered?" I said. "You hounded me no matter what I said. You knew I wasn't telling the truth—you just didn't know what I was concealing."

Acosta abruptly turned and walked toward the window, his fists clenched. He stopped and stared out at the rain-spattered pavement and the blue Buick parked in front of the store, next to Abernathy's magically reserved spot. "What am I supposed to do with that?" he asked.

I exchanged glances with Judy, who looked almost sympathetic. "Nothing," Wallach said, "or, rather, it doesn't change anything for you except that you now know to pay attention when your instincts tell you someone's trying to pull a fast one. If you were a magus, I'd say you could be a front line fighter, but in your line of work you're unlikely to run into many invaders, so there's that."

I decided not to tell Acosta about the *Mind-Call* augury and my theory that the genetic sports might be able to help in the fight against the Mercy. He had the look of someone who'd already heard too much craziness for one day. Instead, I said, "There are several of us. Me, and the stone magus Mangesh Kapoor, and about thirty-five others in North America, except none of them know about the Long War."

Acosta turned back to face me. "Thirty-plus out of all the hundreds of millions living in North America."

"We're very rare," I said.

Acosta continued to stare at me for a few seconds. Then he blinked as if he were waking from a deep sleep. "Genetic sports," he murmured. "I suppose I've heard more unbelievable things."

"Right," I said cheerfully, hoping to distract him. "And it really doesn't make you different than you were ten minutes ago, right?"

He shook his head, slowly, contemplating my words. Then he let out a deep breath and said, "Do you have the augury, Harris? We need to get moving."

"Just like that?" I said, taken aback.

"I can't afford to freak out on duty," Acosta said, and to my astonishment, he smiled. "I'm sure we'll be back later."

I stared after him as the detectives left the store, blinked, and said, "Did that just happen?"

"That's beyond unlikely," Judy said. "You said less than forty in all of North America? And then there are two of you in Portland?"

"Forty that the Athenaeum knew about. That means forty that came to the attention of Wardens somehow, and only in the most general way. Who knows how many there actually are?"

"And it's not like there has to be an even geographical distribution," Wallach said. "Genetics doesn't work that way." He put the lid on the shoebox and put it under his arm. "I'll let you know what else I learn once I've studied the results. I should be able to work out the mechanism your immunity operates by."

"Could that mean being able to alter others in the same way?" Dave asked.

That hadn't occurred to me, but once Dave mentioned it, I couldn't help imagining all Wardens—all humans?—being immune to invader attack. That would change the Long War significantly.

Wallach shrugged. "Depends on the mechanism," he said. "If it's a matter of altering some existing biological function or structure, maybe. But don't get your hopes up. The human body is incredibly complex, and it's far more likely this is something going on at a cellular level that can only be changed at a cost to some other system, probably fatally. I'll know more in a few days."

"Thanks, Mr. Wallach," I said.

Wallach nodded. "Have a nice day," he said, and he and Dave left. I watched them through the plate glass window as they walked to a little white van and drove away.

"Well," Judy said, "this is turning out to be one of the weirder days in the store's history." She picked up the stack of money and squared it up neatly. "At least it doesn't seem to be a bad kind of weird."

"No." I gathered up my two auguries. "And I have something to study."

Judy eyed the books. "The oracle gave you an augury. Two auguries. What about?"

I summed up what I'd discussed with Mangesh and the question that had prompted the auguries, and ended by saying, "I hope I'm not just looking for an excuse to meet these people."

"I don't think so," Judy said. "But you already know I believe they ought to be told about the Long War."

"That just feels strange to me. It's always been such a big secret—"

"Only because the average person wouldn't know what to do with that information." Judy crossed her arms over her chest. "We need all the advantage we can get, we Wardens, I mean. Suppose one of those sports has a magical ability that turns the tide in our favor, either against the invaders or against the Mercy?"

"You've said that before. I'm not sure Lucia would agree."

Judy made a dismissive noise. "Lucia cares about results. She would grumble about it if you brought those people into the secret, but if they were a net benefit, she wouldn't grumble much. And besides, what if that genetic difference made you *more* susceptible to being drained instead? They'd need to know to protect themselves. It's just coincidence that you're all protected instead."

"You make sense." I scowled. "I'll see what these auguries say, but I think it's time to let at least some of them know the truth."

"How do you know a few of them know about magic already?"

I shrugged. "I had Campbell Security investigate all of them, in case that told me more about all of us in general. And there are strong hints that four of them are using their magic deliberately. Like, there's one guy who's a professional gambler, and another woman who tells fortunes for a living."

"That could be coincidence," Judy said.

"*But* they're both precognitives. That's way too much coincidence for me."

Judy pursed her lips. "All right, that's a fair point. Anyway, the more reason to bring them in on the secret. If they know about magic, they're halfway to the truth already, and why not give them a chance to use their powers for something other than themselves?"

"That's an interesting way to look at it."

"The sensible way." Judy turned and retreated into the stacks.

I carried my books to the office and put them into my capacious purse, then stood looking at the photo of Silas Abernathy, former custodian and later stone magus. I thought of him as a sort of guardian of the store, given that he'd overseen its dangerous transfer from its original home in England to its current location. "I wonder what you'd do," I mused. "No, actually I'm sure you'd tell those four sports, because you always followed your instincts. And mine are telling me Judy is right. So maybe I didn't need the auguries, after all." I glanced down at my purse. "Or maybe I needed them to confirm what I already knew. Maybe they'll tell me *how* to go about it, because I'm sure calling those people and blurting it all out is a bad idea."

Silas regarded me in silence, his smile frozen on his lips for eternity, his hat tipped back on his bald head and his hands shoved casually into the pockets of his three-piece suit. "And maybe I need to stop talking to pictures and get back to work," I said, though there wasn't really any work to do. Sit at the front counter and wait for people to come in, probably.

So I did that for about twenty minutes during which no one came in for an augury. It was going to be one of those afternoons. I tried to remember how crazy busy we sometimes got and how frazzled I felt then, but mostly I was just bored. When the door opened, loudly jingling the bells, I sat up and said, "Viv. I'm so glad to see you."

Viv unwound her colorful scarf from around her neck. "Is it that serious?"

"Is what serious?"

"You sure made it seem like Judy's problem was too dire to discuss in front of Jeremiah." She dropped her scarf to puddle on the counter and ran her fingers through her green hair, disordering her chin-length bob.

"Oh, that. I don't know how dire it is, but it's private."

"What's private?" Judy said, emerging from the stacks with the broom in hand.

I blushed. Viv fixed Judy with a sharp stare. "You tell me," she said.

Judy scowled, but her normally rosy cheeks were redder than mine. "It's not a big deal. I'm involved with Mike Conti. That's all."

Viv's eyes widened. "That *is* a big deal. How long has this been going on? Since Helena's wedding?"

"If you knew, why are you asking me now?" Judy sighed. "It's just sex. Really, that's all."

"Except if it was just sex, you wouldn't be so embarrassed," Viv said. "Let me guess. You like him and you're afraid he doesn't feel the same."

Judy leaned the broom against the counter and covered her face with both hands. "Not exactly. It's supposed to be a no strings attached relationship, and he's not interested in changing that."

"Are you sure?" Viv asked. "Maybe you—"

"*Don't* tell me to talk to him," Judy said, glaring at Viv. Then she closed her eyes and let out a deep breath. "I just heard myself say that. I can't believe I'm this pathetic."

"Look, if you like him and you want more out of the relationship than sex," Viv said, "you have to tell him that. At worst, he breaks it off entirely and you no longer have semi-illicit sex in your apartment."

"Why semi-illicit?" I asked.

"Because her father would pop a vein if he knew about it," Viv said.

"That is absolutely true," Judy said. "But I find I don't care about that so much anymore. It's stupid that the factions are so antagonistic toward each other. I mean, what if Mike were my soulmate? Which I'm not saying he is, so don't get excited," she said, heading off Viv's exclamation. "My point is, I shouldn't have to choose who I care about based on how appropriate my father thinks he is. This isn't the nineteenth century, after all."

"So tell him," Viv said. "Mike, I mean. Obviously it's none of William Rasmussen's business who you sleep with."

Judy scowled again, but it didn't look like her heart was in it. "I'll…think about it," she said. "Maybe. I don't know if that's what I want. But you're right, I shouldn't be afraid to bring it up."

"That's right," Viv said. "Girls' night out tomorrow? Helena already said yes."

"Sounds fun," Judy said.

———

I LET myself in by the back door and inhaled the tangy aroma of beef stew. I used the slow cooker a lot during the winter, both because I loved hot meals and because I liked having those hot meals ready when I got home. I kicked off my shoes and padded down the short hallway to the kitchen, where Malcolm was occupied tossing a salad. "Oh, you didn't have to do that," I said. "It's my day to cook."

"I got home early and it's no problem," Malcolm said. He carried the salad bowl to the table in the breakfast nook, which I could see was already set. We never used the dining room, with its table that could seat twelve, when it was just us.

I took the lid off the pot and gave the contents a little stir, releasing more of the delicious smell, and then turned around. "Wait. You said you had an afternoon meeting. How did you get home early?"

Malcolm returned to my side and took me in his arms. "I cancelled the meeting," he said, "on account of another meeting taking precedence. Warden business."

The way he said it made dread creep up my spine. "You're going on the attack."

"Three nights from now, at midnight."

I closed my eyes and rested my cheek against his shoulder. "Can you tell me the details?"

He held me a little more tightly for a moment and then released me. "Let's serve dinner, and we can talk."

I'd thought the knowledge that Malcolm was going into danger yet again would kill my appetite, but the stew smelled so good, and it had been a long time since lunch. I blew on a spoonful of beef and potatoes and said, "Where are you going?"

"Lucia's people have located one of the Mercy's secret hideouts," Malcolm said. "She believes it is their primary stronghold. We intend to destroy it, or at least make it useless to them. At the same time, other nodes around the world will attack the Mercy in their areas. A coordinated strike, intended to cut off the Mercy operatives from their leaders and weaken the organization to the breaking point."

"That sounds huge. Where is it? The one you're attacking?"

"Somewhere in Montana, which is why Lucia is overseeing the operation. Herb Lavigne, who has responsibility for the central north region, doesn't have the resources to mount an operation like this alone. The team leaders met this afternoon to go over the strategy. It's…different."

I took another bite. "That sounds like a bad kind of different."

Malcolm shook his head. "No, but it is interesting. It seems the Mercy has set up a peculiar kind of security on its strong-hold. Humans can't pass through it unless they are accompanied by an invader."

"But—" I stopped with my spoon halfway to my mouth. "Does that mean familiars, too?"

"You're quick," Malcolm said with a smile. "We will use the Nicollien familiars to breach their security, and then we will strike."

"So…the factions have to work together."

"They do." Malcolm took a bite of salad, chewed, and added, "It frustrates me that none of them were happy about it. In fact, some of them argued vehemently that we should find another option rather than work with 'damned Nicolliens.' Their animosity has become ridiculous."

"I agree. We have a common enemy—why can't they see that?"

"Habit," Malcolm said, "and the human tendency to want to take sides in any conflict. But it has become a matter of almost religious zeal, and I'm afraid it's going to get people killed."

We ate in silence for about a minute, me thinking about my friends in both the Nicollien and Ambrosite camps and how I wished they could overcome their differences. When I'd first become custodian of Abernathy's, Ambrosites and Nicolliens had mingled freely on the premises without any more conflict than the occasional insult. Now, the Board of Neutralities had ruled the factions had to come to the store at different times, and even the Mercy's devastating attacks on the South American nodes hadn't done more than create a temporary cease fire.

"Don't worry," Malcolm said abruptly. "The plan is sound,

and I don't think the Wardens will be in any more danger than usual. The Mercy has no idea we're coming."

"Oh. You know I worry anyway."

Malcolm took my hand and squeezed it. "This could represent a turning point in the Long War. If we can cut off the head of the snake, the body will wither and die."

"But what will that mean for fighting invaders?"

He shook his head again, letting go of my hand. "I don't know. We still don't know how long the Mercy has been in existence. It's possible they've been supporting invader attacks for longer than the factions have existed, in which case we should see some difference in how the invaders operate. But it might mean nothing more than eliminating one enemy."

"Which would still be valuable," I said.

"Of course."

I laid my spoon in my empty bowl. "Maybe I need to talk to Lucia."

Malcolm's eyebrows went up. "About what?"

"About these auguries I received. They were in response to me wishing there was something I could do to help in the fight. And with the oracle acting preemptively all those times, I wonder if I'm not meant to participate in Lucia's attack."

Malcolm shook his head. "You're no fighter. I refuse to believe the oracle would endanger its custodian by sending you into battle."

"No, not that, but…my auguries are increasingly clear that the sports are meant to do *something* to fight the enemy. And Lucia knows better than me what that is."

"True. But she'll likely just tell you to stick to your job and let her do hers."

"She needs all the information she can get. I think I should take that chance."

Malcolm shook his head again, this time in resignation. "I just hate the idea of involving you in the war more directly."

"Do you ever wish the war was over?"

"All the time, love." Malcolm stood and began clearing the table. "Though I have trouble imagining what my life would be like if there was nothing left to hunt."

"You'd still be a magus," I pointed out as I picked up the salad bowl. "You could…" My voice trailed off. "You're right, I have trouble imagining what else you might do with magic. Would people even still want magical security systems?"

"Probably, since those work against mundane threats too. I suppose I would eventually fall into new habits. And you wouldn't have any more sleepless nights, waiting for me to return home."

I blushed. "I thought you didn't know about that." Ever since we'd moved into this house, I'd had trouble falling asleep when I knew Malcolm was on the hunt.

"It makes sense, Helena. Hunting is dangerous work. But you've never tried to stop me, even though you hate it when I'm gone."

I loaded our bowls into the dishwasher. "It's not that I don't have faith in your skills."

"I know." Malcolm finished scraping the rest of the stew into two plastic containers that would be my and Judy's lunch tomorrow. "Your faith in me gives me strength."

The look in his eyes, as if he saw right to my core, warmed me all over. "Let's watch a movie," I said. "Naked."

He raised his eyebrows. "I don't know how much movie watching will happen if we're naked."

I put my arms around him. "Then choose a boring movie."

6

"Lucia," I said to her voice mail, "I have an important augury to discuss with you. Call me." I ended the call and shoved my phone into my pocket. Most of the time, I didn't mind that Lucia screened her calls and answered them according to her own ideas of what was important. Today that habit made me want to scream. I'd studied the auguries last night, what was left of last night after some extremely satisfying sex, and I felt increasingly confident that the oracle wanted the sports to play some role in fighting the Mercy, or the invaders, or both. Whether that meant taking part in Lucia's upcoming attack, I didn't know. But I was sure Lucia would. If she ever called me back.

The store brightened as the sun temporarily came out from behind the clouds. The day was overcast, but in a patchy way that made the light dim and brighten as the clouds shifted. It felt like the sky was taunting me. It was one of those days where I craved sunlight. I propped my chin on my hands and watched the shadows on the street outside. At least it wasn't raining.

Judy emerged from the stacks. "Lunchtime," she said. "Unless you're not done with the mail-in auguries."

"No, they're finished." I nodded at the stack of books on the counter next to me. "We can pack them up after we eat."

I hopped off the stool, making it wobble—I hadn't been kidding about the need to replace the rest of Abernathy's furniture—and followed Judy to the break room. I put my container of leftover beef stew in the microwave and watched it slowly revolve. The rich, meaty smell reminded me of my conversation with Malcolm the night before. "I wonder how things would change if the Long War was over," I said.

"You mean, what would all those fighters do, or what would *we* do?" Judy replied. "In a way, I hope—no, that's wrong. I want the war to be over and all the invaders gone. But the Long War gives the Wardens purpose, and if that were gone…it's like how all those men came home from World War II and there weren't enough jobs or housing. The war's end would be hugely disruptive."

"I hadn't thought about that. Mostly I'd thought about what the magi would turn their magic to if it wasn't fighting invaders."

"And would they stop creating new magi?"

I hadn't considered that, either. "No more magi."

"And if there's no more magi, is there any need for the nodes? Or the Neutralities?"

I tried to imagine Lucia out of a job, entering the private sector, so to speak, and my mind came up blank. At that moment, my phone rang. As if my thinking of her had conjured her up, it was Lucia. "Thanks for calling me back," I said.

"I don't have a lot of time, Davies. What's this about an augury? Another unasked-for one? You aren't supposed to read other people's auguries."

"This isn't one for you. It's an augury the oracle gave me."

Lucia made a dismissive noise just shy of a snort. "Sounds like Abernathy's is getting pushy. All right. What does your augury have to do with me?"

"Well…" I'd already discussed the auguries with others, but telling Lucia was different, if only because her irritated impatience was palpable even through the phone. "I…told the oracle—"

"You talk to the oracle?"

She sounded more surprised than disdainful, which heartened me. "Yes, sometimes. It doesn't always pay attention, but now that I know it's a living creature, it feels like the polite thing to do. Anyway, I told it I wanted to do something to help—"

"That astounds me in the sense that it's no surprise. What next?"

"It gave me an augury. Do you know—did Mr. Wallach tell you about me? About the others like me?"

"He might have made a report which is filed with all the other reports on my desk. Why don't you sum it up?"

Filed on my desk meant *in a stack I'm ignoring.* I suppressed a sigh—it felt like I'd told this story a hundred times before— and explained quickly how Wallach had confirmed that I was a genetic sport, how that meant I was immune to being drained by an invader, and that I'd identified others like me. "The augury says that the sports—me and the others like me —can help fight the invaders. Or are important to defeating them. It's not clear on the specifics."

"It does, huh?"

My heart sank, because Lucia's tone of voice was entirely too familiar: slightly sarcastic, a little dismissive, and one hundred percent ready to end the call and move on. "It does. But you know more about the fight than I do. I was hoping you would understand what the augury means in practical terms."

"Davies, you know I don't disregard the oracle. But in this case, I have no idea what use I'd make of a handful of people, most of whom know nothing about the Long War or magic or Wardens, whose sole advantage is an immunity every wood and steel magus has. Or do those magical talents have more usefulness than you suggest?"

"I'm not saying I want us to attack the Mercy stronghold with the front line fighters. I'm saying if the oracle thinks there's something we can do, I want to figure out what that is."

Lucia sighed. When she spoke again, she sounded less impatient. "I don't have time for this. We've planned our attack and it's only two nights from now. Adding an unknown quantity to that attack would push it back several days, and we're already risking discovery by waiting as long as we are."

"I thought you'd found all the traitors. There isn't anyone left to warn the Mercy."

"Leaks happen. It doesn't take a traitor to accidentally give something away. If the Mercy is watching us, they could theoretically work out what we're doing the longer it takes us to act."

"But the oracle—"

"Like I said, Davies, I don't want to disregard the oracle. If you'll sign a confidentiality waiver, I'll send an interpreter to take those auguries and see what he can make of them. This isn't the end of the war, and I doubt it will make much difference if your sports aren't part of this battle." She hung up without saying goodbye.

I sat holding the dead phone to my ear for a minute. "She said no, huh," Judy said around a mouthful of stew.

"Sort of. She doesn't think there's any urgency." I set down my phone and took a bite of stew, which was lukewarm. "I guess I should be grateful she didn't dismiss me out of hand."

"Lucia's not stupid. You've been right too many times for her to ignore your warnings."

I stood, pushing my stew aside. Either I was tired of stew, or I'd lost my appetite for other reasons. "But I'm not wrong about this."

I crossed the hall to the break room and pulled *Mind-Call* out of my purse, riffling through the pages at random. I closed my eyes and stabbed at the page with my finger. Opening my eyes, I scanned the lines surrounding the spot I'd chosen. "Still the same thing," I told Judy, who'd followed me into the office. "Urgency. The need to act now. Lucia can't afford to wait on a professional interpreter."

"So you'll have to act on her behalf," Judy said. "Contact them. Bring them here to meet you and Mangesh."

"That will piss Lucia off beyond measure."

"Not if you get results. She's busy, right? Maybe she'd be grateful to you for taking work off her hands."

I wasn't sure that would be Lucia's reaction, but Judy's logic was still compelling. "All right. But I don't know how. I mean, how to phrase it. This book—" I tapped the pages —"makes it clear that deception is what the bad guy does. So I can't just, I don't know, tell them they have a surprise inheritance. But how are they going to react if I come right out and say 'I know you have magic powers'?"

"You're not thinking clearly, Helena. The oracle's guidance

covers all sorts of contingencies. If it's guiding you to contact these people, it's saying this is the best way to do it." Judy leaned back in her chair and blew a stray strand of hair out of her eyes. "They know they have magic. Telling them you know it too will probably intrigue them."

"Good point." I closed the book and pushed it aside. "Have I mentioned lately how much I enjoy having virtually unlimited resources? It's nice to be able to do things without worrying about the cost. Or to be able to support causes I care about. Or—" I opened my email program and started a new message. "To be able to pay for airfare and hotel rooms for four people I've never met."

I LOVED ITALIAN FOOD, and if I couldn't have my mother's home cooking, I went to Giuseppe's. The deep red of the walls and the maroon carpeting made me feel warm after the chill of the evening air. The restaurant was cozy and dimly lit, filled with little round tables each with their own tiny lamp and larger booths lining the walls. Soft classical music filled the air just at the edge of hearing over all the muted conversations. I didn't think it was Italian, but that didn't ruin my enjoyment.

The server seated me, Judy, and Viv at one of the booths, handed us menus, and disappeared. "You'd think they'd know you by now," Viv said to me. "I swear this is the booth we've had the last three times we've been in here."

I breathed in the smell of fresh mozzarella and marinara sauce and closed my eyes briefly in pleasure. "I think I'll have the fettuccini tonight. I can smell it already."

"It all smells like good Italian food to me," Judy said.

"But you'll still just have basic spaghetti and meatballs," Viv teased.

Judy shrugged. "I know what I like and I stick with it."

The waiter looked a little surprised when he returned for our drink orders and found us ready to order food as well. Maybe we did go to Giuseppe's too often. Viv leaned back and stretched her arms, making the joints pop. I shuddered. "I can't believe that's not painful."

"Feels good," Viv said. "So, I want to know about these people you're flying in from all over. Do you feel like Professor X?"

"We're not X-Men, Viv. Genetic sports, remember?"

Viv waved that away. "Still. Magic talents, immune to invaders…who are these people, anyway? Do they know you had them investigated?"

"I didn't mention it, no. I thought it might come across as creepy."

"No creepier than telling them you know their deepest secret," Judy said. She glanced at the server approaching with our drinks, and added, "How else do they think you learned it?"

I took a sip of my wine and said, once the server was out of earshot, "I implied I had magic that told me. Which is true, just not the way they think."

"So, did it work?" Viv asked.

I nodded. "Three of them responded this afternoon. The fourth may not have seen the message yet. She's an executive with a big company in Vancouver, and I didn't want to send the message to her work email."

"Smart," Judy said. "That was the woman with the Chinese name, right?"

"Her name is Jun Li. Second-generation Canadian, after

her Chinese grandparents settled in Vancouver. She's some kind of vice president of Heritek, which is a medical research firm. Forty-six years old, unmarried, has a substantial fortune but lives very austerely. She's a champion fencer and has two cats."

"That means she's a caring, empathetic person," Viv said.

"Why, because she likes cats?" Judy said.

"She's a high-powered executive who probably doesn't spend much time at home. Two cats means she cares enough about her pets' well-being to give them a playmate."

"That hadn't occurred to me," I said. "Huh. I had the impression she was kind of standoffish because of her talent." I leaned forward, prompting Viv and Judy to lean in as well, though I knew no one nearby could hear us. "She generates this...it's like a personal force field. People can't get too close to her without feeling seriously uncomfortable, she never gets bitten by bugs—"

"You have to be kidding," Viv said. "This is a talent?"

"It is, I swear. She seems to use it to enhance her already intimidating presence. The report I got says she rose in the ranks faster than any other Heritek executive, because people are attracted to her. Not in a sexual way, in an admiring way."

"I don't get it," Viv said. "You said she has a force field, so how are people attracted to her?"

"That's the mystery," I said. "It's like her presence and her talent combine to make her both appealing and unapproachable. Darius Wallach really wants to get his hands on her, so to speak."

The server appeared just then with an enormous tray. I leaned back for him to set my fettuccini in front of me and inhaled deeply. "Oh, I love the smell," I said.

"I love the taste," Judy said, digging into her plateful of

spaghetti and meatballs. The meatballs were huge, almost the size of a baby's fist, and drenched in a rich tomato sauce. "Tell Viv about the others," she added around her mouthful.

"Geez, could you eat less like a truck driver?" Viv said.

Judy swallowed. "That's insulting to truck drivers." But her next bite was daintier.

"*Anyway,*" I said, rolling fettuccini around my fork, "I hope she contacts me. The others were all willing to come to Portland, though Victor Crowson sounded skeptical. But he's only eighteen and I don't think he's ever been out of Atlantic City in his life."

"You mentioned him before. The gambler. He's the one you investigated first," Viv said.

"Yes. He passes for mid-twenties, which is how he's gotten away with his scam for so long. Well, maybe it's not a scam. I don't know what to call it. He can see a short distance into the future and he uses that skill to win at roulette and craps, but he's clever enough not to win so consistently they suspect him of cheating."

"Fortunate for him," Judy said. "What about the other precognitive?"

"Ines Varnado," I said. "She lives in Phoenix. Sixty years old, emigrated from El Salvador when she was in her thirties. Recently widowed—her husband died last year. She earns a very good living telling fortunes, which surprised me until I found out she has a thriving online business as well as the in-person fortune telling. I guess, if you really can see the future, people keep coming back." I took another bite of fettuccini.

"So how is what they do different from the oracle?" Viv asked.

"I'm not sure," I said. "I think the oracle's scope is broader than theirs. Auguries are certainly more complex than what numbers are going to come up on a pair of dice in the next minute. It's something I'm hoping to learn when we meet."

Viv nodded. "Personal force field, two precognitives, and... who's the last one?"

"Nyla Priest," I said. "Twenty-eight, lives with her mother in west Texas. Her mom is homebound and Nyla left school to care for her. I had to arrange for temporary care for the mother to get Nyla to agree to come. She's telekinetic."

"Seriously? That doesn't seem like a minor talent," Viv said.

"I don't know how powerful she is," I said. "I don't think she's any stronger than the average magus—not nearly as strong as a stone magus, definitely. That's another thing I'm hoping to learn about when they arrive."

"If they're cooperative," Judy said. "They agreed to come, but who knows what they'll think when they find out about the magical world?"

"Hey, you were all for this before," I said.

"I still am. But it's a lot to take in. They might not be thrilled at the idea of suddenly being part of a secret organization." Judy forked a quarter of a meatball up and stuffed it into her mouth.

"That's something I'll deal with," I said. "I choose to have faith that it will all work out."

Viv began ticking things off on her fingers. "Two precognitives," she said, "one telekinetic, one personal force field. Two people who can see through illusions. And someone who can detect lies. I still can't believe Detective Acosta turned out to have magic. He's the least likely person I would ever have imagined."

"Me too," Judy said. "Is he coming to your little meet-up, Helena?"

"I asked him," I said. "He said he'd think about it, but I think he'll come. He was trying to act like it didn't matter, but I think the idea intrigues him."

My phone beeped at me, signaling an incoming email. I whipped it out of my purse. "This could be her. Jun Li."

The message was short, almost abrupt, but I didn't mind. "She says there's a flight leaving at five o'clock tomorrow evening," I summarized aloud. "And that I'd better not be wasting her time."

"She didn't actually say that," Judy said.

"No, but there's all sorts of subtext." I held my phone so Viv and Judy could read the message. Judy snorted with amusement.

"I like her," she said. "She's ballsy."

"I don't care what she's like so long as she's willing to listen," I said. I swiftly replied to Jun and equally swiftly arranged for a plane ticket. "I don't know what people did before smartphones."

"They had to use payphones and were always late for things," Viv said.

"Tomorrow night," Judy said. "You think that's urgent enough to satisfy the oracle?"

"I don't know if the oracle cares about what I do with its auguries," I said, "but I prefer to think of it as being decisive."

"Then I'm glad we went out tonight," Viv said. "Jeremiah's on the hunt and he'll probably be out later than me."

"And tomorrow I'm—" Judy's mouth snapped shut, and she reddened.

"Seeing Mike?" Viv prompted. "Are you going to have a talk with him?"

Judy shrugged. "Maybe. If the timing's right."

"You have to be honest with him or you'll just be miserable."

"I know." Judy dragged her jacket on. "Let's get pedicures."

"I thought that was Viv's line," I said, scooting out of the booth.

"The student has become the master," Viv said.

7

The back wall of our living room was all glass windows looking out on the verandah and, past that, the wide sweep of lawn that was the back yard. With the lights on inside and the verandah dark, the windows became imperfect golden mirrors reflecting the living room: the long sofa upholstered in cream-colored suede, the shorter nut-brown love seats flanking it, the square table topped with coffee-and-cream streaked marble at the center of the grouping. The big white stone blocks that made up the fireplace looked yellow in their reflection, as did the screen of the TV above it. I'd lit the fire, thinking it gave the room a homey look, but now I wondered if it wasn't a bad idea. The living room was comfortable now, but it might become too hot when all of us were present.

Freezing rain lashed the windows, and the wind was a distant howl that rose and fell in pitch like a soprano warming up for a performance. I dragged two chairs away from the fireplace and arranged them along the fourth side of the table. That should give us enough room that nobody had to give up their personal space. I surveyed the arrangement with my hands on my hips and tried, for the tenth time, to stop second-guessing myself.

First on my list of worries was my choice of venue. I'd gone over half a dozen possibilities with Malcolm, none of which seemed right. A public meeting spot, like a restaurant, was a bad idea for the discussion we intended to have, and semi-public like a hotel conference room seemed too impersonal, not to mention being still too public. And I couldn't take them to the Gunther Node, because Lucia didn't know this meeting was happening.

That was second on my list, my concern about Lucia's reaction. She hadn't forbidden me to tell the other sports about the magical world, but I was sure she wouldn't be happy about it. She'd want to be in control of that discussion. It wasn't as if she was in charge of all magery...no, she was just one of the most powerful and influential custodians and not someone I wanted to have opposing me. But I knew Lucia well enough to know that even if she agreed to my plan, she'd throw up all kinds of resistance, and delay this meeting, and the oracle's guidance was clear. So I'd decided to take my chances with her.

So, after a long discussion, we came back to my first idea: have the meeting at my home. "It's private, it's comfortable, and it's a controllable situation," I'd said.

"I agree," Malcolm had said. "And I'll be there with you."

That had led to a short...not quite an argument, but a heated discussion, at the end of which my contention that the sports didn't need to feel overwhelmed by Wardens was countered decisively by Malcolm's flat assertion that we weren't going to have strangers in our home unless he was there to protect me against unknown threats. I'd have been irritated by it if I hadn't secretly wanted him there.

"Water bottles," I said.

"You're not going to rethink that again, are you?" Malcolm called out from the kitchen.

"No. Yes. I mean, no, serving something makes people feel more relaxed, and bottles are easier to manage than glasses." I walked around the corner into the kitchen and opened the refrigerator. "I was going to put them on the coffee table. What time is it?"

"7:45," Malcolm said. The doorbell rang, overriding him.

I gathered up an armload of water bottles and shut the refrigerator door with my foot. "That's Mangesh. Would you get the door, please?"

Mangesh and Malcolm entered the living room just as I finished arranging bottles on the table. Mangesh was, for once, dressed for a Pacific Northwest winter in a sweater over a button-down shirt, with an overcoat thrown over the ensemble. "Thanks for coming early," I said. "Is it as nasty out there as it looks?"

"Indeed. What disturbs me is that the weather is supposed to worsen, and as it is already bad enough to make me long for India, I cannot imagine what 'worse' would look like," Mangesh said, handing Malcolm his coat. "But I am eager to meet our counterparts. They all arrived?"

"The planes all landed on time, and Campbell Security says all four cars picked up passengers and took them to the hotel." I wrapped my arms around my waist and hugged myself. "I'm so nervous."

"Understandable. These people could be anything. Including uncooperative." Mangesh warmed his hands at the fireplace. "I choose to be optimistic."

"They were willing to come all this way," Malcolm pointed out, "which means they're unlikely to be antagonistic."

"I could explain everything to them," Mangesh offered.

I shook my head. "I'm the one who contacted them, and I feel responsible. Besides, the oracle gave me the auguries. I'll be fine. But...feel free to chime in if you feel motivated."

Mangesh nodded and took a seat in one of the chairs. Malcolm put his arms around me and briefly rested his chin on the top of my head. "You'll be fine," he murmured.

"I want so badly for this to go well. Even if I don't know why it matters. I hope they don't ask what we expect of them, because neither of the auguries revealed that."

"You are offering them a greater knowledge of the world and their part in it. I think that's enough for anyone." He kissed me and let me go.

"Thanks for staying. I know I said I wanted to do this alone, but I was lying."

He laughed. "It gives me something to think about that is not worrying about the attack tomorrow night."

An icy chill ran down my spine. "I'd almost forgotten. Is everything ready?"

"As ready as it can be. I wanted us to attack last night, but Lucia's information suggests tomorrow night is our best bet."

"Viv and Judy are coming over. I don't want to wait by myself."

"Excellent idea. I would rather you weren't alone."

The doorbell chimed again.

"I'll get it," Malcolm said, which was fortunate because I was frozen in place. After he left, I came to myself and turned around, assessing the room. Where should I stand? Or should I sit? I really didn't have a lot of experience acting as a hostess, and nothing in that experience had prepared me for the kind of meeting I was about to hold.

Distantly, I heard the door open, then close, and the murmur of voices. The front room was prettier even than the living room, but it was too small to comfortably hold eight people. What conclusions would they draw about me based on my home? It was large without being a mansion, in a neighborhood of similarly elegant houses, so obviously I was well-off. *Not* Professor X-wealthy, I reminded myself. Well, we were that wealthy, we just didn't make a show of it.

The noise of voices drew nearer, and I could distinguish Malcolm and an unfamiliar woman speaking with a Spanish accent. What on earth could they have found to talk about? Malcolm's manners were even better than mine, something I had to give grudging credit to his awful mother Madeleine for. Even so—

"—not a lot of time to spare for it, unfortunately," Malcolm was saying as he and a group of strangers entered the living room. He took a few steps toward me and clasped my hand in his. "Everyone, this is my wife, Helena Campbell, the one who brought you all here. Please, make yourselves comfortable."

"It is sad that you do not garden," an elderly woman said. I recognized hers as the voice Malcolm had been conversing with. She was short and round, the very picture of everyone's favorite grandmother—in fact, she reminded me strongly of my own grandmother before she'd gone to the assisted living center. She smiled and offered me her hand. "I am Ines Varnado. Gardening is my passion."

I retrieved my hand from Malcolm's and clasped hers. "I'm afraid my hours at my job are too long for me to be able to care for a yard this size. But I love the results. Thank you for coming."

"What job is that?" the next woman said. Her Asian features were sharp as if they'd been carved that way, but her voice was warm and compelling—or was that her magical talent?

"I'll...tell you all about my job later," I said. "Ms. Li. Thank you for coming on such short notice."

"I was intrigued," Jun Li said. "I hope your story continues to keep my interest."

I swallowed nervously and hoped it wasn't obvious. "I hope so, too. Ms. Priest," I went on, turning to the last woman. "I hope your mother is well."

"She's fine, thanks for asking," Nyla Priest said in a slow, Southwestern drawl. She was about my size, but paler of skin, though it was hard to tell because she was heavily freckled across her face and, when she removed her coat, her forearms. Short red hair curled wildly around her face. "You're younger than I thought." Her gaze flicked from me to Malcolm and back again, but not so swiftly that I couldn't guess what she was thinking: *she's way too young for him*. I wasn't offended. Malcolm was a lot older than me, but we'd found it didn't matter, and I didn't care what other people thought.

"This is quite a house," Victor Crowson said. I immediately saw why he could pass for someone half a decade older than eighteen: he was tall and heavyset without being fat, and his shaved head and trim beard made him look like Denzel Washington's younger and even more attractive brother. He offered me his hand without hesitation, which was at odds with the image I'd built up in my mind based on our email interaction. He was way more confident in person.

"It was Malcolm's childhood home," I said. "It feels welcoming to me despite its size."

"I think my apartment could fit into this room," he said with a smile that didn't hide any resentment. "Very nice."

"Thank you. Would you all like some water? And please, have a seat." Malcolm had already staked a claim to one of the love seats, for which I felt grateful. I took a bottle of water for myself and sat next to him. Jun sat in one of the chairs, while the other three took seats on the other couches. It looked like a casual choice, but my knowledge of Jun's talent made it seem deliberate, as if they were staying out of her range. I hadn't really noticed anything, but I also hadn't come very close to Jun…and now I wondered if that was significant. With luck, she would be cooperative, and I'd have more opportunities to figure it out.

I checked my watch. It looked like Acosta wasn't coming, after all. Just as I thought that, the doorbell rang again, and Malcolm excused himself. He returned almost immediately with Acosta in his wake. I'd never seen the detective in civvies before, and he looked surprisingly normal in jeans and a V-neck sweater under his detective's trench coat. "Detective Acosta," I said, causing the rest of the conversations to come to a halt. "Um, everyone, this is…Greg Acosta." I'd never actually said his first name before, and it felt so strange. "He's a police detective, but tonight he's just one of us."

"One of us," Jun said. "You still haven't said what gives us anything in common."

I took a drink of water to calm myself. "No, I haven't. But since we're all here, I think it's time."

"I thought it was obvious," Victor said. "We all have psychic powers, right?"

"Yes, but it's more than that," I said. "Let me tell you the story of how I found out magic exists, and after that…well, we'll see what other questions I can answer." I took a deep breath. "About two and a half years ago, I answered a Help Wanted ad in the newspaper…"

The story was surprisingly short, stripped of personal irrelevancies like my friendship with Judy and the way Malcolm's and my relationship had progressed from acquaintanceship to marriage. I focused on the general details, such as the beginning of the Long War some seven hundred years ago and the history of the factions, side-tracked into a short description of the Damerel rites that made someone a magus by implanting an aegis in their heart, explained what the oracle did, and concluded by explaining how the Mercy had made common cause with the intelligent invaders and was bent on destroying the Wardens.

When I finished, no one said anything. I immediately fell back into second-guessing myself. Had I said too much? Or, worse, said too little, and now they were all confused? I glanced at Malcolm, who'd kept his eyes on me the whole time. He smiled, and said, "I think that covers most of it."

"Except for what we have to do with all of this," Nyla said. Her accent made her sound like a hick, not very bright, but I'd seen how she watched the others instead of me while I was talking, and I was sure it was a mistake to assume that. "We have magic, but not…aegises, right?"

"Right," I said, relieved that it was a question I could answer. "We all are genetically different in a way that makes us immune to having our magic drained by an invader. That has a side effect of giving us a minor magical ability."

"And we have a strange reaction to being bitten by an invader, or so I'm told," Acosta said.

"How do you know this?" Ines asked. "You sound as if none of this is news."

Acosta smiled, a wry expression. "My introduction to the magical world was a lot more explosive than yours. Though I doubt I'd have believed it if someone had sat me down, all civilized-like, and told me what Ms. Campbell has just shared. For one thing, I didn't know I had magic until two days ago."

"And what magic is that?" Jun asked. She was leaning back in her seat and rolling her unopened water bottle between her hands, a calm gesture rather than a nervous one.

"I can tell when someone's lying." He was seated next to Jun in one of the wingback chairs, leaning a little to the side so his body was angled away from her. It was so casual it didn't even look like he was trying to stay away from her.

"That sounds useful to someone in your line of work," Victor said.

"Then we do not all have the same magic," Ines said.

"No," I said. "Mr. Wallach, the scientist who's been studying my—our situation, says the development of a magical talent depends on a person's individual genetics. He has a test that will identify that talent in genetic sports like us, so anyone else we bring into the secret won't have to guess at what they can do."

"Is that how you found us?" Nyla asked. "Some kind of magical test?"

I blushed. "All of you had come to some Warden's attention in some way to have a record in the Athenaeum—it's a repository of knowledge we use. Then I had Malcolm's company investigate the people I identified, to see if they had anything in common. And you four stood out."

"You invaded our privacy?" Jun exclaimed.

"It was not that kind of an investigation," Malcolm said.

"My people searched specifically for evidence that you had magical abilities, nothing more. And they determined that you knew you had magic and were using it to your benefit."

Jun's expression was hard, her lips pressed tight together. "I don't like being subject to any kind of investigation. It's underhanded."

"I'm sorry," I said. "Would you prefer I'd lied to you about how I found you? I haven't been anything but truthful. And the rest of what I have to say is important enough that I don't regret having invaded your privacy a little."

"Important, how?" Victor asked. "I'm just a small-time gambler who can see about fifteen minutes into the future. I don't see how that benefits anyone but me."

I hadn't had Campbell Security investigate Victor's finances, but I knew enough about his pattern of winnings to know he was a lot more than small-time. But I didn't mention this. "Actually, I don't either," I said. "The oracle gave me an augury that says all of us, all the genetic sports, are important to fighting the Long War. I haven't been able to figure out how yet, but this was the first step—meeting all of you, introducing you to the magical world."

"Which you are all taking in stride to a remarkable degree," Mangesh said. "I expected more refusal to believe."

Ines chuckled. "I have known of my abilities since I was seventeen," she said. "The news that there is more to magic than my simple talent is not news at all. But I would like to know what the rest of you are capable of." She nodded at Victor. "You are a fellow precognitive."

"Fancy word for seeing the future, but yeah," Victor said.

"I've already said Mangesh and I can see through illusions," I said. "And as he said, Det—Greg can tell when someone's lying."

Nyla held her water bottle at arm's length over the coffee table and opened her hand. The bottle hovered in midair, then slowly rotated around its short axis, tumbling gently like space debris. "I can't manage more than a few pounds," she said, "but I've been working on fine control. I have to be careful not to let Mom see me do it."

I swallowed my astonishment. I'd known Nyla's talent, but that wasn't the same as seeing it demonstrated.

Jun's face hadn't relaxed out of its stiff anger. She said, "If this is meant to make me feel like we're a big happy family, don't count on it."

"Ms. Li—" I began.

"I promised to listen. I'm still listening. I want to know what's so important it justified you prying into my affairs."

I took a deep breath. "The fight between the Mercy and the Wardens is not going well," I said. "The Mercy strike from the shadows, and because they used to be Wardens, they know far too much about the Wardens' secrets and their fighting tactics. I may not know how we sports can help in the fight, but I have faith in the oracle, and if it says we're important, I intend to figure out how. And I want your help. All of you."

The four exchanged glances. Mangesh looked impassive. Malcolm had his hand on my lower back, giving me emotional support, but said nothing. Finally, Victor said, "This is going to sound bad, but—what's in it for us? You're asking us to participate in a war that isn't our fight."

"It's everyone's fight. Most people just don't know about it. The point of the Long War, of Nicolliens and Ambrosites pushing back the invaders, is to protect people from being killed—people who don't have to know about the fight to be in danger from it."

"But you don't know what we can do," Nyla said. "I don't

like the idea of flailing around and maybe getting myself killed just because some oracle says I should."

Frustration, and despair, welled up inside me. I refused to let it affect my reaction. "Maybe you're right," I said. "Maybe it was too much to expect you all to feel any responsibility just because you have a magical talent. For me, it was exciting to know I have the ability to make a difference, but I'm surrounded by friends and family who all fight to protect humanity, every day. So all I'm asking is for you to consider it. Think about joining us. If you don't want to, at least now you know you're not alone."

Still no one spoke. I clenched my jaw to keep from babbling a further plea. Then Ines said, "If you have an oracle, why do you need a precognitive?"

She sounded curious, not judgmental, and I said in some relief, "Your talent isn't the same as the oracle's. The oracle can see farther into the future, but it takes effort to work out the auguries it gives. Whatever you and Victor see, it's less ambiguous."

"It sounds as if my talent is not the same as Victor's, even," Ines said, glancing at the young man. "I see some distance into the future, days or at times even weeks, but it is always contingent on events falling out in the most plausible way. Anyone can negate the future I see if they truly wish to."

"And what I see always happens, no matter how someone tries to avoid it," Victor said. He rested his large hands on his knees. "But I have to focus on one thing that's happening now to see its future." His gaze shifted to Jun, and I saw his eyes glaze over briefly, but he said nothing more.

Jun stood. "I want an augury," she said.

I blinked. "Ah…you mean right now?"

"Yes. If this oracle is so determined that we have some part to play, I want a confirmation of that."

I glanced at Malcolm, who shrugged. "I…guess that would be all right. I mean, the store is closed now, but that's more to give me a rest than because the oracle needs down time."

"I'm kinda curious about the oracle myself," Nyla said. She stood as well. "Let's all go. I can think of more than one thing I'd like a prophecy about."

This meeting had spiraled out of my control. I gave up. "All right. The car that brought you all is still out front, isn't it?"

The wind had picked up and now sounded like a whole chorus of sopranos providing mood music for a haunted house. The car, an oversized Ford Explorer, was parked in our driveway. Two other cars, a Subaru and a two-door coupe whose make I didn't recognize, sat at the curb, barely visible past the sleeting rain. The driver of the Ford was a blonde woman I recognized vaguely as a Campbell Security employee. She was doing a crossword by the cab light and got out of the car, pulling the hood of her anorak far down over her forehead, when we all trooped out front.

"Miss Randall will drive you to Abernathy's," Malcolm shouted over the wind, nodding to the driver. "We will meet you there."

"I'll take my own car," Acosta replied, indicating the Subaru. I hadn't thought he drove anything but his stereotypical detective's Buick.

"As will I," Mangesh said. I'd been about to invite him to ride with us, wanting to discuss what had happened, but it occurred to me he might want to be able to go home from the store. It was getting fairly late and I suddenly felt tired. But this had been my idea, and I was bound to see it through. No matter what happened next.

8

M alcolm and I waited for the other cars to leave before locking the house and getting into the Mustang. I slumped in the passenger seat and said, "How bad an idea was this?"

Malcolm laughed. "It's gone better than I expected. Nobody stormed out, and nobody refused to believe the truth."

I cranked the heat up to full and shivered. "That's a good point. I've always hated it in books where the protagonist takes two hundred pages to believe magic is real, no matter what evidence they're shown." I closed my eyes and massaged my temples against an incipient headache. "I guess I might have anticipated at least one of them wanting an augury. Maybe I should have suggested it myself."

"Their desire is not unreasonable. But it occurs to me that the oracle might charge them more than they have money for."

He backed out of the garage slowly. I felt the rear wheels

slide on the slippery driveway and took a moment to be grateful that Malcolm was driving.

"Not Ms. Li," I said. "She's loaded. Well, it doesn't matter. I'll do what I'm sworn to do and worry about the details later. I just wish I'd been able to present them with a specific request. You know—the oracle wants us to mount a vigilante attack on the Mercy's headquarters."

"Don't joke about that. I hate the thought of you involved in any kind of violence, love."

I shuddered. "So do I. I forgot my gun again."

"Helena, if you're not going to carry it, you might as well not have it."

"I know." I sighed and traced the line of chrome beneath the window with my forefinger. "I guess it makes me more uncomfortable than I thought it would. It's not like I object to guns in general, and I appreciate how yours has kept me safe. It just doesn't feel like me."

Malcolm squeezed my hand lightly. "I will never force you to go armed if it isn't what you want. But you've faced enough dangers that *I* feel comfortable knowing you can defend yourself. And...this isn't about my comfort."

"I'll try to remember next time." I pulled out my phone. "I just realized I should warn Judy that we're all coming over. She and Mike—"

I snapped my mouth shut on those words, but it was too late. "She and Mike, what? Mike who?" Malcolm said.

"It's nothing. Just...oh, hell. Judy and Mike Conti have been seeing each other."

"They *what?*" Malcolm exclaimed. "I thought she hated him."

"She doesn't hate him. Well, obviously not, if they're

seeing each other. It—Judy wanted it to be a secret. Promise you won't tell, or let Mike know that you know."

"Helena, how am I supposed to do that? Mike's my best friend. I can hardly pretend I don't know something this big."

I rested my hand on his thigh. "Of course you can. And it's not that big. Just…maybe Mike will tell you himself." If he and Judy worked things out, maybe neither of them would try to keep it secret.

Malcolm's brow furrowed. "Mike and Judy. I never would have guessed."

I didn't feel I should share any more details, but it was a relief not having to keep that secret from my husband. I loved being able to talk to Malcolm about anything.

I tapped out a message to Judy and waited, watching the darkened streets slip past. No response. After five minutes, I tried again; still nothing. I pocketed my phone and said, "Well, I tried. If it's a horrible surprise, it's not my fault."

"We don't have to go upstairs," Malcolm pointed out. "It's not really an intrusion."

"True." It still felt like an intrusion, since I'd once lived in the apartment over the store and could imagine how I would have felt hearing people tromping around downstairs after dark. We'd just have to make this quick.

We pulled into the parking lot at the rear of the store, trailed by Acosta and Mangesh. The Ford Explorer was already there, the engine idling. So was a car I didn't recognize, parked next to the beater nobody in the area was willing to claim ownership of. Malcolm's eyes narrowed as we pulled up next to the unknown car. "That's Mike's," he said.

"I guess Judy said he'd be over tonight." Specifically, she'd said she was going to tell him how her feelings toward him had changed. I hoped Mike's car still being there meant good things for both of them.

My four guests got out when we did. Victor had a gleam in his eye. "Nice car," he told Malcolm as we all hurried inside.

"Thanks. It's one of my indulgences," Malcolm said.

"Mine's a Camaro." Victor's gaze swept from the Mustang's nose to its tailpipe. "Not a lot of places to really open her up in Atlantic City, unfortunately."

I could see Malcolm's own eyes gleaming and forestalled half an hour's automotive talk by saying, "Let's make this quick, all right?"

I led everyone through the back hall, where stairs led up to Judy's apartment and a single door opened on the office. I had to admit Judy had had a point about having the desk facing away from that rear door. It wasn't hard to imagine someone sneaking in, even though the security on the outside door was the best Campbell Security could provide.

Ines regarded the office curiously. "It is not large, is it?"

"We don't need a lot of space for what we do," I said.

Nyla was looking at Silas's picture. I had a momentary urge to snatch it away from her, as if her regard were something disrespectful. But I didn't want to explain the wall safe behind it.

"Who's this?" she asked.

"Silas Abernathy. He was a custodian, years ago." I pushed open the door to the hallway and beckoned to Nyla to follow me. At the end of the hall, I switched on the lights, though they didn't do much more than cast deep shadows over the bookcases. To me, the dimness was comforting, as if someone had turned the store into a blanket fort like I'd made as a child. I wondered how my guests felt about it, whether they, too, were comforted, or just wished they could see more clearly.

I'd never realized just how crowded the stacks were with eight people passing through at once. The corridors formed by the bookcases were narrow enough that only one person could pass at a time, but what made it feel crowded was the noise of all those people shuffling along, breathing loudly enough to echo off the shelves, and their murmured conversations as they stopped to look at the books. I had to suppress impatient comments more than once. "Please, just come through to the front of the store," I finally said. "The books are unimportant unless the oracle has chosen them."

Once everyone was gathered near the counter, I turned to Jun and said, "If you want an augury, you need to write it down in the form of a question." I tore a page from the back of the augury ledger and ripped it in half, then handed Jun and Nyla each a half. I was going to need to buy a new ledger, we'd done that so many times. "And nothing starting with 'who?' or asking how to commit a crime."

"It will answer anything else?" Jun asked.

"No, sometimes it just chooses not to answer, but there's no way to predict those."

Jun regarded me narrowly. She turned away to write her question, shielding the paper with her hand even though no one was close enough to read over her shoulder. She folded the paper in quarters and handed it to me. Nyla, in contrast, wrote in big letters I could almost read from several feet away and didn't fold the paper at all. I indicated she should hold onto it for now.

"Thanks," I said to Jun. "Oh, and be prepared for it to cost a lot."

"Meaning that you'll extort money from me?"

I bit back an annoyed retort. "I don't set the prices. The oracle does. You're just going to have to trust that I don't lie about auguries in any way."

Jun's eyes narrowed again, but she nodded once, a curt gesture that conveyed both the meaning *I agree* and *You had better not be wasting my time.* I nodded back, took three steps, and the oracle's presence rose up around me.

A golden glow filled the air, soft like a sunset. I rarely did auguries after dark, and I'd forgotten how beautiful it was. The air smelled fresh like laundry just out of the dryer, filling me with memories of folding sheets with my mom when I was little. I breathed it in and felt some of my tension melt away. After a few seconds, I came out of my daze and unfolded Jun's paper. *Where is my mother's brooch?* I frowned. I'd expected her to ask something about whether she should trust me, or if joining the Wardens was the right thing to do. I didn't know what to make of this question.

"I hope this convinces her," I said as I paced the narrow corridors between bookcases. "I guess, if you give her an augury, and she interprets it and answers her question, it will be harder for her to argue that none of it is real. But that won't necessarily bring her into the Wardens' fold."

The oracle was silent, only half its attention on me. Ahead, blue light gleamed, and I walked faster. "Tomorrow night is the attack on the Mercy's stronghold, or headquarters, or whatever it is," I went on. "I hope the Wardens succeed. They've certainly received enough auguries…you've been so cooperative, it helps me feel less afraid for Malcolm. I know Lucia is confident that she's chosen the right time to attack, but I can't help thinking how disastrous it would be if some Mercy operative found out and warned them the Wardens were coming. I'll be glad when it's over."

The augury shone brightly in the golden ambience, a hardcover book missing its dust jacket. Imprinted on the tan binding was the title *In This House of Brede*. "It would be nice if Brede was a real house somewhere, and Ms. Li's mother's brooch was there," I said, opening the cover to find *Jun Li, $25* written on the title page in silver ink. "Nice and simple."

I looked around for a second blue glow, just in case, but it seemed the oracle wasn't going out of its way to be helpful tonight. "I was sort of thinking," I said as I walked back to the entrance—though the oracle wasn't laid out to have anything so simple as one entrance— "that maybe Ms. Li wouldn't take us seriously if you gave her a cheap augury. But I won't second-guess you."

No one had moved in the time I'd been gone, though Malcolm and Victor were talking in low voices off to one side, probably about cars. I handed Jun the book. "It's only $25."

Jun raised an eyebrow. "You said it would be expensive."

"I said it *could* be expensive. I never know how much an augury will be, unless the question has something to do with saving a life, and those are generally free. The oracle charges what it thinks is fair." I didn't actually know this, but it was a safe assumption.

Jun had a shiny black patent leather clutch dangling from her left wrist. She opened it and withdrew a twenty and a five. "Cash is acceptable?"

"Yes. We aren't set up to take debit or credit cards."

"Sounds inconvenient," Nyla said.

"Only for our customers, but my co-worker and I have discussed changing store policy to allow it. There's really no reason to reject any form of payment." We'd actually have to get approval from the Board of Neutralities to change that policy, which was the real reason we hadn't already done it—

the Board, with one notable exception involving me, changed for no one. But the sports didn't need to know that kind of detail.

Jun examined the book. "No dust jacket."

"The condition of an augury doesn't matter, only the contents." I felt defensive on the oracle's behalf; Jun had sounded simultaneously critical and amused, like a parent handed a macaroni necklace by a child and asked to pretend it's diamonds.

Jun just nodded and turned away, thumbing through the first pages of the book.

I turned to Nyla and held out my hand for her augury slip. "Should I be worried?" she said. "I didn't bring a ton of cash."

"I'm sure the oracle takes that into consideration," I said.

This time, I saw no blue glow anywhere. The air continued to glow gold and didn't turn red, the sign that the oracle refused to give an augury, so I set off in search of the book. Nyla's question was more in line with what I'd expected: *Should I join the Wardens?* "She's got it tough, though," I said. I folded the augury and tucked it into my pocket next to Jun's. "I don't know if she can afford to pay someone to care for her mother, if she has to be here. Though…I guess she doesn't have to be in Portland to work with the Wardens. She'd help whoever is in charge of her area."

It was the first time it had occurred to me that all these people had lives and jobs and families far from Portland, and discouragement filled me, followed closely by embarrassment. Despite what I'd told them, I'd been thinking, selfishly, that I'd get to know them all and maybe even become friends. But the oracle hadn't said we would be friends; it had said the sports were important to fighting the war. And that could happen anywhere.

I rounded a corner and finally saw the blue glow. This one, by contrast to Jun's battered book, was a hardcover in perfect condition, its dark blue cover shiny with newness. The title was *Jane, Unlimited*, and Nyla's name was inside, along with *$25*.

"Interesting," I said. "Very egalitarian of you, not to charge more or less."

When I handed the book to Nyla, she turned it over a couple of times as if looking for the augury to be printed on the dust jacket. "So I just…read the book?"

"Study it," I said. "Sometimes that means reading it through and taking notes on what pops out at you. Sometimes it means thinking about your question and then opening the book at random to see what a particular sentence or paragraph says. But generally it's more than just skimming it."

A loud clap startled me into looking at Jun, who'd slammed her augury shut and slapped it down on the countertop. "I've seen enough," she said. "I'll be leaving in the morning."

Gaping, I stammered, "But…you have your augury…"

"It doesn't answer my question."

"You have only had it for ten minutes," Mangesh said. "That is not enough time to know—"

"Believe me, I know," Jun said. "I'm not interested in being part of your club, or whatever you call it."

"It's not—" I began hotly, then took control of myself when I saw Malcolm draw breath to respond in anger. "Ms. Li, I'm sorry if we've wasted your time. Thanks for being willing to listen."

"I'm out, too," Victor said. "I won't say it's not interesting to know I'm not the only one with a talent, but it means nothing to me in any practical sense. And you haven't told us what, specifically, the Wardens want us for. So thanks for everything, but I'm going home."

I cast a despairing glance at Malcolm. He turned his attention to Nyla and asked, "What about you, Miss Priest?"

"It's *Ms.* Priest," Nyla said, but without rancor. She looked once more at the cover of her augury, tucked the book under one arm, and said, "I'm not making a decision until I've studied this. I asked a question, and it'd be rude to turn all y'all down without getting an answer first."

"And I," Ines said, "would like to have more information. I think it is remarkable that an oracle sees in me something of value to a greater cause. I would like to know what that is."

In despair at seeing my hopes falling apart, I said, "Ms. Li, Mr. Crowson—"

"You can call me Victor," Victor said. "Look, it's not that I don't believe all of this. I just don't see what it has to do with me. And you don't have an answer to that question."

"But—"

Malcolm put his arm around me, startling me because I hadn't been aware of him coming up behind me. "It's late," he said, "and this is a lot of information to take in. Your hotel is paid up through tonight at least. Give what Helena's said some thought, and return here tomorrow morning at nine. If you're still of the same opinion—" He nodded at Jun, whose chin lifted defiantly— "we'll bid you farewell, and no hard feelings."

"I won't change my mind," Jun said. "But I can give you that much."

"Thank you," I said.

Jun walked past me toward the rear of the store without waiting for my guidance. Rather than annoying me, it sent me into deeper despair. I should have waited until I knew what the oracle had in mind for the sports. Or waited until Lucia came up with something. Now half of them were going to walk away, and the other half were undecided, and none of them had jumped at the chance to be Wardens. I couldn't help feeling I'd let the oracle down.

The storm hadn't let up at all while we were inside. Icy rain stabbed my exposed face like a million needles, and it had crusted the windshield wipers and the door handles. I sat in the car and watched Malcolm defrost the wipers as the Explorer drove away. Mangesh hadn't said anything when he left, just shrugged, but that gesture told me he felt as defeated as I did. Acosta had been silent too, just nodded to me, and *that* gesture, I couldn't read. Well, this wasn't his fight, and he was already a Warden.

Malcolm threw himself into the driver's seat and held his hands over the heater vent. "This is some storm," he said, flexing his fingers. "I hope it blows itself out soon."

"Me too. I don't want to drive to work in this tomorrow."

"I'll take you if it comes to that. I know you don't like driving when the roads are icy."

"Thanks."

Malcolm put the car in gear and backed out of the parking lot. "Do you want to talk about it?"

I sighed and leaned against the window, then thought better of it—the glass was freezing. "What's there to talk about? It didn't work."

"That depends on the outcome you wanted. You succeeded in revealing the Wardens and the Long War without anyone telling you you're crazy."

"True, but…Malcolm, is it bad that I wanted them all to be eager to join the fight?"

"Helena, you have a passion for justice and a driving need not to sit still when evil threatens. It's not unnatural that you hope others feel the same way. But you know not everyone is like you."

"I know." I sighed again. "And Victor was right. I couldn't give them something concrete the oracle wants them to do. I knew that going in, but I guess I didn't realize how much it would matter."

"You have until tomorrow morning for them to think about it and possibly change their minds."

"Do you really think Ms. Li is going to change her mind? Really?"

Malcolm shook his head. "But something happened to her when she studied her augury. I was watching her, and there was a moment when something startled her. Something meaningful. I believe, contrary to her assertion, she learned something from the augury and is resisting admitting that to herself."

That raised my spirits a bit. "I wish I felt more comfortable talking to her. But that's probably her force field at work."

"I wish Victor would change his mind," Malcolm said. "He has the build to be a front line fighter, if not the temperament. If he were sufficiently motivated, that would make up the difference."

"Do you think—no, maybe not. I was going to say, do you think someone could really be a front line fighter without being a magus, but it occurred to me that you use magic in the fight, so it's probably still important."

"Possibly. I don't use magic nearly as often as you might think. Weapons training matters more. So someone like Victor, with the right training, could be as effective as any steel or wood magus."

"Except Victor's not interested."

Malcolm pulled into our driveway and waited for the

garage door to open before parking inside. "Let it go for tonight, love. You've done everything you can. The rest is up to them. Unless you think you should be allowed to make their decisions for them?"

I scowled as I shut the car door behind me. "Of course not. I just wish I'd been more convincing."

"You won't know if you were until tomorrow," Malcolm said. "And for all you know, this is the outcome the oracle had in mind."

I kicked off my shoes in the mud room and put my arms around Malcolm, felt him embrace me tightly. "Thank you for being so rational."

"Always," Malcolm said with a kiss. "Now, hot chocolate, and a warm bed."

"Rational *and* inspired. I knew there was a reason I married you."

9

The storm hadn't let up when I woke the next morning to Malcolm's alarm going off at 6:30. I stood at the bedroom window and looked out at the ice-covered world. The rain had turned to freezing sleet rather than snow, and ice had built up on the eaves and the edges of the roof. When I sat down to breakfast, I got a good look at the fir tree growing outside the breakfast nook. "It looks like someone used a giant flocking gun on it," I observed. "This is one of those days when Abernathy's should just stay closed. Nobody needs an augury so desperately they'd go out in this kind of weather to get it."

"I sympathize," Malcolm said. "Though I can't say the same for Campbell Security. I'll drop you off on my way in to work."

"Thanks." I took a bite of oatmeal. It warmed the deep-down chill I'd been feeling ever since leaving the warm cocoon of my lovely big bed that morning. "I almost forgot I need to be there by nine, to meet with the sports."

"There must be some other name you can give them. 'Sports' sounds a little cold."

"I didn't think I could get them to go along with 'Helena's Hooligans.'"

Malcolm laughed. "Definitely the wrong impression."

Traffic was light even at 8:30 that morning as Malcolm navigated the freeway and then the surface streets to Abernathy's. Mike's car was gone, which meant who knew what. I hoped it was a positive sign, but I was afraid it more likely meant that he'd broken things off with Judy. I suppressed irritation with Mike—how stupid of me to be angry over a hypothetical situation!—and resolved to let Judy tell me the details rather than battering at her.

I kissed Malcolm goodbye and made a dash for the back door, slipping on the icy concrete and nearly smashing my face into the bricks of the back wall. I paused inside the back hall, took off my hat, and ran my fingers through my damp hair to straighten it. Then, when my breathing slowed, I opened the office door. Judy was seated at the desk, typing intently. She didn't look up, didn't say anything, and my heart sank. "How's...you seem busy already," I said.

Judy shrugged. "Mail hasn't come yet, probably because ice skates aren't standard issue for postal workers. How did things go with the sports last night?"

That told me two things: first, that Judy wasn't interested in discussing what had happened with Mike, and second, that Malcolm was right that we needed a better way to refer to people like me. I'd had to explain to both Viv and Judy that 'sports' didn't mean basketball. "It was good and bad," I said. "Nobody ran screaming, but they weren't interested in becoming Wardens."

Judy nodded. She still didn't take her eyes off the screen. "That was always a possibility."

"It was still discouraging."

Judy didn't reply. I thought about my decision not to bug Judy about Mike and realized it was not the decision a friend would make. "So, what happened with Mike?"

Judy's shoulders hunched slightly as if I'd struck her. "Nothing."

"I know he was here last night. Did you tell him?"

Now Judy turned to face me. "How do you know he was here?"

"Some of the sports wanted auguries. Malcolm recognized Mike's car. Didn't you get my texts?"

Judy blushed angrily and closed her eyes as if praying for patience. "Great. So now everyone knows."

"I told Malcolm you didn't want it spread around, and you know he's not the type to blab."

"Yeah. I know." Judy sighed. "I didn't have the nerve to tell Mike. So nothing happened."

"Judy—"

"Don't say it. I know I'm being stupid."

"Not stupid. Just...nervous. But shouldn't that tell you this really is more than sex? If it matters so much how he reacts?"

Judy nodded. "You know what hurts, though? I forgot the Wardens are attacking the Mercy tonight. If something happens to him...Helena, I should have told him how I feel. What if I don't get another chance?"

She looked so upset my heart went out to her. I hugged her and said, "Don't think like that. Their team is strong, and Mike's going to be fine. They all will."

"I never guessed what you must go through when Malcolm goes on the hunt. And it's not even close to the same thing."

"Of course it is." I released her and dropped my purse on the desk. "You're coming over tonight, right? And you and Viv and I will eat chocolate and watch movies and wait for word together."

Judy nodded. Her cheeks were rosier than usual. "But nothing depressing. Something with kissing or explosions or both."

"I'm not sure anything fits that description, but we'll see what we can find."

The mail carrier still hadn't arrived when we went into the front of the store. I checked my watch. "It's 8:47. The sports will be here soon."

"They will?"

I perched on the stool, which was even colder than usual, and told Judy everything that had happened the previous night. Judy leaned against the nearest bookcase and listened intently. When I finished, she said, "It sure doesn't sound hopeful."

"I know, right?" I huffed on the glass countertop and polished a smear with my sleeve. "But they're coming here this morning, so I choose to have hope."

"I don't know. Your Ms. Li sounds like a real hardass."

"Maybe. How much of that is her talent? It can't be easy, always pushing people away without meaning to. I don't think she has a lover, even. Maybe she's just stiff and surly because she's lonely and doesn't know how else to deal with that."

Judy snorted. "That's wishful thinking. You shouldn't indulge in that."

"I know." I sighed so deeply it left another cloud of condensation on the glass I had to wipe away. "I've decided not to expect anything of them, just to make it clear that they can talk to me at any time, no conditions."

Movement on the street outside drew my attention, and my heart gave a thump when I recognized the Ford Explorer and its blonde driver. "This is them," I said, and went to unlock the front door.

Four shapes hurried from the car to the door, which I opened as soon as they neared. "Welcome to Abernathy's," I said. "Again. I almost feel I should apologize for the weather."

"It is very different from Phoenix," Ines said with a smile. "We do not see such rain except for the monsoons, and those are warm rains that last only a short time."

"Mangesh says the same about the rains of India, though those are as persistent as Portland's," I said. "This is Judy, my co-worker." I introduced each of the four, keeping my eye on Jun in the hope I might read her intentions. She didn't look angry or receptive or anything but neutral. I decided I shouldn't take that as a good sign.

"I'm sorry I can't offer you all seats," I said when the introductions were over. "Come back into the office, it's warmer." Abernathy's was never too cold or too hot, but in weather like this, I always felt as if the ice crept inside and made the front room chilly.

Judy and I dragged the chairs from the break room into the office, which made for enough seats for four people. I perched on the desk, and Victor gestured to Judy to take a seat while he leaned against the wall. "So," I said. "You've had time to think about all this. It's still true that I don't know what the oracle has in mind for us, but I don't think that should be a barrier to you becoming Wardens. But it's up to you. I just want you to know that whatever you decide, you're welcome here any time, and if there's anything I can do for you, just ask."

Ines and Victor exchanged glances. Nyla, who'd brought

her augury with her, flipped the pages idly before settling it on her lap again. Jun had her gaze fixed on Silas's photo, her lips pinched and thin like she intended never to speak again. Finally, Victor said, "I don't know. I've given it a lot of thought since last night, and…honestly, I'm not the guy you want. I'm not the hero type. It's cool that you asked me here, and I won't say I don't like knowing there's other people like me in the world. But I'm not your guy."

I opened my mouth to protest, but closed it before any ill-advised words could emerge. Malcolm had been right that the decision was theirs, and it was an insult to try to convince Victor that all his pondering on the subject was misguided or wrong. "I understand," I said instead. "I'm sorry, because I think otherwise, but I understand."

"Me, I do not know what good I am to the Wardens," Ines said. "But I like the idea of being part of this cause. I cannot stay away from home long, but if you learn what the oracle wants, I will help."

It wasn't the wholehearted enthusiasm I'd hoped for, but I'd take it. "Thank you, Mrs. Varnado."

"You will call me Ines," she said with a smile. "And perhaps someday I will convince you to garden."

That made me laugh. "I wouldn't count on it, but it's not impossible."

Nyla cleared her throat. "I spent most of the night studying this," she said, tapping the cover of her book. "It's a weird story even if it's not an augury. And I think it's going to take more than one night for me to really understand it. But the truth is, if I believe what you've told us, and believe this store is really an oracle, then the next step is believing I have a part to play in the war." She shifted in her seat. "Thing is, I've got more responsibilities than this one. My mom isn't well, and

I'm who she counts on to care for her. I don't think I can do both. Sorry."

"I understand," I said. "You have to do what's best for your family."

"Yeah." Nyla really did look as if she regretted her words. I thought about offering to continue to pay for care for her mother, but that would have been too much, not to mention making me a liar. Money couldn't make Nyla's responsibilities go away, not even a lot of money.

I turned my attention on Jun. "Ms. Li? Do you still feel the same?"

Jun was sitting directly to my left, still staring at Silas. "Who was he?" she asked without looking at me. "This Silas Abernathy. Someone important?"

"The store used to be in London, and when World War II began, the oracle instructed him to move it here. It was a huge task, and Silas never gave up on it even when it was dangerous. Then, a few years later, he realized his destiny was to become a magus, which meant he abdicated his position as custodian. He wrote some books that have been a comfort and a guide to me in fulfilling this role." That reminded me that I hadn't read Mr. Briggs' diary yet. I decided to ask Judy later what she'd learned from it.

Jun nodded once, slowly. "So, he gave his life to the Long War," she said.

"Um…yeah, I guess you could say that. He was more or less born to be the custodian of Abernathy's, and when he quit doing that, it was to fight the Long War in a different capacity."

"And you," she said, finally looking at me, "you've also dedicated your life to this fight."

That startled me. "I…hadn't thought of it that way, but

that's true. I'll be custodian of Abernathy's until…well, until something changes, or I die."

"And that's what you're asking of us. To sacrifice our lives to this cause."

"Of course not," I said, and stopped, struck by realization. It *was* what I was asking of them, if only indirectly, because this fight wasn't something you could just walk away from once you were part of it. "I mean—you make it sound like a death sentence."

"Which it is, in a way."

I rallied with, "Aren't there things you've already committed yourself to? How many of them are as important as saving humanity?"

Jun rolled her eyes. "So dramatic. The truth is, you're asking for a commitment I'm not prepared to make. I have a life. This Long War of yours isn't compatible with it." She stood. "Thank you for your hospitality. It's been nice to get to know all of you. But this isn't the life I want."

I stood as well. "I can appreciate that."

Her eyes widened as if I'd surprised her. Maybe she'd expected me to argue more. I offered her my hand, and after a moment's pause, she took it.

"I hope this wasn't too much of an interruption to your schedule," I said, sincerely.

"No," Jun said. "And I really am glad to know I'm not the only one."

It was the nicest thing she'd yet said, and it left me feeling in charity with her. "So…you're all flying out today?"

"Maybe," Victor said. "The hotel concierge said a lot of flights have been cancelled due to the storm and ice."

"I'll let the hotel know you can stay another night if you need to. I hope it won't be necessary." Deep in my heart, I hoped it would be necessary. But that was a foolish hope, because one more night wasn't going to change anyone's mind.

I led the way back to the front door, where I shook hands with everyone and thanked them again for coming. "And remember, you can reach me any time if there's anything you want to talk about, or have questions—just anything."

"I will certainly call you, if you do not call me first," Ines said with a wink. The others said goodbye and hurried out the door to the waiting car.

Judy watched them through the plate glass window, waving half-heartedly. "I know I said you shouldn't get your hopes up," she said, "but now I think they could have been more enthusiastic."

"It was always their decision, Judy."

"I know. But...maybe it's just that I've known about the Long War practically my whole life, but I can't imagine knowing about it and not wanting to be part of the fight."

I leaned against the door. "Why only practically?"

"Wardens don't tell their kids about the Long War or magic or anything until they're old enough to keep the secret. Nobody wants kindergarteners babbling about how their mom can levitate stuff, and maybe get mundane officials or psychiatrists involved."

"That makes sense." Not for the first time, I pictured myself with a baby and wondered what that would be like. I didn't want to hand my child off to a nanny, but I wasn't sure how practical it would be to have an infant in Abernathy's. Or maybe it would be easy, and I'd just wear the kid in one of those baby slings that looked so comfortable. The oracle might even be interested in my child.

The door bumped me as someone tried to open it. I stepped away and held the door for the mail carrier, who wore a yellow rain slicker and looked miserable. He pulled a handful of bills and mailers from beneath the slicker and handed it to me.

"Thanks for being so careful with the mail," I said. "I'm sorry you have to be out in this weather."

"Me too," the man said with a tired smile. "Makes me look forward to July."

When he was gone, I dropped the handful of mail on the counter and sorted through it. "Do you think there will be fewer people in today, or more? What with the attack happening tonight, I mean?"

"I think," Judy said, eyeing the rain-soaked street, "it's going to be fewer, and they're going to be very wet."

My ANXIETIES GREW as the day wore on. Almost no one came in, and none of the people who did wanted to chat. By 3:40 I'd started looking at my watch every ten minutes, wishing I had the power to command it to stand still. By 5:25 Judy and I had stopped talking to each other, each of us caught up in our private thoughts. At 6:00 I said, "Come over at eight, all right?" and Judy simply nodded in reply.

Dinner was a quiet affair. I felt too keyed up to cook, and Malcolm was busy with last-minute preparations, so I heated up some leftovers and we ate in front of the television. I couldn't focus on the show, which was a rerun of some sitcom I hadn't cared about when it was new. When I took a bite of my goulash and discovered it was room temperature, I realized I'd been so caught up in my thoughts I'd forgotten to eat. I set the plate aside and pulled up my legs to sit cross-legged on the couch. "Malcolm?"

"Yes?" His empty plate lay on the coffee table before him.

"You *do* feel confident about this, right?"

Malcolm drew me into his arms and kissed me, the lightest touch of his lips to mine. "I do," he said. "Lucia has planned for every contingency, and my team, for one, is at its peak."

"That's a relief. And success will mean destroying the Mercy."

"Or at least weakening them so they will be less of a threat while we mop up the rest of their organization."

I nestled closer to him. "What makes this location so special?"

Malcolm shifted so we were lying together on the couch and turned off the television. "It's on a large node, Neutrality-sized. How much do you know about how invaders access our world?"

"Not much, except that they slip through cracks between theirs and ours."

"That's mostly true. The larger the invader, the bigger the crack they need to fit through. And the intelligent invaders— we learned from interrogating traitors that the intelligent ones need access to a sizable node in order to cross over."

I shuddered. "Doesn't that mean they could come through here? Or at the Gunther node?"

Malcolm stroked my hair, a calming gesture. "There are many layers of protection to prevent that happening. The wards on Abernathy's, in particular, are set up to stop invaders from getting in. And all the nodes under Warden control are similarly protected. After the Mercy made that big push to take over the North and South American neutralities, the Wardens went to a lot of trouble to regain control over the captured nodes."

That, I remembered. Malcolm had been gone frequently

as part of this effort. "But the Mercy stripped most of those nodes of their *sanguinis sapiens*. Would that make them unusable by the invaders?"

"It does, but what we were concerned about is the nodes they didn't drain. Almost all nodes big enough to be Neutralities are known quantities, but nodes grow and shrink as time passes, and we couldn't be sure we'd regained control over all the big nodes. And as it turned out, that was true. Nobody knew about the node in Montana the Mercy controlled. It took several auguries, Lucia said, to identify it. But that's not what you were asking."

"Right. What makes this node special?"

Malcolm's breath stirred the hair on my forehead. "It's big and it's isolated, meaning the Mercy doesn't have to depend on illusions to protect itself from mundane authorities. That frees up resources for them to devote to fighting the Wardens, like directing invaders to places that are poorly defended, or attacking people high in the Nicollien or Ambrosite ranks. But most importantly, it's big enough to allow the intelligent invaders access to our world. And those invaders are dangerous not just for being large versions of their stupider cousins, but for their ability to organize their attacks more directly. Lucia thinks this is the only node in North America controlled by the Mercy that's large enough to allow the intelligent ones through. And that means if we can shut it down, the Mercy will lose critical resources."

"And it might mean destroying them entirely."

"Right." His arms closed more tightly on me. "I wish I could tell you how long this will take."

"Me too. But I promise I'll be waiting for you when you get back."

"You shouldn't stay up all night, love."

I turned in his arms to face him, though he was close enough that his features blurred in my sight. "As if I could sleep with you gone, under those circumstances."

He smiled, which looked so comical at that distance I laughed. "I can understand that," he said, and kissed me again. This time it was long, and intense, and I scooted up to kiss him back. He ran his hands down my back and lower. "We don't have time," he murmured.

I worked my arms around behind his neck and went on kissing him. "We have *some* time."

I felt him tugging at my sweater and wriggled until he could get it off me. "Upstairs?" he said.

"This is fine right here," I said, and then we were done talking.

Later, snuggled up against him, I sighed in deep contentment and said, "I feel better now."

"I'll take that as a tribute," Malcolm said with a chuckle.

I poked him between the ribs. "You should. And now we ought to get dressed so Judy and Viv don't walk in on us like this."

Malcolm sat up, dislodging me, and handed me my clothes. "I'll call you when it's all over. I really don't anticipate this taking until morning."

"I'm glad. I'll be waiting for your call."

I got dressed while Malcolm ran upstairs to change into fatigues, then I gathered up his discarded clothes and carried them to the laundry hamper. When I returned to the living room, Malcolm was putting on his boots, and his weapons were spread out on the breakfast table. I touched the hilt of one of his steel knives, still his primary weapons against invaders. Tonight, though…

"You'll mostly be fighting humans tonight, right?" I asked.

Malcolm looked over at me. "Does that bother you?"

"I guess what bothers me is that it doesn't bother me more. I should be upset that you'll probably kill other humans tonight, but then I remember what the Mercy has done to people I care about. How some of the people you'll face tonight might have tried to kill you. And then I just want it to be over, whatever it takes."

Malcolm crossed the living room and put his arms around me. The tender gesture made me feel so secure tears rose to my eyes, and I blinked them away so he wouldn't think I was crying from fear or sorrow. "You have a generous heart," he said, "and I have never felt so glad to have found you than I do right now."

I hugged him back. "Be safe. And give the team my best wishes."

He nodded. "I love you, Helena."

I walked with him to the garage door and waved goodbye as he pulled out of the driveway. The rain was still icy, but it wasn't falling as heavily as before, and I chose to take it as a good omen.

10

I went back into the kitchen and got out a bowl and a bag of microwave popcorn. My watch said it was 7:43, and soon Judy and Viv would be here, and we'd watch a stupid movie and gorge ourselves on junk food and pretend this was a normal night.

Viv arrived a few minutes before eight. Her cerulean hair was damp from rain, and her eyes were red-rimmed. "I have the most awful feeling," she said. "I'm afraid Jeremiah won't come back."

"That's just fear talking. Did you bring chocolate?"

Viv held out a paper grocery bag spattered with rainwater. "I might have gone a bit overboard with shopping."

I took the bag and nearly dropped it from its unexpected weight. "I choose to believe there's no such thing as too much chocolate."

"But I'm serious, Hel," Viv went on. She hung her raincoat on a peg in the mud room and said, "I hate it when he goes hunting, but I've never been this afraid for him. I think it's a premonition."

"Viv, you don't believe in premonitions."

"But I do believe in the oracle, and Jeremiah wouldn't tell me about the last augury he got. He went all silent and distant when I asked him about it, and changed the subject. I think it told him he's in danger, and he didn't want me to know."

I set the bag on the center island of the kitchen and pulled out colorful sacks of every kind of M&M imaginable. "Jeremiah's not stupid. If the oracle warned him he might not come back from this, he'd take precautions."

"He's not stupid, but he's also got no sense of self when it comes to the Long War. I think he'd give up his life if it would make a difference." Tears welled up in Viv's eyes. "And he wouldn't tell me if he thought that was likely, because he knows I wouldn't let him go without a fight. He might even think he was doing me a favor by not telling me he's going to die."

Someone knocked on the front door. "He's not going to die, Viv," I said, opening the door. "Judy. Tell Viv Jeremiah isn't going to die tonight."

"I can't do that. There are no guarantees when it comes to a fight," Judy said. She held several six-packs of Diet Dr. Pepper and Diet Coke and the shoulders of her gray wool coat were damp. "My father never promised he'd come back, in the years when he was a front-line fighter. I got used to it."

"Yes, but Viv thinks she's had a premonition."

"Oh, *that*," Judy said. "That's just fear talking. Sure, it's dangerous, but if there's no guarantee that someone will come back, there's also no guarantee that they won't." She set the drinks down on the island, yanked a can free, and drank half of it in a series of gulps like it was alcoholic and she was determined to get drunk as fast as possible.

As if she'd read my thoughts, she said, "I thought about bringing wine instead, but I want to be sober in case anything bad happens. And I don't think any of us want to sleep tonight."

"Good point," Viv said, taking a can of Diet Coke. "Let's watch something stupid. That *Baywatch* movie has sexy guys running around half-naked."

"I like that suggestion," Judy said, swigging the other half of her can and opening a second.

I found the remote control and searched for the movie. Sexy guys…well, I had my own sexy guy now, and he'd proved just an hour ago why I'd never go looking for anyone else, but there was something about looking at an attractive male figure that was fun in a different way. And maybe it would be a distraction.

It only took about half an hour for me to realize it was a disaster instead. The movie wasn't solid enough to keep my attention, which kept wandering to Malcolm and worrying about where he was even though I knew they wouldn't attack until midnight. I ate handfuls of pretzel M&Ms until I felt sick, drank Diet Coke until I was jittery and needed to pee, and wished guiltily that my two best friends were gone so I could curl up in bed and indulge in some anxious crying.

Finally, Judy said, "I'm sorry, but this movie is too dumb even for me," and turned off the television.

I breathed out a sigh of relief. "I'm glad you took action."

"I'm not," Viv said. "Now I have nothing to distract me." She turned on Judy. "So, what happened with Mike? You didn't tell him?"

Judy reddened. "He came over and…we didn't do much talking about anything. I think he was worried about the attack and wanted something good to think about instead. And I thought, what if I tell him I want more from this relationship, and it distracts him so much he makes mistakes and gets hurt? Or gets someone else hurt? But I didn't think—I mean, I was worried enough about him that it slipped my mind that I might not get another chance. If that makes sense."

"Sure it does," Viv said. "But if I can't worry, neither should you. We're talking about experienced fighters who've come through worse challenges than this."

"Is that really true, though?" I asked. "We don't know everything they've faced. Maybe this *is* the worst challenge."

"Nothing we can do about it," Viv said.

"No more worries about premonitions?" Judy asked.

"I'm still worried. But I've gained some perspective. I've done everything I can for Jeremiah, and now it's up to him and Fate." Viv took a drink and looked surprised to discover her can was empty. "And now I need to pee," she said, rising and tossing her can in the recycling bin on her way to the bathroom off the kitchen.

"I guess she's right," I said. "Worrying won't help them. It's just—I really hate this. I feel like I ought to be some kind of kick-ass heroine, facing down monsters by Malcolm's side."

"You do more for the Long War every day just being Abernathy's custodian," Judy said. "And it's not like you haven't faced danger in that capacity."

"I know. But I don't feel very heroic now." I stood and hurried to the bathroom, passing Viv, who looked more relaxed now that she'd relieved herself. I did my business and felt more relaxed myself.

When I returned, the TV was on again, and the credits for *Charlie's Angels,* the one with Drew Barrymore, were rolling. "Not quite as dumb, and it's hot women instead of hot men, which I realize none of us are as interested in, but at least we know what we're getting," Viv said as I took my seat.

I curled up in my corner of the couch and let my mind drift. I didn't know what time it was, and I didn't want to find out even though my watch was right there. If I kept checking the time, it would take forever to reach midnight and the point at which I would really start worrying.

"I forgot to ask," I said to Judy. "Did you read any more of Mr. Briggs' diary?"

"That sounds vaguely dirty," Viv said. "Reading someone else's diary."

"He's dead, and he was a custodian," Judy said, grabbing another handful of peanut butter M&Ms. "That makes his diary fair game. And no, I haven't had time. I really don't think there's going to be anything useful in it. Nathaniel was closemouthed enough that I doubt he'd have written about the blackmail, even in his private journal."

"I was more hoping he'd written why he advertised for help in the paper." I washed down candy with more Diet Coke and burped. "Though I don't know that that matters, either."

"It could tell you if the oracle had guided him, and maybe knew who you were," Viv said. "Maybe you have a destiny."

"Ugh, I hope not. People with destinies often end up dead."

"I agree," Judy said. "I think destiny is just shorthand for being unable to choose your life. And isn't it...I don't know. Better—more noble, maybe?—if you do the right thing without being forced to by destiny?"

"I never thought about it like that before," I said. "Maybe the oracle did know how to manipulate my life to make me custodian, though I have a hard time believing it. But everything I've done since then has been up to me."

"You *think*," Viv said, gesturing at me with her can. "How would you be able to tell the difference?"

"I—" I stopped mid-sentence. "I don't know. I guess because the oracle has given me auguries once or twice, and if it were guiding me, you'd think it would provide them more frequently."

"Or you're just naturally inclined to do what it wants."

That was a creepy thought. "I don't know if I like the sound of that."

Viv shook her head. "No, see, it's like how some people want to be doctors or teachers, right? Their personalities are geared toward taking care of people. And you're suited to being Abernathy's custodian. No destiny, just that tendency you have to leap into action when evil rears its ugly head."

I blushed and ate some more M&Ms. "That usually gets me into trouble."

"And out of it again," Viv said. "Face it, you're one of those people who can't stop being helpful." She ruffled my hair, and I ducked away from her hand, mock-snarling.

Judy rose abruptly and began pacing. "What's wrong?" I asked.

"I'm just anxious. All this talk about destiny and fighting evil...for once I wish I was a front line fighter. Except I don't."

"Was there ever a chance you could be a magus? Or did you start studying to be Abernathy's custodian young?" I no longer felt weird alluding to the fact that if I hadn't come along, Judy would be in my position now.

Judy snagged a handful of popcorn and ate it one kernel at a time, tossing each one into her mouth like she was shooting free throws. "I didn't qualify. That's when my father suggested I train for the custodianship."

"I'd think someone like you, from a long line of magi, would be a no-brainer," Viv said.

"I was physically suited to it, but I didn't want it badly enough. That matters when it comes to the aegis. You have to want to wield magic more than anything." Judy shrugged. "I never did dream of becoming a magus like most Wardens' kids do."

I remembered watching Malcolm go through the Damerel rites to have his second aegis implanted, how excruciating it had looked. "What happens if you go through the rites anyway? I mean, if you're unsuited to being a magus?"

Judy stopped pacing and lowered herself to sit cross-legged on the floor by the coffee table. "Death, usually. That doesn't happen often these days because they're so good at winnowing out candidates. But you get people who slip through the cracks, or people who insist on undertaking Damerel even if signs all point to disaster, and only a fraction of those survive."

I leaned my head back against the couch and stared at the ceiling. "Mr. Wallach said my mutation means the Damerel rites would probably kill me, but Mangesh survived and I don't think anyone noticed anything strange. So we still don't know everything."

"If they ever develop a technique that gives them a one hundred percent survival rate, maybe they'll figure it out," Judy said.

Silence fell. I went back to watching the movie. For all the fight scenes and explosions, it was oddly soothing. I glanced at my watch. Just past nine o'clock. This was going to be the longest night of my life.

We watched the movie, which took us to 10:42, and then my suggestion of *His Girl Friday* was shouted down in favor of *Austenland,* which was funny enough I forgot to check my watch until it was over. Then I felt as if someone had kicked me in the stomach. "It's 12:33," I said.

Viv and Judy went silent. I was sure I looked like they did —mouth slackly open, eyes wide and pupils dilated. I unclenched my hands and said, "It's going to be all right. Malcolm said he'd call when it was over."

Judy nodded. Viv stood and walked to the window, whose blinds were drawn against the freezing rain still pattering at the glass. "Why can't it just be over?" she exclaimed.

"Because the invaders are too stupid to give up," Judy said.

Viv made an impatient gesture. "This war has been going on for over seven hundred years, and nothing's changed. People are going to go on fighting and dying for another seven hundred years because these alien creatures think they deserve to conquer our world. What did you say that invader told you, Helena? That there are millions of the little ones, all slavering to get a toehold in our reality, and all it takes is time?" Her voice was wobbly with tears. "We can't win this."

"Viv, *no,*" I said, jumping up to put my arms around her. "Things *have* changed. The Wardens get smarter and more efficient all the time. You can't think like that or the invaders really will have won."

Viv shook her head violently. "It doesn't matter what I think. I'm just one person, and I'm not even a fighter. It just makes me so mad that some people think the invaders are right, and Malcolm and Jeremiah and everyone are off wasting time and energy fighting *them* instead of stopping the invaders. It really sucks."

Judy came to stand beside us. "It does," she said. "But that's why this fight tonight is so important. If they can break the Mercy, they'll gain an advantage over the invaders. And our Wardens know this. They know what's at stake. That makes a difference."

I hugged Viv more closely, and she put her arms around me, hugging me back. "Malcolm said he didn't think it would take long. An hour, maybe. He says fights always feel long when they're happening, and afterward you realize it was only minutes."

Viv drew in a shaky breath. "I'm sorry," she said. "I'm so worried."

"Let's sit and talk about something else," I said.

"But no more movies," Judy said. "I think that would just drive me nuts."

In the end, we didn't do much talking. I stopped needing to check my watch every few seconds, mainly because I felt I'd reached a point where I was wound so tight I didn't have room for more worry. I wished Judy had brought Mr. Briggs's diary so I could read it; that felt like the right kind of distraction.

Time slipped past unnoticed. I got up and brought us water bottles, which eased the pain in my stomach from too much junk food. I happened to see the clock on the range when I was in the kitchen. 1:24. I closed the refrigerator and headed back to the living room. That might mean the attack was taking longer than expected, or it might just be the beginning of a long night, but either way there was nothing I could do about it.

Somehow, we got on the topic of past boyfriends, current loves being too painful a subject, and that managed to cheer me up. Mainly this was because Viv had a way of making all her past relationships sound both charming and funny. "And then there was Sid," she said. "After Ezra, but before Jake."

"I think I need a diagram," Judy said.

"No, Sid was easy to remember. His real name was Henry, but he liked Sid Vicious, which should have told me everything I needed to know about him."

"I thought you liked the Sex Pistols," I said.

"Yeah, but every poser who thinks he's a rebel idolizes Sid Vicious. It's been done to death."

"I dated a guy named Mick who said he was going to be a rock star someday," Judy said. "That was in my rebellious phase. I don't think Mick knew which end of a guitar to strum."

"I feel so out of place," I complained. "I never went through a rebellious phase. My worst relationship was with Chet, and he was just a loser, not a punk rock wannabe."

"I apologize for introducing him to you," Viv said. "Big mistake."

"Well, it was my fault for sticking with him at all." I giggled and clapped my hand over my mouth.

"That's funny now?" Viv said. "I guess it's been long enough for you to gain perspective."

"Not that. Malcolm dangled Chet off a twelve-story building after he beat me." That beating had been terrifying and nearly killed me, and I hadn't realized the horror of the memory had faded so much.

Viv gasped. Judy toasted the absent Malcolm with her can. "That should have told you right there Malcolm was the man for you," she said.

"It should have. I was so busy being preoccupied with

having a crush on him I didn't realize he felt the same about me." And then we'd fallen in love, and now—

Someone knocked on the front door. It was such a normal sound, not timid, not aggressive, that I sat staring at Viv and Judy for a few seconds without moving. I checked my watch. 2:31. "Who...?" I said.

"Answer it," Judy whispered. She was paler than usual and her hand had closed tightly on her can, crumpling the aluminum. Viv had her eyes closed and her lips were moving soundlessly.

I stood and discovered my legs were shaking enough that I needed to steady myself on the back of the couch before I could walk. Then I crossed the living room to the short hallway that led past the formal dining room into the front room, small and elegantly decorated for visiting with people we didn't really care about. The blinds were drawn here, too, and I couldn't even see lights from someone's car pulled up at the curb. As I put my hand on the doorknob, the person knocked again, more loudly this time, and my heart started trying to break through my ribcage. Swiftly I shot back the dead bolt and opened the door.

Several people stood there, all of them known to me. My eye fell first on Jeremiah, who had a bandage wrapped around his upper left arm but otherwise looked uninjured. Mike stood next to him, his hand raised to knock again. There were traces of blood on his forehead and in the roots of his sandy hair. Behind him, Derrick and Hector hovered. All of them looked grim.

It took me a moment to realize what was wrong with that picture.

"Where's Malcolm?" I said. I craned my neck to look past the four toward the driveway. "What car...where is he?"

Nobody spoke. I felt the blood drain from my face and realized I was gripping the side of the doorway so hard it hurt. "No," I whispered.

Mike took half a step forward. "Helena, I'm sorry," he said in a low voice. "Malcolm is dead."

11

White static filled my vision. In the distance, I heard voices saying my name. I blinked, and discovered Mike had his hands under my arms, holding me up. "I'm fine," I said, stepping away from him before realizing that no, I was not fine, I was never going to be fine again. "I—come in, it's freezing." Why I could think of stupid politenesses at a time like this, I didn't know, but I had to cling to something so I would stop hearing those three words playing a demented chorus in my ears.

"Helena, you need to sit down," Jeremiah said. I obediently sat on one of the blue and gold brocade sofas near the door and clasped my hands in my lap. The cushions were comfortable even though we almost never used this room. Malcolm had—

I sucked in a deep breath and realized I was shaking. "He's not dead," I said stupidly. "He can't be dead. He was here just a few hours ago, he had all those weapons, you must be wrong."

"I saw him go down," Mike said in the same low voice.

"*You're wrong!*" I screamed, and burst into painful tears.

Someone put her arms around me, and I smelled Viv's fruity perfume. "Give her room," she said. I couldn't see for crying, so I didn't know if they obeyed and didn't care.

Over my noisy sobs, Jeremiah said, "He was guarding the retreat along with a handful of others. All of them were overwhelmed. We wouldn't have left them if there was any chance—"

"*You left him there?*" I screamed, and tried to launch myself at him. Viv held me down until I stopped struggling. "Why didn't you save him? How dare you come to me and tell me he—you should have stayed with him!" My mind's eye presented me with the vivid image of Malcolm's bloody corpse clawed and shredded by invaders, and I felt like I might throw up.

"He ordered us to leave, Helena," Mike said. "He didn't want all of us lost. It's standard procedure—never let one man's death be in vain."

Standard procedure. One man's death. Except that one man had been the only one I cared about. I sagged in Viv's arms, crying so hard my eyes and throat hurt. Malcolm. The last thing he'd said to me was that he loved me. According to all the movies, that ought to make this easier. It really, really didn't.

I heard the murmur of speech I didn't understand, Mike's low voice and Judy's higher one, Derrick's deep rumble and the music of Hector's Hispanic accent. Then Viv said, "I don't understand what happened. It was supposed to be a surprise attack, but you're making it sound like they knew you were coming."

I gulped in air, my whole body shaking, and wiped tears

from my eyes. "He wouldn't have died if something hadn't gone wrong," I said. "What went wrong?"

Mike and Jeremiah exchanged glances like neither of them knew what to say. Finally, Mike said, "The first step went off perfectly. I hate Nicolliens, but they were professionals, got everyone through with their familiars. It wasn't until we got to the first building that—Helena, I'm sorry, but I'm still not sure what happened. There were dozens, maybe hundreds of invaders, and the wood and steel magi went after them as planned, but then they just started falling. The magi, I mean."

"Something was different," Jeremiah said, rubbing his bandaged arm. "I've been attacked by invaders before, but this is the first time it was agonizing. It felt like having the marrow sucked out of my bones, and I was dizzy and sick…somehow those invaders were able to drain my magic."

"That's impossible," Judy said. "That's what the wood or steel aegis is meant to prevent."

"Impossible, maybe, but that's what happened," Jeremiah said. "We had to retreat. Malcolm had been at the front of the assault, which put him guarding our escape, and he fought like a demon, but…"

That should have started me crying again, but I felt too numb for tears. "Did they…was it quick?" I said, then shut my eyes tight and said, "No. Don't tell me."

"He told me to leave, Helena," Mike said. His voice sounded strained, as if he were near tears himself. "I can't forget my last sight of him, a dozen invaders tearing at him while he shouted for me to get everyone clear. I'm sorry. I can't forgive myself for——"

I opened my eyes. "So he wasn't dead when you last saw him?"

"Helena," Jeremiah said in a soothing voice, "nobody who

got left behind could have survived. There were too many invaders, and without the protection of the aegis—"

"But you don't know for sure he's dead. You didn't see his body."

Nobody spoke, but Jeremiah and Mike exchanged glances I was sure they didn't mean me to see. "He could still be alive," I said.

"Don't think like that. It will just make this harder," Mike said.

"I've nearly died twice, and Malcolm wouldn't give up on me. I'm not giving up on him. I'm not going to believe he's dead until I see his body." I stood, shaking off Viv. "I'm going to the Gunther Node and I'm going to get someone to take me—"

"Absolutely not," Mike said, just as Jeremiah said, "That's insane. No one is going back there."

I strode through the house to the mud room and rooted around for my shoes. I always swore I'd put them neatly in their cubby and I never did, and then I always had to search for them when I wanted to go somewhere. "I don't believe for one second Lucia has given up on destroying this stronghold," I said, "which means she'll be sending people back, and I am going to be one of them. So you can either come with me, or you can stay here. There's still lots of M&Ms."

Derrick, who'd been silent throughout this discussion, spoke up, startling me. "She's right. Campbell wouldn't leave any one of us there, even if it was just retrieving our bodies. And if Lucia is planning a second assault, I sure as hell want to be part of it."

"Thanks, Derrick," I said.

He smiled at me, an expression that made his bulldog-like face almost handsome. "Don't get your hopes up. I saw the carnage and I don't know if anyone could have survived it. At the very least, Campbell's had his magic drained, and nobody survives that. But even if he is dead, I wouldn't leave his body there."

"That's less encouraging," I said with an answering smile, "but I appreciate the sentiment."

Judy grabbed her coat and slung it around her. "Then let's go."

"Judy—" Mike said, then looked like he was groping for words. "You're her friend. Don't encourage this."

"I'm her friend. That means if she wants to try the impossible, I'm going to cheer her on."

She was standing very close to Mike, and I saw his arm quiver as if he wanted to reach out to her. Instead, he said, "I'll let Lucia know we're coming."

My old Honda Civic, for all it was meticulously maintained, took time to warm up. I gripped the steering wheel and waited for Mike's Land Rover to pull out of the driveway. Beside me, Judy rubbed her hands together and said, "He's right. I shouldn't encourage you. If Malcolm really is—"

"Don't say it," I said, and reversed down the drive. "I'm not giving up hope."

The roads were as icy as they ever were in my nightmares. I wished I'd asked to ride with Mike, or failing that, had Judy drive. My knuckles were white on the steering wheel, my legs and arms were clenched tight with terror, and I was afraid to take my eyes off the road before me, but overriding all of that was the dull ache that said Malcolm was gone and this was a fool's quest. Tears threatened to fall again, and I ruthlessly willed them away before they could blind me and make this that much more hazardous. He wasn't dead. I refused to believe it.

The drive to the Gunther Node took forever, and not just because my fear of the iced-over roads kept me from going as fast as I usually would. Judy didn't speak, not even to suggest that we pull over and switch drivers. When we finally took the turn onto the gravel road leading to the node's entrance, she said, "I texted the node that we're coming. Someone should be there to let us in."

"Thanks. I know this is crazy."

"But you couldn't do anything else."

I shook my head. "I can't believe he's…that he didn't make it. I want proof."

I parked, and we hurried up the low rise to the airplane hangar. Mike and the others, including Viv who'd chosen to ride with Jeremiah, had gotten there first, and stood within the painted circle alongside a black-clad tech I didn't recognize. He clearly knew who I was, because his eyes widened when he saw me and he swallowed nervously. But he didn't address me, just knelt at the center of the circle and dipped a badge hanging from a lanyard into and out of a crack in the concrete, like swiping a credit card.

"Eight," he said. The concrete shimmered glass-bright, and then we were in the great central cavern of the Gunther Node.

The noise of dozens of people shouting orders and dozens more crying or moaning in pain assaulted me. I'd seen the node this busy once before, and that had also been after a failed attack. Men and women lay randomly on the concrete floor, some of them receiving first aid, others being tended to by bone magi. A nearby moan turned into a shriek of pain, startling me into turning around. One of the wounded lay with his back arched as if he were trying to get away from the woman who had her hand on his forehead, and amber light glowed from his shredded midsection. I heard Viv gag as the sickly smell of entrails reached us. It was all so much noise to my numb mind.

"Helena, this way," Mike said, taking my arm. I almost jerked away from him before remembering he was a friend. I didn't want anyone touching me. Instead, I let him lead me across the floor toward one of the painted entrances. Green. I'd never been through the green door before and had no idea what lay beyond it. Then I saw Lucia standing beneath it, talking to a pair of hunters dressed in bloodstained black fatigues. She wasn't gesturing, which was a bad sign. Lucia used her hands as much as her words to communicate, and if she'd gone still, whatever she was saying went beyond urgent into critical.

She glanced past the two hunters in my direction, and our eyes met. She went silent, and her face, which had been animated in the intensity with which she was communicating, went completely impassive. But her eyes…her eyes looked bleak and hollow, as if she'd looked Death in the eye and seen her own mortality slipping away. She made a gesture that dismissed the hunters and waited for me to join her.

Before I could say anything, she said, "He's gone, Davies. Don't entertain any fantasies about rescuing him."

"They didn't see him die," I said.

Lucia's lips thinned. "His survival wasn't a possibility. Without his aegis to protect him, he'd die from having his magic drained before his physical injuries could kill him."

"Then I'll bring his body back." It had never occurred to me that Lucia was the same height as me. She'd always seemed larger than life. Now she looked exhausted and beaten, and it frightened me more than the idea of invaders tearing my husband apart had.

"*You are out of your mind*," Lucia shouted. "You're not going, and that's final."

"I can't have my magic drained, Lucia," I said. "If the wood and steel magi aren't immune anymore—"

"What makes you think you're immune if they aren't?"

"I don't know," I shouted back, "but isn't it worth trying?"

"And lose Abernathy's custodian? Not a chance!"

I looked at Judy, who had taken Mike's hand. It surprised me enough that I almost forgot what I'd meant to say. It didn't look like either of them realized they were touching. "I have a successor," I said, "and if it were me in there, you know Malcolm wouldn't rest until he knew for sure there was no hope for me."

Lucia closed her eyes and let out a deep breath. "Even if I let you go, it's not that simple," she said. "The Mercy will be expecting us this time. You're not a fighter. What you ask is impossible. And I'm not willing to throw your life away on a fool's errand."

Rapid footsteps echoed down the green hallway, and Darius Wallach came into view. For once, his scrubs were plain royal blue, but his hair had come loose from its customary pouf at the back of his head, making him look like a demented dandelion ready to scatter seeds in all directions. He was breathing heavily and held a wadded-up bundle of cloth in his hands. "I found—oh, Mrs. Campbell," he said, sounding surprised. "I didn't think I'd called you yet."

"You didn't," I said. "Why would you?"

"Because we need you for the second assault," Wallach said. "You and as many sports as you can round up."

Lucia turned on him. "What are you talking about?"

Wallach shifted his burden to beneath his left arm and dug his battered smartphone out of a pocket in his scrubs. "I have the information from the ansible Ms. Valentino took into battle, all the way up to when it was destroyed. The Mercy reverse-engineered the protections on the steel and wood aegises so they could bypass them. But they didn't alter their invader allies—that would be impossible, given how many there are."

"That doesn't explain how the invaders were able to drain our steel and wood magi," Lucia said.

"It's—" Wallach looked around as if searching for something. "Come with me and I'll explain it," he finally said.

"I don't—"

"*Don't* say you don't have time for this, Lucia," Wallach said impatiently. "This is the key to defeating that Mercy stronghold."

Lucia's lips thinned again, but she nodded curtly and gestured for Wallach to proceed. Wallach crossed the central hub, deftly avoiding the injured Wardens. Lucia followed him with equal ease. I had more trouble keeping up, but I wasn't about to be left out. Lucia cast an irritated glance at me, but said nothing. The rest of my friends brought up the rear. I didn't look back to see what they thought of this, since it wouldn't matter even if they thought I was crazy. Hope had threaded its way into my heart for the first time since I'd opened the door to see Malcolm's team on my doorstep without him.

Wallach exited the chamber via the red door, but instead of going to one of his labs, he opened the first door he came to and ushered us all inside. The room was full of gray padded chairs in neat rows facing a lectern and a whiteboard. It reminded me of those rooms in TV cop dramas where the police chief explains the situation to the officers.

Wallach strode to the front of the room and swept up a red

marker. "This—damn," he said, as the marker failed to do more than make a pale pink streak on the whiteboard. He tossed it aside without recapping it and found a green marker that was more effective. "This is what their stronghold looks like," he said, sketching out a bunch of rectangles in a loose grouping around a central circle. "A lot of outbuildings with that prefab greenhouse at the center."

"I know this, Wallach," Lucia said irritably.

Wallach ignored her tone. He drew a big circle enclosing all the rectangles and labeled it PERIMETER FENCE. "Mrs. Campbell, this is the first line of defense," he said, tapping the circle. "We used familiars to get our Wardens through it. Easy enough."

"Maybe too easy," I said. "Don't you think the Mercy would have considered that familiars could get through?"

"They were counting on Ambrosites and Nicolliens being unwilling to work together for that solution," Lucia said. "Do you have any more comments?"

I shut up.

Wallach found another marker, this one purple. "This is where we ran into trouble," he said. He drew a second circle with the purple marker between the green circle and the rectangles, and roughly shaded in the space inside the purple circle. Lucia took a step toward the whiteboard, then subsided.

"Like I said," Wallach continued, turning to face us, "they couldn't alter the invaders because there's just too many of them, and the alteration takes days for each one. So we got lucky in that respect. The bad luck is that they were able to create a field in which the protection of a steel or wood aegis is negated. That's this purple zone. It covers the entire compound."

"But it doesn't destroy an aegis," Lucia said.

"No. More like it suppresses its protection. Leave the field, and everything is fine." Wallach flipped the marker around and over his fingers deftly. "What's more, based on the ansible data, I have a good idea of what's generating the field and how to disable it."

Lucia let out a long breath. "Let me guess. The generator is within that circle. And the field is still full of invaders who will drain or tear apart anyone who enters it. So we can't reach the field generator."

Wallach shook his head. "*We* can't. *She* can." He pointed at me.

"I'll go," I said promptly.

"You will not," Lucia said. "The Mercy will be waiting for us this time. You might be immune to having your magic drained, but you're not immune to bullets, knives, or the claws and teeth of an invader."

"Neither is anyone else, and I'm willing to take the risk."

"Well, I'm not. I've already lost one Campbell today and I'm not going to lose another." Lucia's eyes were shadowed and weary, but her voice was as strong and as acerbic as ever.

"There's a chance Mr. Campbell is alive," Wallach said.

My heart beat faster. Lucia shouted, "Don't you *dare* give her false hope, Wallach!"

"It's not false hope." Wallach was unperturbed by her tone. "The tungsten alloy steel aegis is enough different from the old steel aegis that it provides partial protection from the field. There's no way to make the field perfectly functional against both at once. So any of the new steel magi, like Mr. Campbell, can't have all their magic drained. And they're all powerful fighters who aren't likely to be overwhelmed by invaders. It comes down to whether the Mercy needs information, or hostages, to the point that they'd capture rather than kill."

I turned to Lucia. "You see?" I felt as numb as I had when Mike had told me Malcolm was dead, but this time it was from excitement. "We have to get our people back."

Lucia closed her eyes briefly. Then, to my surprise, she put her hand on my arm and gripped it gently. "Helena, it's madness. You think I don't want to believe those Wardens are still alive? I'm not risking more of our people on a slim hope."

"Then change the odds," I said. "Get the glass magi to find out if they're alive, now that you know it's possible not all of them were drained. Besides, I need time."

"Time for what?"

I looked at Wallach, who was smiling. "Time to recruit my allies."

12

I ended the call and let out a deep breath. Judy, sitting in one of the gray padded chairs beside me, said, "Well?"

"I am *never*," I said in tones of deep relief, "going to complain about ice storms again. Not even if I have to drive in every one of them from now until I'm eighty."

"So…they're not gone?" Viv said. She'd been drawing pictures on the whiteboard for the last half-hour and winnowing out the markers that didn't work anymore.

"They're not gone. Ines said all their flights were cancelled and every one of the sports is still at the Grandison. Doesn't that feel like Fate is on our side? Or God?"

"I won't think that until you've convinced them," Judy said. She rose from her chair and stretched. "Did you tell Ines you wanted to speak with them?"

"Yes, and she said she'd ask them to meet in her room in half an hour. Which means we have to go now."

Judy held out her hand. "Keys. I was willing to put up with

your driving before, because you clearly needed a distraction, but I'd like to see my next birthday."

I handed over my keys. "It's just as well. I need to call Detective Acosta. I don't think I'll ever be able to call him Greg."

We hurried through the node until we found someone who could send us back to the airplane hangar. There were fewer people lying on the floor of the central chamber, and the noise had quieted to a dull murmur punctuated by a few louder moans. A lot had happened in the three hours since we'd arrived at the Gunther Node, and if I let myself think about it, I started feeling overwhelmed. There was still so much we didn't know. The glass magi were still working on the "status"—such a cold, horrible word to describe a person—of those lost in the attack, and no one had been able to tell me if Malcolm was still alive. But after my conversation with Wallach, I felt more positive about our chances.

Outside, the storm had dwindled, though at six o'clock in the morning it was still dark. Judy, Viv, and I got into my car and drove toward the freeway. Jeremiah and Mike and the rest of Malcolm's team were somewhere in the Gunther Node, working on a new plan of attack. Watching Viv and Jeremiah kiss goodbye had made my heart ache, and I'd had to tell myself that it was only a matter of time before Malcolm was back.

After that one moment of hand-holding, Judy hadn't said anything to Mike, and he'd barely acknowledged her presence, which made my heart hurt in a different way. I'd caught Judy looking at Mike once with an expression of terrible indecision, and it made me wish I could shut them into a room all by themselves until they talked this out, whatever this was. But now was not the time.

As we proceeded south toward the city, I reflected on everything Wallach had told me while we were waiting for it to be late enough to justify waking Ines. Half of it, I hadn't understood, but I hoped the rest was enough to convince the sports that they could do what I was going to ask of them. I'd found Mangesh at the node, and he was willing, and Acosta might be convinced to stick his neck out for the Wardens, but I was sure we would need more than three people. Even getting one of the sports on board would help.

I called Acosta and got his voice mail. "Hi, it's Helena," I said. "Um. This is too much to explain in a message, so would you call me? It's urgent. Warden business."

"Remember when he thought Abernathy's was a Mob front?" Judy said with a sideways smile.

"I remember being afraid he'd figure out a way to make some criminal charge stick," I replied.

"The Wardens wouldn't let that happen. Even if you'd been guilty of something, we prefer to police our own."

I leaned against the window and warmed my fingers at the heater vent. "So there would have been private justice for Mr. Briggs and his blackmailing?"

"If he was blackmailing people about Warden business, absolutely. It's not like we could let that become public knowledge."

My phone rang. "Detective, thanks for calling me back."

"Isn't this early even for urgent Warden business?" Acosta said.

"You have no idea. Do you remember the Wardens were attacking the Mercy at midnight today? Or last night—six hours ago, anyway?"

"I remember."

Suddenly everything I had to say felt like an avalanche of

information. "They were…the Mercy had a trap prepared. A field that made magi vulnerable to an invader's attack. But the sports aren't affected by it, and I'm going back to disable the field generator. I need your help."

There was silence. "Detective?" I finally said.

"You want me to walk into a Mercy trap?" Acosta said. "Isn't that certain death?"

"Darius Wallach doesn't think so. And I have faith in him. Besides," I drew in a deep breath, "Malcolm is in there, and if there's any chance he's still alive, I have to try to get him back."

"I see." Acosta was silent again. "So you want my help to rescue your husband."

"That, and to defeat the Mercy."

"Huh."

This time, he was silent for so long I almost thought he'd hung up. "I know it's not your fight, but…*please*, Detective. I can't do this if it's just me and Mangesh."

"What about the others?"

"I'm going to ask them now. But none of them know anything about fighting. You do."

"Interesting." Acosta sighed. "Where are you meeting the others?"

"At the Grandison. They couldn't leave because the airport's iced in or something."

"I'll meet you there. Convince me, and I'm in."

"Thank you. That's all I ask."

I hung up and pocketed my phone. "Am I being selfish?" I asked.

"Why selfish?" Viv asked.

"Selfish because all I care about is getting Malcolm back. Maybe I should be more worried about the survival of the

Wardens in general, or winning the Long War." I stared out the window at the taillights of the cars ahead of us. They looked wobbly in the rain, which was less icy now.

"You're a little selfish, true," Judy said, "but if everything about this situation was the same except that Malcolm was here—if you knew your genetic difference could help the Wardens in this attack—wouldn't you still want to help?"

I nodded slowly. "Yeah. I guess I would."

"So don't worry about it. And besides—" Judy shut up so abruptly I could guess what she'd been about to say: that Malcolm was probably dead.

"Do you wish you'd said something to Mike?" I asked.

Judy shrugged. "There was never anywhere private. It's no big deal." Her cheeks were pink enough I was sure that was a lie. I couldn't think of anything to say to that.

The Grandison Hotel was on the riverfront a short distance from the red brick building that housed the Board of Neutralities. I'd stayed at the Grandison two Christmases ago for the Conference of Neutralities and been impressed enough by its comfort and style that I'd chosen it to host my fellow sports. It was a tall, narrow structure of pale gray stone that was darker in the rain, and the green awning over the door dripped icicles on all sides. We pulled up to the front door, and Judy handed the keys to the valet at the parking stand. I wasn't sure the valet service was for non-guests, but I was paying enough for these rooms I didn't care.

The Grandison looked barer without Christmas trees decorating its foyer, and the smell was more flowery and less piney, but it was still as elegant as ever despite its age. The foyer was dimly lit and quiet, and the carpet, though worn in places, swallowed our footsteps. I hurried to the elevator, ignoring the woman at the front desk. I remembered how torn up the place had been when the conference was attacked by rogue familiars bent on killing custodians and marveled at how there was no trace of that damage now. Maybe the woman at the front desk hadn't even been there that night and knew about the attack only from hearsay.

"Wait up," someone called. I turned to see Acosta crossing the foyer toward us. "Good timing," he said. "I didn't know where to go from here."

"Thanks for being willing to listen, Detective."

"I think we know each other well enough for you to call me Greg," Acosta said with a wry smile. "And at this point I've seen enough crazy not to dismiss you out of hand."

I smiled back. "It can't be stranger than disappearing polar bears, right?"

"Don't be so sure," Judy said. "What you're going to tell them requires an awful lot of faith."

We rode the elevator to the fourth floor and walked in silence to Ines's room. I hoped Judy was wrong, and all of them would see the sense in my argument and agree to help immediately, but that was pushing it even for my famous optimism.

The plush royal blue carpet swallowed our footsteps, sending a deeper hush over our silence. Doors spaced relatively far apart bore brass numbers, and arrangements of flowers that almost looked real hung on the walls between the doors, their creamy petals and dusty green leaves coordinating with the pale gold stripes of the wallpaper. I hadn't sprung for the top floor suites, reasoning that it would be overwhelming in addition to arrogantly throwing my money around, but I'd gotten rooms slightly nicer than average and hoped they were comfortable.

At room 412, I knocked and waited. Moments later, Ines

opened the door. She looked as fresh as if I hadn't woken her at an ungodly hour and smiled like she was actually happy to see me. "Come in," she said. "And—who's this? I don't believe we have met."

"This is my friend Viv. She's a Warden, too."

Ines looked as if she didn't believe Wardens could have blue hair, but she was polite enough to say nothing more. She gestured for us to enter.

The room was a mini-suite divided into two living spaces, one with couches and a coffee table, the other with a king-size bed and a chair drawn up to the window, whose drapes were closed. The other three sports sat in the living area and looked up when we came in. Victor's normally cheery expression was closed off, his eyes were puffy, and he cradled a steaming mug of coffee in his large hands. Nyla also had coffee and looked as if she wished she was still asleep. Jun, on the other hand, gazed at me with bright, alert eyes. "I hope this is important," she said. "I have a plane to catch in four hours."

"It's important. Thank you all for being willing to meet with me."

Viv and Judy, after a glance at Ines, took seats on the couch next to Victor. Ines sat beside Nyla. Acosta, after establishing that there was nowhere left to sit, leaned against the wall with his hands shoved into his pants pockets. Victor started to rise and offer me his seat. "No, don't," I said. "I need to stand for this. Actually, I might need to pace. It's okay."

"Well?" Nyla drawled. She sipped her coffee and added, "If this is to ask us to change our minds, I'll tell you that I for one am gonna need some convincing."

I took a deep breath. "Six—nearly seven—hours ago, the Wardens attacked a Mercy stronghold they think is their primary base. They hoped by destroying it, they could either destroy the Mercy completely or make them vulnerable to more attacks. It went well right up until they ran into a...a field, an area that cancelled out the protections of a wood or steel aegis—you remember I told you how those aegises give a magus the protection the seven of us all have naturally? And it was a rout. A lot of magi died, and some were left behind, including my husband, Malcolm."

I closed my eyes briefly, hearing again Mike's voice saying *Malcolm is dead* and the mental image of his torn and bleeding body. Nyla said, "He's dead?"

"He is *not* dead," I insisted, opening my eyes and staring her down. "And I'm going in there after him."

"And you want us to come with you, is that it?" Jun said. "First you couldn't give us a reason to fight, and now you give us a selfish one?"

"I'd do this even if Malcolm were safe beside me," I snapped, "and don't you dare think you understand my motives. I'm asking you all to help because this is something only we can do, and it's something that is going to change the course of this war. It may ultimately save millions of lives. I think that's a cause worth fighting for. Whether you agree is up to you, Ms. Li."

Jun stared at me with narrowed eyes. Ines cleared her throat. "Surely there is more to the Mercy's defenses than just this," she said. "We are not fighters. I am not saying I do not wish to help, but I don't want to throw my life away."

"Neither do I," I said, "and we have a plan." I shrugged out of the heavy black knee-length cardigan I wore over my coat and held it out to Ines. It was big enough that if I hadn't had my coat on underneath, it would have looked like I was wearing a blanket with a cowl hood. The cardigan was woven of some strange fiber halfway between wool and plastic that smelled faintly minty, but not real mint, the fake mint some outdoor trash bags were scented with to drive off rodents. I hoped the smell would fade into the background soon.

"Mr. Wallach at the Gunther Node developed these based on research he's been doing on why invaders and familiars are so drawn to custodians like me. This has magic woven into it that makes someone…maybe not invisible, but at least unattractive to invaders. The thing is, it's never been field-tested, and there are only eight of them, so he can't outfit all the Wardens. But it will get us past most of the invaders prowling the area, and if it fails, we've got our immunity to back us up."

"Yeah, but the Mercy isn't going to stay back and let the invaders do all the fighting," Victor said. "And if the Wardens failed once, the Mercy will be on alert. Unless that thing works on humans like it does on invaders."

"No, but that's where these come in." I pulled out a two-inch-wide gold locket that was hopelessly gaudy with filigree and popped it open. "There's a kind of magic that makes someone invisible—I've used it and it's really effective. We'll have those, and communicators to keep from getting separated, and weapons—"

"I do not like weapons," Ines said. "I will not kill another person."

"Even if he's trying to kill you?" Nyla said.

Ines shrugged. "It is a weight on my soul I do not want. I would rather go to God on my own terms."

"The Wardens have a lot of different weapons," I said. "Some of them are non-lethal. But if you don't want to, that's fine. Our goal isn't to kill people, it's to find the field generator and shut it off so the Wardens can finish the job." I didn't say that my personal goal was to find Malcolm. They didn't need to be involved in that and maybe get themselves killed. "And the glass magi will locate it so they can direct us straight to it. If this goes right, we might not have to fight at all."

Nyla stood. "And you think all this is enough? That we few ordinary people can succeed where dozens of trained fighters failed?"

"We're not ordinary," I shot back, "and yes, I do."

Nyla let go of her mug, which drifted down to rest on the coffee table. "It's crazy," she said, "and I like crazy. I'm in."

"I told you I am willing to help," Ines said. "I do not know how much help a sixty-year-old Latina grandmother can be in this, but I will join you."

Acosta stirred from where he leaned against the wall. "When do you want to do this?" he said.

"Um…Lucia said as long as we couldn't go in immediately after the first attack, we should wait a few hours so the Mercy isn't on full alert. Something about them losing their edge. 11:00, maybe?"

Acosta nodded. "I'll need to make some calls, but…you've convinced me."

"Not me," Victor said. "I'm no fighter. And I'm not embarrassed to say this whole thing scares me. Those people are willing to kill to get their way. I don't want to put myself in danger."

"Yeah, it really sucks that you have no way to see into the future to know the safest path to take," Judy drawled.

Victor's eyes widened.

"She's right," I said. "Victor, Malcolm told me you've got everything it takes to be a front line fighter but the temperament, and if you cared enough about a cause, that would make up for it."

"He said that?" Victor sounded shaken, but pleased.

"He did. I promise you this is a cause worth fighting for. I'd really like to have you along."

Victor shook his head, but he was smiling. "You people are nuts," he said. "I can't believe I'm talking about magic and commando raids on enemy compounds and invisibility like it's all real."

"Of course it's real!"

"I know. But anybody listening to this would have us all committed." He shrugged. "All right. I'm in."

I turned to Jun. "Well?"

"You're not serious," Jun said. "You know how I feel."

"Yes, and I also know your talent is the one most likely to get us where we need to be," I said.

"Wait, what *is* her talent exactly?" Nyla asked. "She never said."

I ignored her. "Ms. Li, I know your augury answered your question. I'm certain you know how important this is. So what's stopping you? It's not fear—I don't think you've ever feared anything in your life, and if you have, you didn't let it get in your way. This is the last time I'll ask, and then I swear I'll never speak to you again. Will you help me?"

Jun met my gaze fearlessly. Then she stood. She was taller than I was, but I didn't feel intimidated—just uncomfortable from her nearness. It felt my skin no longer fit, and I wanted to crawl out of it. "This isn't about one attack on one enemy compound," she said. "I don't know why no one else has seen it, but you're asking us to commit our lives to this cause. No, don't argue," she said to Victor, who'd opened his mouth to say something. "When you know there's evil in the world, and you know you can do something about it, you can't just fight while it's convenient to you. You fight to the very end. Something you understand, Ms. Campbell. Don't think I don't realize your husband is more important to you than any of the rest of this."

"That doesn't mean I don't care about the Wardens," I said.

Jun waved that off. "That wasn't a criticism. You'd be inhuman if your personal issues weren't important to you. I'm saying if we join you, this is only the beginning." She drew a deep breath. "I won't explain what I learned from that augury. It's personal and complex and it's none of your business. But I can say that it told me this is a cause worth fighting for. I just didn't want to believe it." She shook her head slowly as if she couldn't believe she'd just said that. "I guess I'm taking a few more days of personal leave."

Relief made me weak at the knees. "Thank you," I said. "You won't regret it."

"Oh, I'm sure that's not true, but I can deal with a few regrets." Jun smiled. She had a nice smile that softened the stern lines of her face. "So what do we do now?"

13

I'd long ago given up trying to guess how big the Gunther Node was, but this room surprised even me. It was the size and height of a high school auditorium, with rows of metal chairs rather than permanently-installed folding seats, and it smelled of oil and exhaust like the node's airplane hangar even though there were no doors big enough to admit a vehicle bigger than a moped. It could probably hold two hundred people with a handful of others standing along the walls. At the moment, there were fewer than thirty.

The seven of us genetic sports sat near the front of the room. We were bundled up in those oversized black cardigans with cowl hoods that made us look like medieval monks from the knees up. The fake mint scent was fainter, but not gone completely. Wallach assured me that only someone wearing one could smell it, but I could imagine the odor giving us away and hoped he was right.

Viv and Judy sat next to me. I'd tried to say it wasn't their fight and they'd just glared at me, so I'd given up. It wasn't as if they were going into battle just because they were here for this briefing.

Briefing. That sounded so…military. So not me. But I would do anything, including not be myself, if it meant getting Malcolm back. I'd called Ariadne Duwelt and informed her Abernathy's would not be opening today. I was betting on the Board of Neutralities not being willing to challenge me, but I didn't much care if they did.

Off to one side sat four stone magi. They would get us to what Lucia called the deployment point in Montana, a safe area where wards had been installed for ward-stepping. They were chatting quietly among themselves just like none of this mattered to them. It irritated me.

On the other hand, the two glass magi who stood near the door were silent and alert. One held a clear plastic box full of tiny things that glittered in the light. The other had a glass cornucopia tucked under one arm and what looked like a clear crystal Rubik's cube in her other hand. They looked like they took their responsibilities seriously, which reassured me. We were counting on them even more than on our gadgets to get us through this.

In the row behind us sat three fighting teams, including Malcolm's, bristling with weapons. They were our backup, and the first line of fighters for when we'd shut off the generator. I'd greeted them when we all entered the room, but now my attention was on Lucia, who stood at the front of the auditorium next to Wallach. There were dark circles beneath her eyes, but she moved as if she'd had a full night's sleep.

"The plan is simple," she told us. "You'll all ward-step to outside the compound, and the teams will take Davies and her people to where they'll infiltrate the compound, guided by Stentson and McGee." She gestured at the glass magi, who nodded alertly. "You'll have communicators to talk to each other, but use them sparingly. None of the illusions we were able to produce on short notice can do anything about sound, and you can't count on the enemy being too stupid to realize someone's there when they hear an invisible person talking. So —whisper when you have to talk, and keep quiet when you don't."

She snapped her fingers in the direction of the glass magi, and the woman holding the Rubik's cube handed it to her. "Davies has this one's twin," she said. "McGee will enter directions on this one, and they will show up on Davies's cube. It will lead you straight to the generator. Then all you have to do is smash it, or shoot it—anything to disrupt it."

I saw Victor, to my left, run his hands over the odd-looking gun they'd given him. It looked like a toy rather than a real gun, if Nerf made toy guns that weren't made of plastic in primary colors, and one that shot fist-sized rocks rather than bullets. I'd once more forgotten my own gun at home and had accepted an identical replacement, a Sig Sauer P320 I'd practiced with enough to be…not comfortable, guns never made me feel comfortable, but I wasn't afraid I'd shoot my own foot off. I touched it where it hung at my right hip and made myself imagine using it. To save Malcolm, I could do anything. Even shoot another person.

"Once the generator is disabled," Lucia was saying, "use the communicators to tell the teams, and get out of there as fast as you can. Make your way back to the deployment point and the stone magi will take you home."

"You make it sound like we might get separated," Nyla said. "I thought we were working together."

"You should stay together, but with those illusions active, only Davies and Kapoor will be able to see you all. You need to be prepared with a plan for if you are separated." Lucia looked suddenly tired. "If any of you do get separated, and you can't find the others, get out. Don't be a hero."

"No worries there," Victor said with a grin.

"Then…good luck," Lucia said.

We all stood, and I approached Lucia, saying, "Thanks. I know you don't believe he's alive—"

"What I believe doesn't matter," Lucia said. "Now get out of here. I have to see how many fighters we still have so they can follow once you've cleared a path."

I smiled. "So you do have faith in me."

Lucia pursed her lips in thought. "Your God-given reserves of luck haven't run out yet. I'll let you know what I think tomorrow."

She walked away. I was about to return to the others when Wallach grabbed my arm. "Mrs. Campbell," he said, holding something small out toward me. I took it reflexively and nearly dropped it when I realized it was Malcolm's wedding ring. Shock and horror shot through me. They'd retrieved Malcolm's body and hadn't told me. He was dead and all of this was pointless.

"Mrs. Campbell—oh, no, it's not what you think," Wallach said, converting his grip on my arm to a supportive hold. "I was told Mr. Campbell never wears his wedding ring when he goes on a mission. Something about it catching the light at the wrong time."

I breathed out shallowly to dispel the white static before my vision. Of course. Malcolm never wore it when he went hunting, either.

"I've worked a little sympathetic magic on it," Wallach went on. "It will warm up the nearer you are to him. It should guide you straight to him—well, not *straight*, but you shouldn't have any trouble finding him."

"But Lucia said to leave as soon as the field was disabled," I said stupidly. The gold of Malcolm's ring was smooth and warm to the touch, and I could imagine it having come right off his finger.

Wallach smiled and tapped his forehead knowingly. "That compound is a warren of little buildings," he said. "Easy to get turned around. Good luck, Mrs. Campbell."

I slid the ring over my left thumb, where it fit loosely, and returned to my team. What an odd sensation, having a team. The sports looked so uniform in their bulky cardigans with the gold pendants hanging down in front they managed to make Judy and Viv, in civilian clothes, look out of place. Viv hugged me. "Don't get killed," she whispered. "I say that to Jeremiah every time he goes on the hunt. It's like a mantra."

"I know," I said, and hugged her back. "We'll be back in no time."

I got a more tentative hug from Judy. "Talk to him," I whispered in her ear.

Judy shook her head. "It's the wrong time."

"There's never going to be a right time." I released her and looked at where Mike stood, quietly talking to Hector and Derrick.

Judy followed my gaze and turned pink. She shook her head again. I sighed. She knew best, probably, but I couldn't help thinking it was a mistake to let things go on like this.

Mike waved off the other two and came toward me. "Be careful," he said. "Mal would kill me if I let anything happen to you."

"That means you believe he's still alive."

He smiled, a wry expression. "Your faith is infectious."

He turned to Judy, who was watching him, her expression totally neutral. "You're waiting here?" he said.

Judy nodded. "I couldn't bear waiting at home and not knowing…you know."

"I know."

The air between them was so charged with words they weren't saying I felt scorched. I wanted to back away, but I was afraid of drawing attention to myself. Neither of them seemed to remember I was there. Then Mike took two quick steps toward Judy, caught her up in his arms, and kissed her so passionately I thought the air might actually ignite. Judy, after a startled second, threw her arms around his neck and returned his kiss. I took the opportunity to step back, but I couldn't stop watching them even though I knew it was rude.

Mike finally released her, but Judy didn't let go her hold around his neck. "When I get back," Mike murmured, "we have to talk."

"I'm counting on it," Judy said.

I quickly turned away, though I was sure they knew I'd been watching. Everyone still in the room except the stone and glass magi had their eyes on the little tableau. "Um," I said, "I think we should have those glass communicators now. Mr. Stentson?"

The male glass magus looked up when I said his name. "Communicators. Yes." He came toward me holding the plastic box with its glittering contents. "These work like typical wireless earbuds," he said, extracting one from the pile and handing it to me. His brusque tone made me wish Lucia had brought in Harriet Keller, whose presence was always so soothing. I wondered whether she and Harry were somewhere in the node. The magus continued, "Though of course they're powered by magic. It will fit to your ear and latch on for extra security."

I didn't like the sound of "latch on," but I took the small glass earbud and inserted it into my ear. It wiggled unpleasantly, swelling just enough to be painful, then shrank until I could barely feel it was there. I touched it and felt hair-fine filaments growing from it, clinging to the arch of my ear and wrapping securely around my earlobe. I tilted my head, shook it, and felt the earbud move not at all.

"It's not hard to use, but it has a lot of features, so it can be complex," Stentson said. "Tap it once to activate it and double-tap to turn it off. These are set by default to communicate with everyone on the same band, which is all seven of you. However, if you want to speak to just one person, tap and hold the earbud while you say the person's name. That will let you communicate individually not just with your team, but with any of the other teams' members. Stop touching the earbud to end the communication and go back to your team's band. Any questions?"

"How do I get it off when we're done?" Victor said. He looked profoundly uncomfortable and kept raising his hand to almost scratch his ear.

"You just pull it out. The filaments break easily and dissolve in seconds. Don't worry, it can't implant itself in your ear canal." Stentson grinned. "These are top of the line glass magus creations and won't fail."

"What about invisibility?" Nyla asked. She touched the gold locket hanging around her neck like she was afraid it might fall off.

"Ward-stepping can interfere with illusions," Derrick said, "so I've got the origamis and will activate them when we're in Montana. They're good for three hours, but if you need to dispel the illusion before that, you just open the locket and take out the origami. Touching it will break the magic."

"I hope nobody needs to do that," I said. "Any other questions?"

Nobody spoke. "Then I guess it's time to go. Don't forget what I told you about ward-stepping, how it can make you sick." I offered my hand to Mangesh. "How far outside the Mercy perimeter are the wards?"

"Far enough that we will not be seen," Mangesh said. He took my hand, and something wrenched at my stomach, turning it inside out. The stink of hot gunmetal surrounded me, though there was no air for it to fill. I resisted the urge to breathe deeply and relaxed, knowing from experience that fighting made the sickness worse. Then there was solid ground beneath my feet. I staggered a few steps away through ankle-deep snow, closing my eyes against the frigid air that wanted to freeze them, and bent over with my hands on my knees, breathing deeply to keep from throwing up.

With my eyes closed, sounds were sharper, and I heard what sounded like dozens of people tromping through snow whose frozen crust crunched like broken glass. Knife-like wind sliced my face, making me grateful for my gloves and the coat I wore under my cardigan. I shook snow off my boots and stood, slowly, still feeling a lingering nausea. The wind blew loose snow in drifts across the field we stood in, and the sun, which hung as high in the sky as was possible in late March, was partly obscured by thin, wispy clouds. I saw nothing man-made anywhere nearby, just scattered conifers weighed down by blankets of snow.

"That's some view," Victor said.

I turned to face him and was struck temporarily mute at the sight of a wide river, dull blue despite the overcast, flowing sluggishly behind us. The ground on the far side of the river sloped steeply upwards, and a snow-crusted range of mountains towered over it. I'd never seen anything so casually majestic, as if the mountains had no idea how beautiful they were. This would be an extraordinary place to vacation, for someone who was the outdoorsy type.

"Helena," Mike called out. I trudged through the snow to where he waited near the riverbank. "Open your locket."

I cracked it open with some difficulty and held it flat on my gloved palm. Mike had the box of tiny origami butterflies open and extracted one with tweezers. He carefully placed it in the center of the locket. Its tiny wings fluttered once, and then it lay still. I closed the locket and tucked it away beneath my cardigan. I heard someone gasp, and turned to see Nyla looking about in all directions, searching for something.

"I'm still here," I said. I wasn't invisible to myself, something I'd insisted be part of the illusion; it didn't matter for me, because I'd see through the illusion regardless, but I could imagine how disorienting it would be to the others not to be able to see their own hands and feet.

One by one, everyone got their origami butterfly illusion. "Turn on your earpieces," I said, and tapped mine. I felt the swelling sensation again, and then a tense feeling on the back of my neck, like someone standing behind me breathing on it. "Can you hear me?"

"*I can,*" Ines's voice sounded in my ear, soft but clearly audible and sounding as if she were standing there speaking to me.

"*This feels very strange,*" Jun said. "*It's too bad it's magic, because I can think of half a dozen uses for it if it were tech.*" Jun was actually standing next to me, so I heard her voice both through the earpiece and with my natural ears. *That* sounded strange.

"Time for the perimeter," Mike said. "I'm telling them to bring through Paradox now."

I was about to ask what Paradox was when the air a few feet away distorted, and an enormous familiar, four feet high at the shoulder with a hard exoskeleton that glimmered like an oil slick, twisted into being. I sucked in a deep breath to control a scream, but the creature ignored me despite being essentially right in my face. I fingered the stiff wool of the cardigan, then took a step toward the monster. It didn't move, didn't even sniff the air. I might as well not have been there for all the attention it paid me. I decided right then I was keeping the cardigan.

The air distorted again, and a familiar red-headed figure appeared. "This is stupid," Brittany Spinelli said to Mike. "They're all going to get killed."

Mike's upper lip curled in a sneer. "Spinelli," he said. "I wonder why they sent you."

"Because I'm the best, Conti," Brittany replied. "Where are they?"

"Already concealed," I said, making Brittany jump—I was close enough to touch her.

Brittany's hard expression softened. "I won't say I don't think you're crazy, but—good luck, Helena."

I figured Brittany, who hated Malcolm, would be less generous if she knew my actual intentions. "Thanks," I said. "Will you be part of the attack when we take down the field generator?"

"Heh. If that happens, I'll be at the head of the line."

"After me," Conti snarled.

"Figure it out later," I interposed. "Let's go."

Our trip across the snowy, pine-studded field was more difficult than I'd imagined, though I'd anticipated the invisible sports running into each other. I just hadn't realized how easily that would happen. Finally, Mangesh and I took charge of the others and told them where to walk and when they were about to run into another invisible person, and the trek became easier.

"Stop," one of the other fighters said. I didn't know her name, but she wore elaborate goggles tinted pink and a matching anorak that made her look like Steampunk Barbie. "Spinelli, it's your turn."

I had thought, from Wallach's description, that the perimeter of the Mercy compound was a physical fence, but as far as I could tell, the field stretched out for miles untouched by man—all except for a distant blotch with sides far too regular for Nature. It might have been a large farm or a small settlement. I held perfectly still in fear of accidentally wandering across the perimeter line. It wasn't invisible, or I'd have seen it, but whatever it was made of, Steampunk Barbie could see.

Brittany led Paradox forward five steps, then six. Eight. Twelve. "Shouldn't we have reached it by now?" she said.

"I don't get it," Steampunk Barbie said. "The line's still there, but it's not reacting to anything."

Brittany dropped Paradox's leash and strode back toward us, making the others cry out. The sports didn't react, probably because they didn't realize how potentially fatal her action was.

Nothing happened. Steampunk Barbie walked forward and drew a line in the snow with her toe, then waved her hand in the air above it. "It's been turned off."

"Isn't that good?" Nyla asked.

"No," Acosta said. "If they aren't counting on this perimeter anymore, it means they've got different defenses up elsewhere—defenses we don't know to protect against. This mission just got a hundred times harder."

I clasped my hands together. Malcolm's ring pressed into my thumb, cool as water now despite being close to my skin under my glove. "We can call it off," I said. "This isn't what you signed up for."

"Not a good idea," Acosta said. "This is still the perfect time for an assault. It's been enough hours since the first attack that the edge has worn off their alertness, and not enough hours for them to change their strategy completely. Unless they've decided to evacuate—"

"They need this base too much to evacuate it," Mike said. "If anything, they'll have stepped up whatever they've been doing here and won't be paying close attention to anything else."

"We should go now," Victor said. "They have someone walking the perimeter, and when he gets here, he won't find anything."

"How do you know that?" Brittany exclaimed.

"I see the future," Victor replied. "I don't know how you people are going to clean this up so it doesn't look like anyone's passed—"

"Leave it to me," Mike said.

"Is everyone okay with that?" I asked my team. Everyone nodded, even Jun, who I'd thought would put up more of a fight. I guessed she really had been sincere when she committed herself. "I'll contact you soon," I told Mike, who nodded in the direction of my voice.

"Now is the time to stay close," I said. "Mangesh and I will keep you from getting too far away or running into anyone. Let's go, and…good luck."

I pulled the glass Rubik's cube from beneath my cardigan.

It was clear enough that I could see the warped shapes of whatever lay beyond it. Deep in its heart, a tiny pink light pulsed like a heartbeat, pointing toward the distant angular shapes. I closed my left fist tight so I could feel Malcolm's ring again and started walking.

14

Almost immediately, I saw the flaw in our plan. While our illusions made us invisible, they didn't do anything to conceal our footprints or the sound of feet crunching over snow. The Wardens clearly hadn't come this way during the first assault. I stopped and told everyone else what I'd noticed. "They'll see us coming."

"*I think not,*" Ines said in my ear. "*I see the place—the compound —in vision. The snow here is unmarked, but closer to the buildings, it is trampled as if many people walked over it. In some places the snow is completely gone.*"

"*What else do you see?*" Acosta asked.

"*Not much yet. The seven of us, no longer invisible. The field generator, I think. It is inside a building, but I do not yet know which one.*"

"Then I guess we keep going," I said. I hadn't realized how hard it would be to trust someone else's magic. Continuing to walk into danger unconcealed, sort of, with only Ines's assurance that it would work filled me with trepidation. But they were trusting my magic right now, and I couldn't do less for them.

I directed everyone wide around a copse of pine trees where birds sang loudly and the wind rustled the needles. The sound of the wind made me feel even colder than the actual wind did. I burrowed deeper into my layers of outerwear and wished I'd worn a scarf as well. Or goggles. My eyes watered from the chill in the air.

I blinked the tears away and discovered our distant target had grown close enough for me to make out individual buildings. They were small, maybe the size of a mobile home or smaller, and they were all painted a drab gray-green that blended with the pines surrounding them. As we drew closer, I realized they *were* mobile homes, or at least prefab huts. Beyond them rose a white dome—the greenhouse Wallach had referred to, but bigger than any greenhouse I'd ever seen. Battered pickup trucks, a few of them six-wheeled monsters, but most of them typical Ford vehicles or smaller Toyotas that looked dainty by comparison, were parked here and there between the huts, providing the only spots of color in the area. Except for the dome, it looked so much like a survivalists' camp I almost imagined us in some postapocalyptic nightmare, sneaking up on the warlord's camp to steal supplies.

"*I see it*," Nyla whispered.

"See what?" I whispered back.

"*The bare spot. We're close.*"

I couldn't see anything that clearly because there were trees between me and the first buildings, but the blue pickup parked between the trees and the nearest building had torn up the ground, and I could imagine the rest of the space looked the same. From somewhere nearby came a whiff of sulfur, and I froze. That was the smell of—

A long-limbed creature came around the rear of the truck, its violet carapace glowing like a black-lit shell. I held my breath. Surely the invader would notice us. To my horror, the thing walked directly toward me, its oblong head drooping as if its thin neck couldn't hold it up. I made myself breathe quietly so I wouldn't pass out. In my ear, someone said, "*What is that?*" and I heard a muffled gasp. I couldn't take my eyes off the invader.

It came to within three feet of me before curving off to the right, strolling unconcernedly in the direction of an even smaller building. I put my hand on the nearest tree trunk and waited for my knees to stop trembling. "It's all right," I said. "I take it you didn't see a dog?"

"*I see familiars only rarely in my work, and free invaders never,*" Mangesh said. His voice was as shaky as my knees. "*It is no wonder the Nicolliens use illusions.*"

"*There's another one,*" Victor said. His normally deep voice sounded shrill. "*What do I do?*"

"Hold still," I whispered. "The first one came really close to me and didn't perceive me at all. The cardigans work." I walked slowly around the trees to where Victor stood. The invader he'd seen was smaller than the first, but had spider-like legs and a dozen blood-red beady eyes and looked altogether more terrifying. "I'm right behind you, and everything's going to be fine."

"*Two more,*" Nyla said. "*They may not be able to see us, but we can't just stand here.*"

I checked the cube and discovered the pink pulsing light was brighter and throbbing faster. There was also tiny lettering on the central square of one of the six faces. I held it closer to my face. TWENTY STEPS FORWARD AND TURN LEFT.

"I think we should join hands," I whispered. "Mangesh—"

"I am to your right," Mangesh said. *"Meet opposite the red truck."*

I hoped he was talking about the truck that had once been red and was now a patchwork of primer gray and orange rust spots.

I touched and held the earbud. "Victor, I'm right behind you and I'm going to take your hand, so don't freak out." I took two steps forward and clasped his big gloved hand. Victor jerked, but managed not to make a sound. The spider invader had headed off to the left and disappeared around the corner of a building. I wished it had stayed where I could see it. The idea of it being out there loose somewhere it could jump me made me queasy.

I tugged on Victor's hand and walked to where Jun stood, giving her the same private warning before taking her hand and passing it to Victor's. That had to be weird, holding hands with someone you couldn't see.

More invaders came into view, and the smell of sulfur increased. I helped Nyla find Victor's hand and took hold of Jun's free one so my right hand would be free to hold the cube. Feeling like the head of the world's weirdest conga line, I led everyone in the direction of the red pickup. Mangesh had Acosta and Ines by the hands and was standing about twenty feet from the truck. Four invaders moved slowly through the intervening space. The brisk wind carried their scent to me and I felt like throwing up.

"Hang on," I said quietly, and examined the cube again. The writing had changed to FIFTEEN STEPS FORWARD, THREE STEPS SIDEWAYS TO THE LEFT, TEN STEPS FORWARD. "Follow me."

I took a few steps forward, five, six. If I kept going straight, I'd run into the truck's bed, which told me the glass magi were alert to environmental hazards as well as the prefab trailers.

One of the invaders passed within inches of me, and I stopped, making the conga line bump against my leg. I didn't want to touch the invader and test the extent of the cardigan's protection.

Eight steps. Nine. Where were all the people?

I'd barely had time to think that when the door of the nearest prefab building opened and a couple of people emerged. "Back," I whispered, but getting four invisible people all pointed in the same direction is hard at the best of times, and I had to stop moving for fear I'd knock someone over and make a noise the Mercy operatives were sure to hear.

One of the people, the man, said, "I'll drive." The woman just grunted in acknowledgement. Neither of them seemed to care that the place was full of invaders, which made me wonder how the Mercy kept the stupid small ones from attacking them. I stood perfectly still as the man walked past, close enough for me to touch him without fully extending my arm. He opened the truck door, then paused, half turning around with his chin lifted as if he were scenting the air. I held my breath, sure he would be able to smell it if I breathed out. The others were behind me, and I hoped they wouldn't do anything stupid to make a noise.

The man turned again so his face was visible. He looked puzzled, like he'd forgotten something that was niggling at his awareness. Then he shook his head and climbed into the truck. I let out a shallow breath, conscious that its condensation could still give me away, and breathed in the exhaust as the truck drove away. It had never smelled sweeter.

Without the truck in the way, the directions were simpler, and pretty soon we were all gathered in a relatively narrow space between two huts. I let go of Jun's hand and checked the cube again. My heart sank. "This is going to be complicated," I said.

"And the space between these trailers is tight," Acosta said. "We're going to get separated."

"So maybe we ought to do it on purpose. Separate, I mean," said Ines. "I now know what the building looks like. I can guide some of us, and the rest can go with Helena."

I hated the idea of splitting up. With all of us invisible, that could lead to disaster. I looked out over the rest of the compound. The trailers, or huts, or whatever you called them, didn't have any pattern to their locations. From above, they would probably look like a handful of 2x4 Lego bricks scattered across the field. The greenhouse dome was visible only as a white bubble against the overcast sky. The one thing I was sure of was that Acosta was right, and we'd be threading our way between the trailers, probably single file.

"Ines," I said, "you're sure you know where you're going?"

"Very sure," Ines said with a smile that calmed me somewhat. "We will wait for you outside."

"I guess it's no crazier than anything else we've done today," I said. "Everybody join hands."

I helped Victor, Nyla, and Jun link hands, took Victor's free hand, and with a nod for Mangesh trotted out into the open.

Trying to keep track of my team while reading the cube's instructions *and* avoiding contact with anyone soon had my nerves wound tighter than a violin string. Once we were past the open space of the aegis-neutralizing field, there were fewer invaders, but more people. We had to make frequent stops to keep from bumping into Mercy operatives, none of whom were as alert as the first guy had been, but who were all prone to walking rapidly and darting in and out of buildings. I learned to avoid walking anywhere near doors, even if the instructions told me otherwise.

I discovered early on that the cube was about as responsive as a GPS system, if more accurate. If I had to detour away from the directions, it only took the glass magi McGee and Stentson a few seconds to recalculate my route. I hoped the reason I wasn't seeing very many humans was that they were leading me around most of them. If that were true, it meant there were a lot of people in this camp, and at some point we'd need to find a way out past them. I eyed the pistol holstered on the hip of the next woman I passed and decided not to worry about it. Time enough to plan for an exit when the generator was disabled and I'd found Malcolm.

The ring on my thumb remained cool, which was a relief. I didn't know if I had the fortitude to stay on task if it started picking up signs that Malcolm was near. My shoulders ached with tension, my armpits were sweaty despite the cold wind, my nose was runny, and my eyes ached from having to read the tiny print. We'd been walking for a much longer time than I'd anticipated, because I'd thought for some reason the generator would be close to the edge of the compound, and I was starting to worry that the directions were wrong and we'd passed the generator five minutes ago when the pink light flared and began pulsing hard enough I could feel it, like holding someone's living heart in my hand.

I looked up. The building in front of us looked exactly the same as all the others, gray-green paint, metal roof painted black, three wooden steps leading up to the door. STRAIGHT AHEAD, the instructions read.

Movement to one side of the building caught my eye. There were people there, three of them—it was Mangesh,

Ines, and Acosta. Relief washed over me, and I trotted over to meet them.

"This is it," I whispered. "Any idea if it's occupied?"

"Greg looked through the back window," Ines said. "There is no one there."

I dropped Jun's hand. "I'll go. When the door opens, Jun will lead her group, and Mangesh will follow when they're all through." The illusion was starting to get on my nerves. I hurried up the steps to the door, cast a quick look around, and turned the knob.

The door was locked.

I stupidly tried turning the knob again, with the same results. Locked? After everything we'd been through to get here? I turned and ran back to where everyone crouched. "Guess what," I said.

"I can't believe it's locked," Victor said. "What do we do now?"

Nyla stepped forward. "Give me a minute," she said.

"You can pick locks?" I said.

"It's one of the things my talent is good for," Nyla said. "I don't even need to see the lock anymore."

I gaped. "So you've done this often? Should you admit to that in front of a detective?"

"Sometimes you have to bend the law a little," Nyla said with a wicked smile. "And I doubt anyone here will press charges for breaking and entering."

"No, because they'll be too busy shooting," Victor said.

Acosta shrugged. "I'll pretend I didn't hear that. Besides, you're out of my jurisdiction, all the way down there in Texas."

Nyla grinned and hurried up the steps. Her body blocked the doorknob, so I couldn't see what she was doing, but in only a few minutes, the door swung open. I grabbed Victor's hand. "Hurry!"

We were getting better at moving invisibly together. Everyone was inside without mishap in seconds. Acosta shut the door and leaned against it. His mouth fell open. "Damn," he said. "This is not what I expected."

The room was full of steel cabinets like giant fuse boxes, lining three of the four walls. Computers on plastic folding tables displayed moving graphs that reminded me of medical monitors, as if the Mercy were keeping track of people's heart rates and breathing, except the graphs were labeled POWER1 and NODECENTRAL and a bunch of other things that did not sound at all medical. There were no chairs, not even the cheap folding kind, which relieved my mind because it meant there probably wasn't a computer operator somewhere who would be coming back after his coffee break.

Victor opened one of the cabinets at random and whistled in astonishment. "I never saw so many wires in my life."

Hundreds of thin red or black wires filled the cabinet, some of them bundled together with zip ties, others threaded through silver-rimmed holes running top to bottom along the right edge of the cabinet. A row of green lights ran across the top. Some of them were blinking, but most glowed a steady green. I drifted closer, mesmerized.

"They are all the same," Ines said. She'd opened another cabinet and revealed more wires and lights. "How do we know which is the one?"

"Are we sure this is it?" Nyla asked. "This doesn't look very magical."

"The wires don't go anywhere," Acosta pointed out. "Not even underground. They're just for show."

Now that he mentioned it, I remembered that there hadn't

been any wires or anything leading from the roof. "We can't just destroy all of them," I said. "It would be disruptive, but it would also alert the Mercy that we're here. Taking out just the anti-aegis field will be quiet enough that the Wardens can surprise attack them."

Victor looked as if he'd been about to suggest destroying all of them. Ines said, "I did not see in vision which of these is the right one."

"There is one computer for each cabinet," Mangesh said. "If one of these computers shows the display for the field, we can match it to its cabinet."

I immediately scanned the labels. "POWER1, POWER2, NODECENTRAL—" I stopped, my heart in my throat. "DETENTION."

"Helena, stay focused," Nyla said. "Here it is. PERIMETER2."

"How do you know that's it?" Jun said.

"Because there's a PERIMETER1 next to it, and that graph has flatlined, like there's no power going to it." Nyla pointed at one of the cabinets. "That's the one."

Mangesh opened it, then hesitated. "I do not think it is safe to simply tear out the wires."

"Back up," Victor said. He shrugged his absurd-looking gun off his back and hefted it in both hands. "This will do the job."

I backed all the way next to Acosta, who still stood leaning against the door. "Um, how noisy—"

A *pah* of sound no louder than someone blowing out birthday candles came from the gun. A streak of black shot away from it, impacting with the cabinet with a sound like a fist hitting flesh. Lightning flashed, sizzling along the wires and grounding itself in the floor and wall. The green lights all went out. The moving line on the graph marked PERIMETER2 plummeted and vanished.

"Yes!" Victor shouted, punching the air, then ducked as we all shushed him.

I pressed and held the glass communicator. "Mike, it's done. You can send in the teams."

"*Hold on, Helena,*" Mike said. I waited, my hand still to my earbud, until he said, "*Confirmed the field is down. Good work. Now —get out of there. If Malcolm's there, we will find—*"

I lowered my hand. "All right. We've done what we came for. It's probably best if we all split up to get out of here. You remember how we came—just follow that path backwards."

"You're not leaving, are you?" Jun said.

"Don't worry about me." My eyes were already on the DETENTION monitor.

"Helena, you don't even know if he's alive," Acosta said.

"I'll find out. Go on, get out of here."

"And leave you alone? Not a chance," Nyla said.

"Well, I'm going," Victor said. "I'm no hero. Sorry, Helena."

I looked at each of them in turn. "Don't worry about it, Victor. I need you all to leave. This is my problem, and I can't rescue Malcolm if I'm worried about the rest of you."

"Then only some of us will stay," Nyla said.

I focused on her, on how intent her freckled face was. "It's not your problem."

Nyla shrugged. "You were willing to risk your life and do this on your own if we didn't help. I respect that. Plus, I'm thinking we might be able to do some more damage, and I'm starting to think Jun has a point about this being a fight you give your life to."

My chest felt tight with stupid tears. "Thanks, Nyla. Okay. Everyone else——"

"I'm coming too," Jun said.

My mouth fell open. "You didn't even want to come!"

"I know. But my talent works against humans as well as invaders, and where you're going, you may need that."

"Did she ever say what her talent is?" Victor murmured.

I couldn't help laughing. "All right. But that's all. More than that, and it will just get confusing. Mangesh, Greg, can you get the others back to the wardstones?"

"Of course," Mangesh said. "Victor, what do you see?"

Victor's eyes glazed over briefly. "We'll make it back. But we should leave in…two minutes."

I took a moment to clasp each person's hand. "Thank you. For everything."

Ines held onto my hand when I would have let her go. "Helena, I do not always see the future clearly," she said, "but I know you will not be alone. I believe your husband is alive."

Joy filled me, and I hugged Ines. "I believe it, too."

"I think I know where to go," Nyla said. "Sort of."

I joined her at the PERIMETER1 computer. The graph display had disappeared, and instead the screen showed a top-down map of a handful of 2x4 Lego bricks—no, it was the compound. Nyla was scanning a list displayed down the right-hand side of the screen. "Detention is here," she said, pointing, "and we are…I think this is us."

The detention building was on the farthest side of the compound from where we were. Of course it was. I closed my eyes and prayed briefly for success. I was getting better at praying, though probably anyone with real religious experience would tell me I was doing it wrong.

When I opened my eyes, Jun had her phone out and was

taking a picture of the screen. "We need to hurry," she said. "If the Wardens are on their way, there's no telling what the Mercy might do with prisoners."

"We'll see you all soon," I said. I double-tapped my communicator to turn it off—I didn't want to confuse the others while they were escaping, and Jun and Nyla and I would be close together—and led the way out the door.

15

Nothing had changed in the few minutes we were inside the power station, as I thought of it. Icy wind still blew between the buildings, and we saw no humans and no invaders. Jun had her phone out and was staring at the little screen. "This way," she said, pointing.

"I can't see you," Nyla said. "We need to hold hands."

I grabbed her hand and Jun's free one. "We have to go slowly so we don't get separated," I said, though my heart was pounding fast enough I wanted to grab Jun's phone and run.

Jun led us between buildings, through spaces as narrow as Abernathy's "aisles" that forced us to sidle along with our backs to the wall. The smooth vinyl siding rubbed my hood, dislodging it, but I didn't dare reach up to pull it back into place. Windows that glowed with a light stronger than the dim sun looked down on us, and once or twice I saw shapes moving in the rooms beyond. It was hard to remember that anyone looking out would see nothing but wall.

We stepped out from between two very close buildings, and

with a final tug, my hood slid off my head and sagged loose around my neck. "Hang on," I said, letting go of the others' hands.

"What's wrong?" Jun asked.

"My hood slipped." I reached up to adjust it, and froze. Not two feet away, an invader with a bright red shell like a cooked lobster and four fat, sucker-covered tentacles came out from between buildings. It was looking right at me, its bulbous head cocked like an inquisitive terrier. I slowly lowered my arms, letting my right hand rest on my gun. "I think it knows I'm here."

"But you're invisible," Nyla said. "It can't see you."

"Invaders rely on senses other than sight." I remembered Wallach's pet familiar sniffing without interest at my T-shirt. "I don't know why it hasn't attacked."

"Stand still," Jun said. She took a wide step to the right, then another.

"What are you doing? What is she doing?" Nyla demanded, her voice a little too loud.

"Shh," I said. "Jun, what—"

Jun drew a white baton about a foot long and a couple inches around from beneath her cardigan. "I hope this works like they said it would." She twisted the baton, and it telescoped to a length of three feet. Now it looked like a cane a blind man might use, but she held it like a sword.

The invader shifted its weight. I flicked my gaze back to it, willing it to pay attention to me and not Jun, who had worked her way around behind it. My breath was coming too fast, and my heart beat hard enough I was sure the thing could hear it. It took a step, or whatever you called the rolling, rocking gait as it moved forward on those tentacles—

Jun lunged like a fencer, extending the pole to touch the

invader on the back of its head. It squealed, a shrill sound that carried far in the quiet air and made me jump. It leaped for me, I drew my gun, Nyla shouted, and the invader collapsed in a heap, its white eyes staring blindly at the sky. I shakily lowered my gun. "Is it dead?"

"They said this would kill an invader if I could get a head shot," Jun said, "and wound it if I hit anywhere else."

I drew in a deep breath. "Thanks."

"Somebody had to hear that," Nyla said, "between my stupid shouting and its death screech. We need to move."

"I think it's time we cancelled the invisibility illusion," I said. "We need to move fast. We'll just have to take our chances that we don't look odder than the average Mercy operative." I cracked open my locket and pulled the origami butterfly out, then stomped it into the ground. I didn't think anyone would see it and draw the right conclusion, but it wasn't a chance I wanted to take.

Nyla and Jun followed my example, and their bodies shimmered briefly as the illusion vanished. Somewhere close, someone shouted—thankfully not so close that their words were intelligible. I grabbed two of the invader's tentacles. They were sticky and squishy and I swallowed to keep from throwing up. Quickly I dragged the body back into the narrow space between buildings, pulled my gloves free of the stickiness, and said, "Time to run."

Jun led the way, glancing at her phone every couple of steps. We made it as far as the next three buildings before running into someone, nearly literally, who emerged from one of the buildings in front of us. Jun dashed around him, not saying anything, and Nyla and I followed. "Hey—" the man said, but we ignored him and heard no more words, no sound of footsteps following us. I tugged my hood on more securely.

It might not look like standard-issue Mercy gear, but I didn't want to face another invader without its protection.

Jun slowed to a halt. "That's it," she said, gesturing to a building set a little ways from the rest. It didn't look like a jail —didn't look any different from the other Legos. "What do we—"

An ear-splitting klaxon blasted the still air, and the wail of a siren went off immediately after, rising and falling like an air raid alert from a World War II movie. "So much for stealth," I said. "That's the Wardens. Let's go before whoever's in that detention building figures out they're not under immediate attack."

Now I took the lead, running full out. My hood slipped again, and this time I let it fall, not wanting to waste time dealing with my wardrobe malfunction. I pounded up the three steps, yanked the door open—not locked, thank God for small mercies—and shouted, *"Up against the wall!"*

The space just inside the door was tiny, barely big enough to hold the IKEA student's desk and chair taking up the far side. A man dressed in olive green fatigues was just rising from it. My gun was in my hand before I consciously decided to draw it, and I pointed it at him, shouting, "I mean it! Face the wall!"

We stared each other down. The man looked terrified, his eyes wide and his lips moving nervously. My hand on the gun was steady, but that wouldn't last long—only until my brain caught up with my reflexes. Just as I was thinking I would have to shoot him, he slowly turned and spread his hands wide, pressing his face against the wall.

I calmed my breathing and looked around. There were no decorations on the walls, which reassured me. If the Mercy went in for kitten posters, I'd be completely unnerved. The space was tiny because they'd built a wall just ten feet from the end of the trailer, with a single door in the middle of it. "Check that," I said, more abruptly than I'd meant because my brain had just realized I was holding a man at gunpoint. Helena Davies Campbell, Abernathy's custodian, with a gun aimed at some man's head. At some point, the weirdness was going to catch up with me, and I was going to have a meltdown. But not until I'd found Malcolm.

I listened as Nyla and Jun opened the door and disappeared beyond it. My captive turned his head so I could see his face. "Don't move," I said, holding the gun more steadily.

"Shoot me," he said. "You'll have to, because I'd rather die now than be executed by the Wardens."

Footsteps told me Nyla and Jun were returning. "He's not here," Jun said. "The cells are empty."

My heart sank. Then I felt stupid. The ring on my thumb was still cool. I should have known Malcolm wasn't in this trailer. "Where are the Wardens you captured early this morning?" I asked.

The man stayed silent. I took a step closer to him, not so close that he could turn around and grab my gun, and said, "Tell me where they took the prisoners, and no one has to know we were here."

Still nothing. My adrenalin rush turned sour, and despair swept over me. I didn't know what to do. I might have been able to shoot him if I'd done it when I came through the door, but I was too weak and cowardly to shoot a man in cold blood, not to mention if I killed him, I might never find out where Malcolm was. This had been a stupid idea, and I needed to get back to the wardstones and return to the Gunther Node, let the trained Wardens handle this.

That thought banished my despair. I was *not* going back

without Malcolm. I eyed the man in front of me, then shifted my aim to point at the back of his knee. "Fine," I said. "Let's see how far you get with only one leg."

The man's gaze met mine. I hoped he saw resolute fury in my eyes and not nervous terror. My finger tightened on the trigger.

"No!" the man shouted. "They all went to the node. Kill me, make it quick, just don't—"

There was a zapping sound. A full-body spasm struck the man, and he folded. Jun withdrew her baton. "I guess it works on humans, too."

"Did you know that would happen?" Nyla demanded.

Jun shrugged. "No. But I could tell Helena had run out of bluffs."

I holstered my gun and drew in a deep breath. "I shouldn't have brought the gun. Malcolm always says a weapon you're not willing to use is a weapon in your enemy's hands."

"I don't know," Jun said. "That was some effective bluffing. Where's the node?"

It hadn't occurred to me until that moment that the unconscious Mercy operative had done what no one in the Wardens had achieved: confirmed that our people were still alive, or had been when the attack failed. "The node is inside the greenhouse dome," I said, pulling my hood back on. "It's going to be crawling with the Mercy."

"Then let's go," Nyla said.

Over the last two years, I'd watched a lot of movies with Judy and Viv, most of them ones that weren't the sort I'd choose for myself. Viv loved rom-coms, and from those I'd learned about the meet-cute, and second-chance romances, and the dark moment—everything about two people coming together. Judy's movies usually featured explosions rather than life lessons, but there was one thing I'd learned that helped me now more than a thousand romantic comedies: if you walk with purpose, don't meet people's eyes, and carry a clipboard, no one will question your presence no matter how much you're not supposed to be somewhere.

I didn't have a clipboard, but it didn't matter; most of the people we passed on our way through the compound carried guns instead. The siren had shaken the hornet's nest, and men and women in black or olive-drab fatigues ran in every direction. I got nervous when we fell in behind someone headed the same way we were, then realized we just looked like part of that person's team. Since she never looked back, she didn't know she was trailing Wardens like a comet's tail, and we followed her all the way to the center of the camp, where we veered off and made a wide circle around the greenhouse.

I could see why Wallach had called it that, but to me it looked more like a semi-permanent sports arena. It was made of white fabric draped tautly over a rigid oval frame the same shape as a football stadium, with doors at each end and in the center of both long sides. The brisk wind made the fabric between the frame's struts ripple, but despite that it looked remarkably stable.

We kept walking with intent as we sized it up. "I don't know how it looks inside," I said. "I've never seen the actual Gunther Node—the part that generates magic, I mean—so it could be anything. Or it could be the node is somewhere else, and that's just the place that takes you there." I rubbed my thumb against the glove's palm and felt Malcolm's ring press into my flesh.

"We have to go inside and look around," Jun said.

I rubbed my thumb again, and stopped walking. "It's

warm," I said. "Malcolm is close!" He was alive. I wanted to cry with relief.

"Well, bursting in unannounced has worked for us so far," Nyla said.

We made one more circuit before heading for the northern door, one of the ones on the narrow ends. It had had the least amount of traffic in all the times we'd passed it. As we approached, a squad of men in black fatigues burst through it, running in eerie silence past us. I successfully kept from cringing in fear and led the way through the door as it slowly swung shut.

Then we all stopped, awestruck. In the back of my mind, I knew we needed to keep moving, but what was inside the dome stunned us into frozen stillness. I'd been expecting the area inside to be divided into rooms, maybe even cubicles, but the Mercy had built *up*—taking advantage of all that open space between the floor and the dome roof. It looked incredibly unsafe, with platforms attached to long white poles and walls made of translucent plastic, and it looked like it was in motion as well. As we watched, a cube of plastic detached itself from what in a real building would be the third story and gracefully drifted to the ground, where it was disassembled and the parts spread out to join other sections of the structure.

High up near the center, the plastic walls glowed with purple light, the kind I'd only ever seen in flashes when I'd hit my head hard on something. But this glow was persistent, and the longer I looked at it, the more it made my eyes water and my head hurt as if I really had hit it. "That's the node," I said.

"We don't have to go near it, right?" Nyla said. "It looks dangerous. Like a hole in space."

"I don't know." I stripped off my left glove and held up my hand, turning slowly. The ring warmed fractionally when my hand was pointed directly at the structure, but I already knew Malcolm had to be in there somewhere. "I guess we'll find out."

No one paid us any attention as we approached the flapping plastic sheet that appeared to be the entrance. I tucked my glove beneath my cardigan and surreptitiously held my left hand in front of my body. We ducked past the plastic into a...I couldn't call it a room, really, because it was nothing but lightweight PVC pipe about two inches in diameter and more of the translucent plastic sheeting. A man-sized hole to the left led to a plastic-walled tunnel.

"This makes me think of isolation camps and infectious diseases," Nyla said. "Like we ought to be wearing those sterile suits."

I held up my left hand and turned. "Great. It's saying he's straight up."

"We'll have to work our way around," Jun said. "Besides, the tunnel is the only way to go unless you have a big knife on you."

I ducked into the tunnel, which was barely tall enough for me to walk upright, and even then my hood rubbed against the roof. It smelled strongly of plastic and the sharp ozone scent of a lot of magic in one place. The tunnel snaked along upward, swaying free with every step, until it let out in a room identical to the first except for having two more exits. One led directly to another room, and the other was a new tunnel. I stomped my foot on the floor. It looked like plastic with nothing beneath it, but it felt like stone.

I waved my hand around and then pushed aside the plastic draped between the rooms. The new room had a couple of chairs and a filing cabinet with all its drawers flung open. I looked down and couldn't see how high we were. It was still unsettling, because it looked like the cabinet ought to plummet straight through the plastic to the ground beneath.

I turned back to Nyla and Jun. My eyes widened. "Look out!"

A huge woman dressed in ordinary clothes had come through the tunnel behind us. "Why aren't you," she began, then said, "You're not—*Intruders!*"

"Run!" I screamed, and turned to flee, hoping the others would follow but not daring to look back to see if they had. I dashed through the only other exit, another tunnel that sloped downward, and ran as fast as I could. I didn't even pay attention to the ring. My only thought was to get as far from the Mercy operative as possible. I could not let myself be captured.

I took turn after turn, rushing through plastic-sheeted rooms and up swaying tunnels, until I realized no one was following me. Nyla and Jun had vanished. I stopped, breathless and with a stitch in my side. The air glowed purple, and I looked up at the node, which was only one or two of the strange plastic levels away. Through the plastic, I saw people moving around the node, though thanks to the purple glow I couldn't tell what they were doing. The air sang with a high-pitched whine, like a wet finger on the rim of a crystal glass, that rose and faded in no rhythm I recognized. The room I'd ended up in was one of the bare ones, and I wished I had time and distance to analyze the structure so I could understand the reasoning behind it. It had too much complexity to simply have been built at random.

When my breathing had slowed, I felt the ring on my thumb. It was warm, almost hot, and when I swung my arm around, it pointed me up and left. There was a tunnel going that way, so I took it. After all my running and rubbing my head against the tunnels, my hood had turned sideways, and I impatiently pushed it off my head. If I met an invader in these narrow spaces, being free to fight would matter more than not being perceived, not to mention that I hadn't seen a single invader in all my running around in here.

The ring continued to warm as I slowly made my way up the tunnel, which swayed underfoot like a rope bridge. This one, however, let out on an aluminum platform open to the air that gave me a very clear view of how high up I was, which was maybe twenty feet from the roof of the dome. The node was visible now as a purple-rimmed hole in space that sucked at my eyeballs until I had to look away. The whining hum had been joined by others until it became a harmony that was almost beautiful, even as it set my teeth on edge.

I stood very still until I regained my balance. The platform was about ten feet wide and twenty feet long, and I immediately knew this was the Mercy's prison, because hanging along both sides of the platform were giant clear plastic spheres like hamster balls without the air holes. Shorter platforms extended beneath each one. And every one of them held a crumpled human form within.

I walked down the platform slowly, conscious of how long a fall it would be even though the platform was solid and didn't shift underfoot the way the tunnels had. Bright lights illuminated the platform and each ball, and I couldn't help thinking that was a kind of torture, never giving a prisoner a chance to sleep. The ring had grown painfully hot. I ignored it, examining the figures until I reached the sphere at the end of the platform, where a man in black fatigues lay sprawled on his back, as still as death.

Malcolm.

16

I flung myself at the sphere and pressed my face against it, wary of crying out his name but desperate to know if he was alive. He looked dead, his normally tan complexion waxy pale and his eyes closed. His fatigues were torn and blood-stained as if he'd been attacked by wild animals—well, that was almost true. I stared at his chest until I convinced myself he was breathing, though the motion was so slight I was afraid I was lying to myself. Then I stepped back and examined the sphere.

I couldn't see a door. The sphere looked smooth and unbroken all the way around. How had they put him in there? How was he breathing, with no air holes? I closed my eyes and ran my fingers over the surface, thinking maybe my fingers could find what my eyes couldn't. Nothing. It was a seamless whole.

I opened my eyes and looked around. There had to be some way to open it. Maybe there were controls, or a teleportation circle, or, hell, even a diamond-tipped glass cutter like they had in movies. I backed all the way to the mouth of the tunnel and searched around it. There was a button to the right of the tunnel, but when I pressed it, all that happened was a seal slid shut across the tunnel's mouth. I hurried back to the sphere, in case closing the tunnel had triggered something else, but nothing had changed.

I decided to leave the tunnel closed—if anyone came up here, it would give me a few seconds' advance warning—and sat on the platform with my arms around my knees. I was *so close* and yet I might as well have stayed at the Gunther Node for all the good I could do here. From this position, the spheres' bottoms were above my head; there was a good four feet of clearance between the spheres and the platforms beneath them.

I looked up at Malcolm, sprawled helplessly in the bottom of his hamster ball. Then I looked closer. His body blocked out the details, but there was something else at the bottom of the sphere. I crawled out onto the short platform and peered up at it. The plastic was warped slightly, barely noticeable. I felt along the base of the sphere, and my fingertips found a seam. Thin, barely enough for me to fit my fingernails inside, but definitely a seam.

I prodded at it until I established that it made a square with rounded corners. A hatch, maybe? I still couldn't figure out how to open it, but knowing it was there gave me added resolve. I lay back beneath the sphere and had a moment's claustrophobic fear that it would break free of whatever was holding it and crush me. I distracted myself by tracing the outline with my gaze.

It definitely looked like a hatch, so what did that tell me? It couldn't open outward, or Malcolm would be able to open it. If he were conscious. I shuddered and sat up on my elbow so I could trace the line with my fingers. What would make sense, I decided, was if you could only open the hatch by pushing *inward*. Have the seal, or whatever the edge was like, be flush with the inner curve of the ball, so only someone on the outside could open it.

I lay back down and pressed my feet against the square. Drawing a deep breath, I pushed upward with all my strength. The square moved. Not much, not more than a fraction of an inch, but it moved! I suppressed a yelp of excitement and pushed harder. Once again, there was that fractional shift, but nothing else. I looked through the plastic at Malcolm's recumbent form. Moving him was going to be impossible. I needed him to wake up.

Maybe.

The more I thought about it, the more I realized it would be poor planning if the Mercy couldn't access their cells when the occupant was unconscious. I was thinking about this the wrong way. Brute force might be useful in some circumstances, but the mind that had designed this elegant prison wouldn't have wanted any solution that crude.

I clambered out from beneath the sphere and stood in front of it, just where someone coming to retrieve a prisoner for interrogation would stand. I let my eyes go unfocused and looked, not through the plastic, but at it, looking at my faint reflection rather than at Malcolm. Then I laid my palm against the faintest smear on the plastic, right at head height.

With a whoosh of displaced air, the plastic square swung inward on hinges I hadn't seen, pushing Malcolm's body up. As the door rose higher, Malcolm slid off it and fell half-in, half-out of the opening. I stifled a shriek and threw myself under the sphere, supporting him as he slid out until he fell on top of me. I rolled him onto his back, stripped off my other glove, and with shaking hands felt for a pulse. Nothing. I grabbed his shoulders and shook him. "Malcolm," I whispered in his ear, "Malcolm, wake up. Wake up!"

A faint groan escaped his lips. My heart near to bursting with happiness, I threw my arms around him and pressed my cheek to his chest. His heart beat faintly but with regularity, redoubling my joy. I wiped away tears and shook him again, more gently this time. "Malcolm, we have to get out of here. Can you stand?"

It was a stupid question, because Malcolm was clearly not capable of moving more than his lips. I remembered, too, that he'd had some of his magic drained, and that had to have weakened him before whatever the Mercy had done to him. I tried hoisting him to his feet and immediately gave that up as a lost cause.

Malcolm moistened his lips, moved them once or twice soundlessly, and then breathed out, "...Helena..."

"It's me. The Wardens are attacking. We have to get out of here." I spared a thought for Nyla and Jun, who I hoped had escaped, and tried not to feel guilty that I hadn't worried about them sooner.

"...can't move...why..."

"Don't talk. It will be all right." It would be all right if I were Victor, bigger than Malcolm and probably capable of lifting him. But I was an average-sized woman, and Malcolm outweighed me by a lot. "Hold still."

I got my hands under his arms and dragged him onto the main platform. He gave me no help, but I saw him move his head and decided to take it as a good sign. I'd shut the tunnel; maybe we could wait here until he was recovered enough to walk. Maybe nobody would think to check on the prisoners in the middle of fighting a battle with the Wardens.

I heard another hiss of displaced air and looked around, wondering which of the spheres was opening. I hadn't done anything to release the other captives, being preoccupied with Malcolm, but I really ought to get them free. Maybe some of them weren't as incapacitated as Malcolm, and could help me.

None of the spheres had opened. Instead, white fog had begun to collect in the top of each sphere, gradually spreading downward. A sickly-sweet smell drifted to me from Malcolm's open sphere. I walked to the next sphere, confused. The fog was drifting lower, brushing the face of the woman lying within. Suddenly, she jerked as if electrocuted. So did the man in the next sphere. Then all of them were convulsing as the white fog wrapped around them.

Realization struck me just as the white fog began trickling out of Malcolm's sphere. Without thinking, I slapped my hand against the sphere and watched the door swing closed, far too slowly. The sickly-sweet stench filled my nostrils, and my vision tunneled as my muscles jerked involuntarily. I held my breath and ran for Malcolm, dragging him away from the sphere toward the tunnel as best I could with my body convulsing. Well away from the fog, I gulped in clean, ozone-rich air and collapsed next to Malcolm, breathing deeply and willing the fresh air to cleanse my body of the poison. Tears filled my eyes at the thought of the Wardens who'd died in that poisonous prison, even as I knew I couldn't have saved them without killing myself.

When the convulsions slowed, I put my arms around Malcolm and held him tight. His arm quivered beneath me. "...leave me..." he whispered.

"Right, I'm going to leave you after I did all this to find you." I hugged him again, then sat up. "Someone will find us, though I wish—oh, Malcolm, I'm so stupid." I tapped my communicator and said, "Where is everyone?"

A chorus of voices filled my ear, shouted down by Acosta, who said, *"We made it back to the wardstones. Where are you?"*

"I found Malcolm. Jun, Nyla, are you there?"

No answer. I remembered they'd turned off their communicators when I had and cursed quietly. Well, there was nothing I could do for them now. I pressed my finger against the earbud and said, "Mike?"

There was no answer at first. Then Mike said, *"Helena, where the hell are you? You're not with the others!"* His voice was loud enough to hurt, though it was only my imagination that it was audible beyond my own head, because Malcolm didn't react as if he heard Mike.

"I found Malcolm. We're stuck inside the dome, near the node." I felt such relief at saying this. Mike would rescue us. It was what he was made for. I hoped he and Judy would make a go of it.

There was another pause. *"It's going to take a while to reach you,"* Mike finally said, *"but if you can get outside—"*

"Malcolm can't walk yet. I don't know what's wrong with him."

"…paralyzed…nerve disruption…wears off…eventually," Malcolm managed.

"He says it was nerve disruption. Does that mean anything to you?" I asked Mike.

Mike cursed. *"Someone's coming for you,"* he said. *"Do you still have the glass cube?"*

I'd nearly forgotten about it. "Yes."

"Hang onto that. We can track it. Fifteen minutes. I—" Mike's voice cut off like a dropped signal. I waited, but he didn't

finish his sentence. Finally I lowered my hand and clasped Malcolm's inert one.

"He said fifteen minutes. It's going to be all right," I told my husband.

Malcolm's fingers twitched. "...shouldn't have... come...dangerous..."

"You would have come for me if the situation were reversed. Besides, I remembered my gun." That wasn't strictly true, but I thought it would reassure him.

The corner of his mouth curved up in a smile. "...not sure...you are...able to shoot...in cold...blood," he whispered.

"Me neither, but the Mercy didn't know that."

Malcolm's smile widened fractionally. Then his eyes flew open, and a thin whistle emerged from his lips. It took me a second to realize it was a shout. He was staring at something behind me. I turned to see a really big knife, almost a small sword, stab through the plastic covering the tunnel and slice downward.

I threw myself over Malcolm and had my gun in my hand before the person wielding the knife could cut an opening big enough to get through. "Stop right there," I said, cursing my shaky voice. At least my hand was steady. "Stop or I'll shoot."

The person stopped, and the knife withdrew. Then a hand reached through the slit and pulled the plastic aside. I froze. I knew that hand. Tanned skin, well-shaped fingers with trimmed nails—all except the pinky, which was missing down to the first joint. A man ducked through the slit and stood just outside the tunnel, far enough away that he couldn't grab my gun. I knew that did not make him any less dangerous.

"Ms. Davies," Rafael Santiago said. "You are the last person I expected to see here."

"You thought I'd burned to death?" I said. The last time

I'd seen Santiago, he'd forced me to perform an augury for him and the Mercy, and when I'd fought off his minions with the oracle's help, he'd set the store on fire. I hadn't given him another thought since, but in truth, it made sense that he would be here. If he wasn't the Mercy's top man, he was surely very close to it.

"We knew you and the oracle survived," Santiago said. "But surely you are too valuable to the Wardens to send you into the heart of danger like this. Did you think to rescue your prisoners? How sad for you that you were not fast enough."

"You murdered them," I said.

"Disposed of. We are preparing to leave this place and cannot afford to take prisoners along. A pity, because I would like to know how they resisted having their magic drained. I don't suppose you are willing to tell me?"

So they didn't know about the new steel aegis. At the moment, that seemed irrelevant. "You know I won't tell you anything."

"Mmm." Santiago's gaze fell on Malcolm. "But you rescued one man." He looked from Malcolm to me and back again, and a smile touched his lips. "Your lover? How sweet."

I glared at him. "Back away now, or I'll shoot."

Santiago laughed. "I don't think you have it in you to shoot anyone."

"You saw what I did to your people when you tried to force the oracle against its will. I don't know why you'd say that."

Santiago took a step forward. "Ah, but that was when you were in your center of power. Now you are in mine. Your lover is helpless to defend you, you cannot hide within the oracle… and your hand is shaking."

I brandished the gun and wished he weren't right. "I said stay back."

He took another step. "This does not have to end with violence. I bear you no ill will for what you did to my people. I challenged you, you fought back—it is what happens in a war. It is not too late for you to make a different choice."

I stared at him. "You're kidding, right? You think I'd be willing to join the Mercy? You're crazy."

"Crazy, to invite you to join the winning side?" He took one more step. I aimed my gun at his heart, and he stopped, five paces from me. "You are strong, Helena Davies. You want to win the Long War. I am giving you the opportunity to do so."

"Winning?" I laughed. "The Wardens are going to take this place apart around you. You're retreating. That's the opposite of winning, Mr. Santiago."

Santiago smiled. It was such a cruel, knowing expression I shivered. "We have what we want from this node. We are leaving with perhaps a little more alacrity than we expected. But we are leaving on our own terms." He pointed toward the purple glow. "Our allies have already arrived, and the node is simply a liability now."

I reflexively glanced up—and Santiago pounced. I got off one wild shot before his hand went around my wrist and squeezed, his fingers digging into the space between my bones. I screamed in pain. The gun fell from my nerveless fingers, bounced, and slid toward the tunnel, well out of my reach. Then Santiago's other hand was around my throat, choking me. I dug into his hand with my nails, twisted my other hand out of his grip and clawed at his face. He cursed and threw me back, away from Malcolm. I hit my head on the platform, bit my tongue, and lay still for a few seconds, sucking in air.

"You are a fool," Santiago said, his voice tight and pained. He was clutching his arm, and blood spread across the sleeve.

So my shot hadn't gone completely wild, after all. "I do not know what they see in you, but my…masters…do not think like humans." He smiled, one corner of his mouth quirking upward. "But they are not here, and I think what they do not know cannot hurt them. A tragic accident, I think."

I scrambled to my feet, breathing heavily. Fifteen minutes, Mike had said. I didn't think I had fifteen minutes. "The Wardens will be here any second," I bluffed. "If you start running now, you might escape."

"Your defiance bores me," Santiago said. He wasn't smiling anymore.

He took a step forward and came up against Malcolm, lying helpless at his feet. Malcolm's hands twitched as if he were closing them on an invisible gun. "More useless dead-weight," Santiago said. He crouched and lifted Malcolm like a baby, grimacing in pain as his injured arm flexed.

I knew what he intended in the moment before he stepped to the edge of the platform. "*No!*" I screamed, flinging myself at Santiago with both fists raised. I rammed into him, making him stagger, but it wasn't enough. As if he were tossing a bag of garbage off a balcony, Santiago heaved, and Malcolm went flying, loose-limbed and inert, over the edge.

My vision went red and tunneled almost to nothing. Screaming and kicking, I pounded Santiago's chest and throat, breaking free of his efforts to restrain me as if he were a child. My fist found his face, and his head rocked backward from the blow. He shoved me away. I skidded backward toward the tunnel, coming up hard against its frame. The back of my head smacked against it, making tiny specks of light fill my vision. The frame felt more like steel than plastic.

My hand fell on something hard and angular and cold, and without thinking I wrapped my fingers around it. Santiago rose from where he'd gone to his knees on the platform. He swiped blood away from his nose with the back of one hand. "Don't worry," he said. "You will follow him soon." He took a step toward me, haltingly as if it hurt, then another.

I raised my gun, steadied it with both hands, and fired.

17

The first bullet took Santiago in the chest. He jerked, his eyes wide and startled. I squeezed the trigger again, round after round, my terror and despair sending every shot home. Santiago collapsed, blood pooling around him, but I couldn't stop shooting even though the bullets started ricocheting off the metal platform.

At some point I realized the gun was making an empty clicking noise and finally lowered it, breathing as heavily as if every shot had been torn from my body. Then I sagged helplessly against the tunnel and cried, clutching the gun as if it were my salvation.

When I ran out of tears and my body stopped shaking, I made myself go to the edge of the platform and look down. Malcolm had landed on one of the modular cubes about twenty feet down and lay sprawled there, as lifeless as he'd been when I took him out of the sphere. I fell to my knees and then lay on my stomach, staring at my husband's body.

I couldn't understand why so many stories ended with the

202 | MELISSA MCSHANE

hero getting vengeance for his girlfriend's death by killing her murderer. There was no satisfaction in it. Santiago's death had saved my life, but it wasn't going to bring Malcolm back. More tears rose up, and I swiped them away. Mike should have been here already. If he hadn't been so damned slow, Malcolm might still be alive.

I closed my eyes and cursed myself for even thinking that way. Malcolm's death was no one's fault except Santiago's. Blaming Mike wouldn't bring Malcolm back, either.

The harmonic whine that had faded into the background while I rescued Malcolm and fought Santiago drew my attention again. I wasn't sure, but I thought it had grown higher in pitch. I rolled onto my back and looked at the node. It was definitely smaller than before, which was strange; I'd thought nodes changed size very slowly, over long periods of time. Maybe it was going to destroy itself and take this whole place, and me, with it. The idea was a dull ache in the pit of my stomach, not even capable of rousing my fear.

There was a black spot at the edge of the node, blocking out the purple radiance. Unlike the node, it was growing larger. I watched it in idle curiosity as it grew larger and sprouted tendrils that waved like seaweed. Then I realized it wasn't growing larger, it was getting closer. Fear I'd thought I'd never feel again surged through me, and I clambered to my feet and backed away toward the tunnel. My hand felt around for the button, but all I found was the frame. I was afraid to turn my back on the thing, but I had no choice. I spun around and mashed the button. The plastic over the tunnel jerked, moved a few inches, ran up against the slash Santiago had made, and stuttered to a halt.

"*Helena Campbell,*" the thing said. Its voice was scratchy, like insect legs on tile. I turned to face the invader, not trying to conceal my fear. It was man-sized, black and purple-rimmed like the node, with dozens of flailing tentacles and no visible face. I couldn't tell where the voice was coming from or even if I was hearing it with my ears. It might just as well have been inserted directly into my brain. It hovered over the pool of blood Santiago lay in, completely indifferent to his dead body.

"*You have taken a life,*" it said. I waited for more, but after those few words, it was silent.

"Don't expect me to apologize," I finally said. My defiance sounded thin and pointless in my ears.

The invader waited, staring at me—at least, it felt like it was staring. It was certainly aware of me even if it didn't have eyes, because I could feel its attention on me in the same way I knew when the oracle noticed me.

Finally, my nerves giving way, I shouted, "You can't drain my magic, so if you're going to kill me, give it your best shot! I won't make it easy on you!"

"*Your death is not essential,*" the invader said. "*We have already had our revenge on the Wardens. You, though, might take that one's place.*" It flicked a tentacle in the direction of Santiago's body.

"You're sick," I breathed. "I'm never going to join you."

"*No?*" Its tentacles writhed around it. "*Not even if it meant victory for your Wardens?*"

My mouth fell open. "What...I don't understand. This is a trick."

"*No tricks. We warned you, Helena Campbell. You will be given one last chance, when all hope is gone. Remember.*" The tentacles flew through the air, dizzying me. The purple glow around the invader's edges brightened until it was too painful to look at. I shielded my eyes, and just as quickly as it had come, the light vanished. When I lowered my arm, the invader was gone.

The ringing sound in the air vanished. Then a noise like *fwooomph* shattered the stillness, and the sky caught fire.

I flung myself flat on the platform and covered my face. The fire was close enough to scorch my skin, but after a few terrified moments, I realized the heat was gone. I rolled over and saw, instead of the white cloth covering the dome, pale blue sky covered with high, thin clouds. Dark shapes plummeted through the bare frame, halting as if cushioned by the air just before they would have fallen to the ground, and came to rest on the plastic and PVC of the structure.

Two figures dropped to light gently on the platform's far end. "Helena," Mike said. He released a switch that turned off the rushing jet of air coming from the pack on his back and rocked a little, getting his balance. "Where's Malcolm?"

My throat closed up. I'd managed to forget, in the terror of facing my enemies, that my life was over. "He threw him," I managed, and pointed over the side. "He's down there."

Mike looked over the edge and swore. "Stevens, get her down from here," he said to his companion, a blonde woman with powerful shoulders who was examining Santiago's body. "I'll get the—I'll get him, Helena."

I nodded. Stevens helped me into a harness that hooked me onto her like a parachutist in training, only facing toward her instead of away. "It's perfectly safe," she told me. "You don't even have to hang on, though most people like to."

I nodded. I'd reached a state beyond fear. Obediently I put my arms around her shoulders and held still as she turned on her air jet and we drifted gradually downward. I didn't know why she hadn't just carried me all the way to the wardstones and didn't really care. When we landed, she unfastened me and I nodded to her and walked away. There didn't seem to be anything to say.

The Wardens had burned the entire dome, so I could have stepped through the frame at any point, but my numb mind steered me toward the door Nyla, Jun and I had entered by. I hoped they were still alive.

The place was crawling with Wardens, none of whom intercepted me or even seemed to notice I was there. I decided to walk wide of the compound, skirting its perimeter. All the invaders were gone, though I saw some bodies here and there. A few of the bodies were human. I steered clear of all of them. I didn't need any more close encounters with death.

I remembered the look on Santiago's face when I'd shot him, that stunned, disbelieving look. Was it shock that I'd managed to pull the trigger, or an inability to believe he was mortal? It didn't really matter, but it was something to think about that wasn't remembering Malcolm's broken body lying so still— I went to my knees behind a bush and threw up.

Empty, drained, and exhausted, I wiped my mouth and continued on my way. Back to the wardstones, back home, and then…I hadn't slept in over twenty-four hours, and maybe that would help. It probably wouldn't, but even now I hadn't lost all of my famous optimism.

None of the sports were at the wardstones when I arrived. That was good. They deserved rest after what they'd accomplished. I hoped Jun and Nyla were safe. Someone at the Gunther Node would know. I accepted the hand of the stone magus on duty, not someone I knew, and endured the stomach-wrenching transition more easily than ever before. Of course, I'd already vomited up everything that was in me, so that might have made a difference.

The central chamber was as busy as it had been after the failed attack, but this time there weren't any moaning injured people. I was sure they hadn't made the second assault without casualties, but it was reassuring to know there weren't so many that they couldn't use the node's infirmaries instead of the central hub. I started walking, realized I didn't know where I was going, and stood still in the middle of the spaghetti tangle of colored lines on the floor. I traced the blue one with my eyes until I lost its thread, then focused on the red one. If I could find the right line, maybe it would take me to the place where Malcolm was still alive.

"Davies!"

I turned at the peremptory sound of Lucia's voice. She strode toward me across the hub, Dave Henry at her heels. "Is your communicator working? Conti's been trying to raise you for ten minutes."

I tapped the communicator, which responded by falling out of my ear into my palm. "I—it stopped in the middle of a communication. I thought it was Mike's that was damaged."

"Looks like yours had a flaw. Some of that batch did. I'm going to have words with the magus who created them." Lucia took my elbow in a supportive grip that confused me. "Conti was trying to tell you that Campbell is alive."

I stared at her. Campbell who? Then it hit me. "Malcolm fell," I said stupidly.

"Not far enough. Cracked his skull, broke a few bones, but—"

The white specks filled my vision again, and the last thing I heard before I fainted was Lucia saying, "Henry, catch her—!"

I came to on the hard, cold concrete, staring up at the distant ceiling of the central hub. My mouth was filled with a coppery taste, like I'd bitten my tongue, but it didn't feel bloody. Cold sweat had broken out on my forehead and scalp, and my whole body felt numb. I blinked, slowly, and drew in a deep breath of air scented with gardenias.

THE BOOK OF WAR | 207

"Sorry about that," Lucia said. She was crouched beside me and didn't sound any sorrier than she ever did. "It was going to be a shock no matter how I told you, so I figured, better to get it over with."

"He's alive."

"Barely. Half his magic's been drained, he's lost a lot of blood, and the broken bones are just the beginning of his troubles. But none of it except the magic is anything a bone magus can't fix. Conti was afraid to move him, so they were waiting on a healer. Should be another half hour."

I sat up. "I have to go to him."

Lucia put a restraining hand on my shoulder. "You'd be in the way. The Mercy compound is overrun by Wardens and Mercy fighting. Or did you want to get yourself killed?"

I closed my eyes and breathed out. "Where are Jun and Nyla? Did they make it back?"

"I don't know. I've been busy." Lucia converted her grip on my shoulder to an extended hand, and I let her help me up. "Try looking in Yellow 15. They might have gathered there."

"Thanks."

Lucia held my hand a few seconds longer. "I've never been so glad to be wrong."

I resisted driving home the point that I had been right and headed off along the yellow painted line.

Yellow 15 was the briefing room where we'd received our instructions and the earbuds. I hurried down the hall toward it, my heart aching with impatience. Malcolm was alive. They'd heal him. I'd already saved his life and I couldn't do anything more for him. I still couldn't bear being separated from him, even if it was only for half an hour. I focused instead on the sports—my friends, really. Now that the excitement and terror of finding Malcolm had passed, I could worry about Jun and Nyla.

How could we have become separated so easily? It wasn't like there were a ton of places to go in that plastic hamster habitat.

By the time I reached Yellow 15, I was running. I threw open the door and halted just inside, more dramatically than I'd intended. Victor stopped midsentence, turning to look at me, and then everyone started talking at once. I breathed out a sigh of relief when I saw Jun and Nyla both.

"That was a foolish thing to do, running off alone," Ines said, approaching me with her hands outstretched. She clasped mine gently and added, "I hope you were successful."

"Malcolm's alive, and they're healing him now," I said. Just saying the words made me feel giddy with happiness. "Nobody's hurt?"

"We made it back to the wardstones without incident," Acosta said. "We wanted to wait for the three of you, but the Wardens insisted we return immediately."

"What happened to you?" Nyla said. "We tried to follow you, but there were more of the Mercy in the way, and you were gone before we could get you to wait."

"Though that probably would have been fatal for all of us," Jun said. "Nyla and I headed for the ground, but then I got tripped up, and *we* were separated."

"I didn't realize you weren't behind me until it was too late," I said. "But it was probably just as well you weren't with me. I...it's a long story."

"Mine isn't," Jun said. "I reached the ground and took off running. Had to use the baton on a couple of people, but when I reached the edge of the camp, there were a lot of Wardens and I ended up having to dodge them too. These cardigans aren't Warden standard issue. At least the magi by the wardstones knew I was an ally."

"I got turned around in the plastic maze," Nyla said, "but aside from that one woman, none of the Mercy soldiers paid any attention to me so long as I kept moving. Then I used my talent to distract a couple of them at the exit and just ran for it."

"It took you a lot longer to get back than it did me," Jun said. "You were lucky not to be noticed."

"Yeah." Nyla ran her hands through her hair, disordering her red locks. "But—damn, y'all, we did it!"

A spontaneous, ragged cheer went up, though Acosta and Mangesh didn't join in. Mangesh was his usual calm self. Acosta looked like something was bothering him. I caught his eye, and to my surprise he gave me a tiny shake of the head, as if to say, "ask me later." So I didn't push.

"So, you found Malcolm," Victor said. "It can't have been that easy."

"It wasn't," I said. "He was nearly gassed by the Mercy, and thrown…it was awful." I told them the basics of what had happened, though I left out the invader entirely—that was an interaction I wanted to discuss first with Malcolm, and then with Lucia.

"I didn't think you'd be able to shoot someone," Nyla said at the end.

"I was semi-insane at the time. Maybe that's what it takes," I said. "I've never been so furious and terrified and miserable as when Mr. Santiago threw Malcolm over the edge like that. I hope I never feel that way again."

"It is a miracle your husband survived," Mangesh said.

"I feel like I've exhausted my lifetime supply of them," I said.

I glanced at my watch. I couldn't remember when Lucia

had told me it would be another half an hour, didn't know if I could justify leaving to search the node for Malcolm.

"So now what?" Victor asked.

That silenced us. It was a good question. We'd accomplished what the Wardens needed of us, and accomplished my personal quest, but I didn't feel like that meant the sports were finished. "I don't know," I said. "I mean…you all have lives to return to…"

"But the world is a much bigger place now than it was seventy-two hours ago," Ines said. "I do not believe everything the Wardens do is so dramatic as this, but surely there is not nothing for us to do?"

"There are other nodes, right?" Victor said. "All over the country?"

"All over the world," I said.

"Then maybe we introduce ourselves at the nodes near where we live, ask them what we can do," Victor went on.

"Or have Lucia tell us what else she wants," Nyla said. "She could talk to the other node custodians, right?"

"I'm ready to return home," Jun said. "I want some time to absorb all of this before the magical world sucks me in again."

"I thought you said it was something to commit your life to," I said.

Jun's smile was tired. "It is," she said, "but not something to kill yourself over. I think we've earned a break."

"Amen to that," Victor said.

I felt a little dizzy at their enthusiasm. "I never expected this," I said. "I thought…I don't know what I thought. I hoped you'd want to be a part of all this, but I didn't think it would be so easy."

Everyone laughed. "If this is what you call easy, Helena,"

Victor said, "I gotta ask what you normally see in a day's work."

"Okay, I guess easy is the wrong word." I glanced at my watch again and decided I was through waiting around. "I'm going to go find Malcolm. You should all go back to the hotel for some rest, and then…Jun, didn't you have a flight to catch?"

"I already missed it. I'll get a later one. I don't feel like rushing."

"I should get back home to Mom, see how she's doing," Nyla said. "But I'd like to know what Lucia thinks, you know, whether she can tell us anything about the nodes where we live."

"If we can find her." I turned toward the door and felt a hand grip my elbow. Acosta stood right next to me, his expression unreadable, but his grip unmistakably telling me to wait. Surprised, I let the others pass me until Acosta and I were the only ones in the room.

"Sorry," he said, letting me go. "But there's something you should know. Jun lied about what happened when she was alone in the Mercy stronghold."

"What?" I blinked at him. "She lied—what did she lie about?"

"She said she reached the ground and took off running. That was false." His lips thinned in frustration. "Maybe it's nothing. This talent isn't precise. But if she was alone in the Mercy stronghold, and something happened that she felt she needed to lie about—"

"That could be a problem, yes." I sighed. "But what can we do about it?"

"Watch her. If she's made common cause with the Mercy—"

I gasped. "You think she's a traitor?"

Acosta shook his head. "That's just one possibility. Like I said, it could be nothing."

I almost asked him why he'd told me, but even I knew I'd become the sports' leader. "Thanks. I hope it's nothing."

Acosta smiled, a tired expression. "I'd thought the Wardens were done having to look over their shoulders for spies and traitors."

We headed for the door. "So, do you think of yourself as a Warden now?" I asked.

He shrugged and held the door for me. "If I really was a Warden," he said, "it could be a huge conflict of interest. It's better if I'm a cop with some unusual allies. But...I could be wrong about that."

"Well, for what it's worth," I said, "I'm glad to be one of those allies."

We caught up with the others in the central hub. They looked as if they didn't know where to go. "I need to go to the infirmary," I said. "I'll find someone to take you back to the—"

"Helena!"

The cry had come from my left. I turned to see Judy and Viv racing toward me. Viv threw her arms around me, nearly bowling me over. "We heard the news," she said. "I'm so glad he's alive!"

"Mike told us," Judy said without a blush at saying his name. "It sounds like it was close."

"It was. Do you know where he is? Lucia only said they couldn't move him, and had to heal him where he lay."

"No. We thought you'd be with him." Viv released me.

Impatience surged over me. I touched my ear before remembering the communicator was gone. Lucia, of course, was nowhere in sight. Dave would be with her, wherever she was. I needed my husband and there was no one who could tell me where he was!

Jun touched my elbow. "Helena."

"What?" I snapped, and immediately felt bad that I'd let my impatience loose.

Jun pointed. Across the chamber, a handful of men in black fatigues were walking through the purple gate. Mike, Derrick, Hector—

—and Malcolm, striding along as if he'd never been injured.

I sucked in a painful, heartrending breath. Then I sprinted across the hub, dodging people too slow to get out of my way, stumbling once and righting myself through pure force of will. I threw myself on Malcolm, knocking him back a step, and buried my face in his shoulder, crying so hard I almost couldn't breathe.

His arms went around me, and he rested his forehead against my hair as he held me tight. Neither of us spoke. I couldn't think of any words that could mean more than the two of us embracing as if we'd never have the chance again. His fatigues smelled of blood and sweat and a trace of the sickly-sweet poison, and they were still badly torn, which made me cry harder at the memory of his limp body sprawled atop that plastic cube.

"I ought to be angry that you risked your life for me," Malcolm murmured in my ear, "but it's no less than I would have done for you, so I choose to be grateful instead that my wife is fearless in my defense."

"You nearly died twice," I sniffled. "Three times, if you count the Mercy's poison. Can you try not to do that again for a while?"

He laughed and held me tighter. "I'm exhausted, and I want nothing more than to go home and sleep for a year, preferably with you beside me."

"I can handle that." I lifted my head so I could look him in the face. "I love you."

He pushed a lock of my hair out of my face where it had come free from my ponytail. "You'd better," he said, "because you are my heart." He lowered his head to kiss me, and I wrapped my arms around his neck and returned his kiss with all my heart.

I lost track of time, of where we were, of who was watching. Nothing in the world mattered except kissing the man I loved and feeling my heart nearly burst with joy that he wasn't dead. But eventually we separated, and when we did, I heard Lucia say, "About time. You need to take him home, Davies, and let him recover from the healing."

"That's a wonderful idea." I took Malcolm's hand and squeezed it. "But the sports wanted to talk to you, if you've got a minute."

Lucia raised an eyebrow. "All right." She and Dave, who was grinning like he approved of our extended kiss, followed me back across the hub.

The sports hadn't moved in all the time I'd been with Malcolm. Ines and Nyla looked as if they'd been cheering me on. Victor whistled in astonishment. "They told us you looked like you'd been hit by a train," he said to Malcolm. "I didn't know magic could heal so thoroughly."

"It is a perfect healing with side effects," Malcolm said. "The body still hurts afterward. I have a terrible headache that will last for a day or so. But since the alternative was having my brains spill out on the floor, I'm not going to complain. It will also take time for my magic to fully regenerate, and there's nothing healing can do about that."

"Some of us were wondering," Nyla said to Lucia. "We can't keep coming back here when there's stuff we can do for the Wardens. And this can't be the only magic place in the world. So we were thinking, who do we talk to? And maybe, if there's other node custodians like you, you could explain to them about us."

"Not a bad idea," Lucia said. "Where are you from? Texas? Ginger Rubio at the Bonaventura Node isn't the kind of woman who deals well with change. She'd only believe your story if it came from me."

"Thanks," Nyla said, extending her hand. Lucia looked skeptical, but shook it politely.

"I'm surprised you all seem so eager now," she said. "Davies made it sound like you were all mentally on the plane home."

"Some of us were," Jun said with a smile. "I've always been stubborn when it comes to change. I needed time to get over myself. I understand I live within the range of this node's authority?"

"You do," Lucia said. "I've got a few ideas on how to use your talent."

"Wait, how come *Lucia* knows what her talent is and none of us do?" Victor muttered to me.

Jun nodded. "My schedule isn't very flexible," she said, holding out her hand for Lucia to shake, "but I'll do what I can."

"Sounds reasonable," Lucia said, "and..."

Her voice trailed off, though her hand continued to shake Jun's, pumping up and down automatically. She was staring into the distance past Jun's left ear, and her pupils had shrunk to tiny points.

"Lucia?" I said.

Jun cried out and snatched her hand away. Sharp red crescents like nail marks bloomed on the back of her hand. Lucia's hand remained outstretched, though it was closed into a tight fist. Dave put a hand on her shoulder. With a sigh, Lucia closed her eyes and folded at the knees, hitting the floor too fast for anyone to catch her.

18

"Lucia!" Dave shouted, dropping to his knees beside her. He eased her into a more comfortable position, though it was clear she was past feeling anything. He leaned over with his cheek to her mouth, then felt along her neck for a pulse. "Her breathing is shallow, and her pulse is thready," he said. "What the *hell* did you do to her?"

Jun looked bewildered. "I didn't do anything. She dug her nails into my hand—look," she said, displaying the sore red crescents.

Dave touched his ear. "I need a couple of bone magi in the hub immediately. Lucia is—she's ill." He glared at Jun, who flinched. "No, I don't know what's wrong, that's why I need the damn bone magi." He lowered his hand and looked up at all of us. "You," he said to Jun. "You touched her, and she collapsed."

"I didn't do anything," Jun protested. "*She* clawed *me*. Look!" She waved her hand in his face again. Dave grabbed it and turned it over, examining it, then thrust it away.

"Don't move," he said. "Any of you. I—it's about time," he shouted to a couple of tall, muscular men who looked more like bodybuilders than doctors. They said nothing, just went to their knees beside Lucia. One of them lifted her head to rest on his knees, and the other took her left hand as if taking a pulse, though he used his thumb instead of his fingers.

The one holding her head let out a hiss of surprise almost immediately. "Poison," he said. "Jerry, give me a hand."

"Poison?" I said.

The two bone magi ignored me, which was just as well because I hadn't meant that as a query, just an expression of surprise. I looked at Jun, whose face was rigid and expressionless. But Jun couldn't have poisoned Lucia. She barely knew her, so what would be the point?

The invader's words came to mind. *We have already taken our revenge on the Wardens*, it had said, and I'd been so afraid and overwhelmed I hadn't thought to ask what it meant. Lucia dead would be a tremendous blow to the Wardens, not just at the Gunther Node, but all over North America and probably beyond as well. And Jun had lied about her escape. If she'd been suborned by the Mercy, been given something she could poison Lucia with...no. I couldn't believe it. And yet, what other explanation was there?

Lucia's darkly tan skin was even darker than usual, and her lips were blue around the edges. The bone magi had clasped hands and didn't appear to be doing anything else. I held Malcolm's hand and kept my gaze locked on Lucia's face as if that would keep her from dying. The idea was ludicrous. Lucia was too much a force of nature to be discommoded by something as banal as death.

A trickle of blood ran from Lucia's nose down her face to pool in her ear. She didn't appear to be breathing. I wiped away tears and ordered myself not to be stupid. I wasn't going to grieve for her when she was still alive.

"Watch it," the bone magus named Jerry said, but again nothing happened—nothing visible, anyway. I couldn't begin to imagine what the magi might be doing beneath Lucia's skin. Then Lucia's chest rose as she drew a deep breath and released it in a long, slow sigh. I sniffed. The air smelled of onions. The bone magi sat back, sagging as if exhausted. "That's all we can do for now," the one said. "But it's good news. We've put her into a coma—"

Viv gasped. I held on to Malcolm more tightly. A coma was a *good* thing?

"And as soon as she's stable, we can get a team working on extracting the poison," he continued. "It resisted being converted into something neutral, so right now it's in stasis with her."

"How was it administered? Something she ate? Or topical?" Dave asked.

Jerry shook his head. "Slipped beneath the skin. It would have been encapsulated, so when it entered her body, it didn't start poisoning her immediately—not until the encapsulation dissolved."

"How long would that take?"

"No idea." Jerry shrugged. "A few seconds, half an hour… no way to tell because her body absorbed the encapsulation vector."

Dave grunted acknowledgement. "Take her to the infirmary, and let me know when you start work on removing the poison." He stood and faced Jun. "You and I are going to have a talk."

"You don't think she did it?" Victor exclaimed. "Why would Jun want to poison Lucia?"

"I'm supposed to believe it was a coincidence that you touched her, and almost immediately she's poisoned?"

"Nyla touched her first," Jun said, pointing at Nyla. "It wasn't just me."

Acosta cleared his throat. "But you're the one who lied about what happened when you were escaping the Mercy compound."

Jun's eyes widened. "What?"

Dave said, "What are you suggesting, Detective?" He'd turned his furious gaze on Nyla after Jun's first words, but now he looked back at Jun, his eyes narrowed.

"I'm not suggesting anything except that Jun is hiding something, and it might be something deadly to the Wardens." Acosta's dark, lean face was impassive.

Jun took a step back, and Dave grabbed her wrist. She stopped. "I didn't do it," she said.

"We'll find out. Come with me."

"You have no authority to hold me. Let me go."

Dave smiled. There was no amusement in it. "The laws of the Long War aren't the same as those of the mundane world. If you're innocent, you have nothing to fear."

Jun matched him mirthless smile for mirthless smile. "That's about as reassuring as it would be coming from a real cop."

I looked from Dave to Jun and then at Lucia's body, being carried out of the hub by the bone magi. "Jun, please cooperate," I said. "We just want to know the truth."

Jun looked at me. Her eyes were dark and distant. "You don't believe me."

"I—you need to tell us the truth about what happened in the Mercy compound. Please, Jun."

Jun's lips thinned. "It was no one's business but mine," she said, "and I'm not telling you anything."

"That's enough for me," Dave said. He tapped his ear. "Send enforcers to the hub. Yes, now."

Jun tried to pull away from Dave, but his grip was implacable. Victor said, "Uh, maybe this is the wrong idea. You're not cops."

"Stay out of this," Dave said. He waved at a trio of people who were even more musclebound than the bone magi. "Jun Li, I'm ordering you bound over for investigation. Cooperate, and you won't be harmed."

"Dave—" I said.

"Get the rest of them out of here, Helena," Dave said. "Ms. Li, give me your earbud."

"But this is still just circumstantial evidence."

"Then the investigation will prove that." He pocketed the piece of glass Jun handed him.

I didn't like the hard, cold look in Dave's eyes. For all I'd never known him to be less than impartial, this was *Lucia* we were talking about, his lover, and I wasn't sure his impartiality would hold up under these conditions. "I'll stay with Jun," I said.

Jun's eyes widened again.

"Helena, you need to let Henry deal with this," Malcolm said.

"She's only here because of me," I said. "I want to know the truth."

"Sounds like you don't have any faith in our system," Dave said.

I squared up to him. "Systems make mistakes."

Dave's eyes narrowed. "Are you suggesting I'd engineer some kind of accident?"

"I'm suggesting that you're angry and looking for someone to blame. That's natural. But you have to stay impartial, and I think if I'm there, you'll remember that." I kept my gaze on his face, willing him to see reason.

"Helena—" Malcolm said.

Dave held up a hand. "Fine," he said. "You can babysit and make sure she doesn't accidentally fall on some bullets. Happy?"

I wished I dared touch him in reassurance. Under that anger was a wellspring of hurt trying to get out. "Dave," I said, "they'll save her. And we'll find out who did it."

Dave let out a deep breath. "We will," he said, glaring at Jun. She stared back at him with no expression. "Take them both to detention. I'll be there shortly."

"You are *not* locking Helena up," Malcolm growled.

"It was her idea, Campbell, weren't you paying attention?" Dave nodded to the enforcers, who surrounded Jun without touching her. If her force field made them uncomfortable, they didn't show it. "I'll join you shortly." He turned on his heel and walked away toward the green door.

"I'm coming with you," Malcolm told me.

"It's all right, Malcolm, nothing's going to happen to me," I said. "You need to make sure the—everyone gets back to the hotel. Oh, and they need to return the cardigans and the earbuds."

Malcolm took me by the shoulders and turned me to face him. "If she's a traitor, you could be in danger."

"She's not a traitor."

"And you know this how? Helena, this is a bad idea."

I shook my head. "I just know. She's not going to hurt me."

With a scowl, Malcolm said, "Then I'm coming with you."

I hugged him, rejoicing in how warm and strong and living

he was. "I think it would be overkill if we both went with Jun to detention. Go. It won't take long."

Malcolm's lips thinned in disapproval, but he nodded. I kissed him once more and turned back to face the enforcers and Jun. Jun still looked expressionless. The enforcers looked confused. "It's all right," I said. "I've been in the cells before. Should I lead the way?"

The enforcer on the right, a man whose dark skin reflected the fluorescent lights, let out a little snort of amusement. Jun looked confused now, which relieved me; I'd thought she was going to stay impassive forever. Surrounded by the enforcers, we set off in the direction of the detention cells, following the black line.

I caught Jun casting furtive glances my way as we walked along the corridors. "Let me guess," I finally said. "You're wondering why I was ever locked up here."

"It crossed my mind," Jun said. Her mouth barely moved, as if she were afraid the enforcers might crack down on her if she talked too loudly.

"You remember I told you about the Accords, how they govern all the Neutralities, including the custodian of Abernathy's? I was arrested for violating the Accords."

Jun raised an eyebrow. On her, the gesture looked sinister, possibly because her eyebrows were thin and flexible enough nearly to reach her hairline. "You were? I thought you were the most law-abiding person the Wardens had ever produced."

"I had my limits. Specifically, I was in love with Malcolm and I didn't care that the Accords said we couldn't be together. I admitted to our relationship in a situation where I couldn't keep it secret anymore."

"You're married. Something must have changed."

I smiled in memory. "I convinced the Board of Neutralities

that it was an unjust law." And then the oracle had extorted five million dollars from the Board so I could afford to pay the fine they'd imposed. The memory still warmed my heart, almost a year later. I knew I was in the right, but having the oracle back me up felt like the ultimate vindication.

The dark-skinned enforcer looked at me as if he wanted to order me to silence, but didn't quite dare to speak like that to Abernathy's custodian. I fell silent anyway. The enforcers were doing their jobs, and I didn't want to make that harder.

The magenta line, which had paralleled the black line, made a sharp left turn. After about twenty more steps, the cyan line turned right. Now it was just the black line, snaking down a curving tunnel. Ahead, I saw a steel door painted beige I remembered. Even though I wasn't here as a prisoner —or at least was a voluntary, temporary prisoner—my heart still beat faster at the sight.

One of the enforcers withdrew a key card from his breast pocket and dipped it into the reader beside the door. The light went from red to green, and the enforcer pushed the door open. Beyond was a short corridor lined with more beige metal doors, their steel riveted together. Each door had a key card reader next to it. All of them glowed with tiny red lights like malevolent stars fallen to earth.

The enforcers marched inside and closed the door. Two of them took up guard positions on either side of Jun and me, and the third, the one who'd opened the door, continued down the hallway to the far end and did his door opening trick again. We waited. I was starting to feel stupid about my grand gesture. Dave was a good guy—he wouldn't arrange for Jun to be tortured or killed in custody. *You don't know that*, I told my sensitive, trusting self. The Long War was hard, and Dave had executed or ordered the execution of dozens of traitors just a year ago. Staying with Jun was the right thing to do.

The enforcer returned, holding a key card—black, not white like the first. He stopped at the fifth door on the right and beckoned to us to join him. Jun and I walked toward him without waiting for the enforcers to prompt us, which made me angry with myself for being cooperative with my jailors. I reminded myself that they weren't the enemy and waited patiently beside the door.

The enforcer swiped the key card, and the door swung open. Jun entered the cell without looking at anyone. "Thanks," I said, then hurried inside before I could feel too stupid about having thanked them for locking me up. The door swung shut beside us, not with a clang, but with the faintest click as the lock engaged.

The cell was just as I remembered from last year—a concrete cube about twelve feet on a side, lit by a single bulb, with a bench attached to one wall and a sink with one handle on the tap attached to the wall next to it. Jun had already taken a seat on the bench. It was long enough for someone to lie down on, but with no pillow or blanket, it wouldn't be very comfortable.

I worked the tap at the sink and filled my cupped hands with water, which I drank down thirstily. Then I dried my hands on my pants beneath my cardigan and freed my hair from its ponytail. It was messy and frizzy from all the running and how my head had rubbed against the plastic tunnels of the Mercy compound. I combed through my hair with my fingers and put it back up again. "So, what should we talk about?" I asked. "It might be a while before Dave comes back."

Jun was staring at me as if I'd gone crazy. "Why did you do

it?" she asked. "You barely know me. And I might be a traitor who'd try to kill you next."

I leaned against the wall and crossed my arms over my chest. "I know you're not telling the truth. Det—Greg said you lied about what happened to you in the Mercy compound. But I don't think whatever happened made you a traitor. Tell me, Jun. Why did you lie?"

Jun looked away, her lips thin and straight. "You believe that detective?"

"Strangely, given our history of mutual antagonism, I do. Come on. Whatever it is could clear you of attempted assassination!"

Jun was silent. She crossed her arms the way I was doing and stared at the door.

"Thirty-one," I said.

She turned to look at me. "Thirty-one what?"

"Rivets in the door. In case you were counting them. I did that when I was here before and there's thirty-one. Seems like a strange number, huh? Why not an even thirty or thirty-two?"

Jun's lips curved in a reluctant smile. "You're an odd one," she said. "You volunteered to be locked up to protect the life of a woman who might have killed your friend. And you put your life on the line not just to save your husband, but to stop an organization you're not even remotely qualified to fight. I don't understand you at all."

"I think you do," I said. "You want to make a difference in the world. You just don't know how. And you're alone because your talent makes it hard for people to be close to you, and you wish that was different but you don't know how to change that either. I think you wanted a reason to join the Wardens that would be...incontrovertible, maybe. Something you could point to and claim it was inevitable, that you couldn't fight it. I wish I could prove to you that I can be trusted."

Halfway through my speech, Jun's smile disappeared. When I finished, she said, "You think you know me? Part of the investigation you conducted?"

"*No*, of course not!" I threw up my hands in exasperation. "Why is it people always object to other people understanding them? Like you're too...too special for mere mortals to comprehend your motives? Jun, I don't know for sure that's what your life is like. It's just a guess I feel comfortable making. Would it really be so bad to let someone else in?"

Jun looked away again. "You don't understand."

"Because you won't explain. Just tell me what happened in the Mercy compound. I'll defend you to Dave—I'll even explain it to him. But don't think you have to hide anymore."

Jun said nothing. I walked to the door and leaned against it with my face pressed against my arm. I couldn't force Jun to talk, and for all I knew she actually was a traitor and would attack me next, never mind what I'd told Malcolm.

"If I tell you what happened," Jun said quietly, "you really will think I'm a traitor."

I turned around. She had her hands clasped loosely in her lap and was staring at them. "Why is that?"

She shook her head. "Honestly, I'm not totally sure what happened. Whether it didn't make me a traitor without me knowing it. But I didn't agree to its terms."

I held my breath and suppressed a dozen questions.

Finally, Jun said, "I tripped, and Nyla ran past me. I thought I followed her immediately, but when I got through the next tunnel, she'd vanished. I had no idea where I was, so I just took as many down-sloping tunnels as I could find. And after about the fifth one, I ran into it."

She let out a deep breath. "I'd never seen anything so terrifying. It had arms and legs like an insect, multijointed, but thick and muscled like a bodybuilder's. Other than that, it looked almost ridiculous, all those rainbow colors...it looked like the offspring of a goliath beetle and a unicorn. But it didn't make me want to laugh. I stood there staring at it because I was afraid to turn my back on it to run. And it called me by name." Jun finally looked up at me, and I was caught even more breathless by the look of bleak despair in her eyes. "How did it know my name?"

"I don't know. They seem to know a lot of things they shouldn't. The—" I'd been about to tell her the one who'd spoken to me had known I was married now even though Santiago hadn't, but I decided that would derail the conversation. "What did it tell you?"

"My name. My talent. How it feels to always keep people at a distance." The corner of Jun's mouth went up in a half-smile. "Do you know why I hate it when people say they understand me? It diminishes who I am. If someone understands me, that's like saying I'm not unique in my trials. I hate that. But I also know it's stupid, because who am I to be—what did you say? Special?—to be too special in what I've endured? There's only so many kinds of misery in the world."

"But you're the only one with that talent," I said. "I *don't* understand how that must feel. I can only imagine it, and maybe I'm wrong in my imagining."

"It doesn't matter. That...thing...knew exactly how I feel. It told me details I've never shared with anyone. And every word it spoke sickened me more, made me feel smaller and more terrified. Maybe it did that on purpose, so its offer would be more compelling."

"It made you an offer?" Despite what I'd said to Malcolm,

fear touched my heart. If Jun was a traitor, we were trapped together in this cell and she, for all she was twice my age, was taller and stronger than me.

Jun looked away again. "It said it could remove my talent from me. Make me normal."

"That's impossible."

"Is it?" Jun shrugged. "Maybe. It was very convincing, and you know I'm not easily convinced. I believe it could do what it promised. And it chose exactly the promise guaranteed to make me consider its bargain."

My muscles tensed, preparing to fight. "But you didn't."

She glanced up at me, and this time her smile was real. "You're afraid," she said. "Smart of you. No, I didn't agree. I've been part of enough negotiations to recognize when the person across the table from you isn't showing all his cards. That creature might have been able to free me from this curse, but once I did as it asked, it would go on asking me to do more, until it stopped asking and went to ordering instead. I'm nobody's puppet."

"Even though it offered you your heart's desire?" I hadn't relaxed, though part of me knew Jun was telling the truth.

Jun sighed. "This talent has benefits as well as drawbacks. I'm not sure I could adjust to being normal. So even if the creature had been completely honest with me, I probably still would have said no." She stood and stretched. "Besides, I draw the line at poisoning someone."

I shifted my position so I wasn't quite so tense. "That's what it wanted, then. Poison Lucia. Which means somebody else took that bargain." I paced a short circle in front of the door. "It has to be Nyla. If it was someone Lucia touched earlier today, the invader wouldn't have tried to get you to do it. But Nyla didn't lie about what happened to her."

"She also wasn't very specific," Jun pointed out. "She might easily just have left out her encounter with the creature, and Greg wouldn't have picked up on that."

I sighed and sat on the bench. "We just have to convince Dave. Which means waiting—"

The light went out.

I froze. In the distance, I heard a faint *thunkthunkthunk* sound, like an airplane engine stuttering to a halt. Then the light came back on, dimmer than before. A voice I recognized as the woman who made recordings for the Athenaeum and the Gunther Node's elevators said, *The node has been breached. Prepare for invasion. The node has been breached. Prepare for invasion.*

19

J un and I stared at each other. "Invasion? What does that mean?" Jun said.

"It means invaders have found a way past the Gunther Node's protections," I replied. "I thought that was impossible."

"If there was one traitor, there could have been more," Jun said.

"You mean someone let them through? Maybe. But anyone who knew how to let the invaders in would know how to do it without setting off the alarm. I think something else is going on. It can't be coincidence that the one time Lucia is out of commission, invaders manage to enter the node."

"We have to get out of here," Jun said. "If that man, Dave, is preoccupied with an invasion, he's not going to come here any time soon. And who knows what kind of damage Nyla might be able to do with no one suspecting her?"

I jumped up and ran to the door, pounding on it. "Let us out!" I shouted. My voice echoed through the cell in a way that told me it hadn't penetrated the solid steel of the door. I pounded some more, hoping that noise would reach someone.

"That's not going to work," Jun said. "Someone would hear it only if they were in the hallway outside, and why would they hang around the cells like that? The enforcers are all somewhere else in the detention area."

I stepped back and glared at the door. "Well, crap. We're stuck. I bet they think these cells are proof against invaders, so they won't let us out the way they would if there were a fire or something."

"I have a solution," Jun said. "I can unlock the door."

"You what?"

"I intended to do it as soon as the enforcers were well away, see if I could sneak out, but *someone* nobly insisted on being locked up with me, and I didn't want to give away my secret." Jun frowned at the handle. "I think I can do it, anyway. If this was a mechanical lock, it would be impossible."

"What do you mean?"

Jun gestured to me to step away from the door. She placed her hand flat against the wall beside the doorknob and closed her eyes. "My personal force field can interfere with electronics. The more sophisticated the system, the more vulnerable it is. Fortunately, I have to concentrate on making it happen. Imagine if I needed a pacemaker or something."

"Right," I said, staring at her hand. I felt as if I ought to be able to see something, an aura or white sparks or whatever. But all I saw was Jun's hand, loosely pressed against the wall. Jun said nothing more, so I stayed silent, in case my chatter disrupted her concentration.

After about a million years, the faintest *click* came from the door, and it popped open about half an inch. Jun removed her hand and wiped away sweat beading her forehead. "That card reader was almost too far away for me to affect it. Where do we go now?"

"We need to find Malcolm." I checked my phone, but found what I already knew I'd find—no bars in the detention area. "And warn him about Nyla."

Jun pulled the door open and carefully closed it behind us. The latch didn't engage, and the tiny light burned green, so it would be immediately obvious the door was unlocked. So long as we got out of here quickly, it wouldn't matter.

The door leading out of the cells had no card reader on this side, and we opened it easily and ran for it. The lights outside were tinted red, like emergency lighting, but everything was eerily silent—no screams, no alarms, no people running around in a panic.

"Where would they go?" Jun asked. "You said they have to return the cardigans and the earbuds. Where would that be?"

"I have no idea. And I don't think we should go chasing around the node, trying to guess, especially if the node is under attack. I think we need to find Lucia."

We reached the point where the cyan line joined the black line and kept going. "They took her to the infirmary," Jun said. "Where is that?"

"I've never been there. I guess we can ask someone."

"Who's likely to want to help a couple of fugitives?"

Somebody pounded out of a side corridor, a man in white fatigues who paid us no attention even though we had to look strange in our cardigans and non-standard-issue snow boots. "You see that?" I said when he had vanished down the hall. "Nobody knows we're fugitives. But they do know who the custodian of Abernathy's is. They'll be helpful."

The magenta line joined the other two. Noises had become audible from up ahead, and now I heard the shouts and screams I'd thought would be natural in an invasion. Jun and I slowed our pace as we neared the corridor's exit. It wasn't one of the giant painted doors, but a smaller service tunnel like the one that led to Lucia's office, and through it we saw confused motion and flashes of gunfire. We stopped at the exit and peered out from the sides.

It was carnage. Invaders of a dozen different unnatural hues clung to the walls and ceiling, gouging holes and making bits of concrete rain down. Men and women in fatigues or the black jumpsuits of the node's techs ran in all directions, those in fatigues shooting the invaders, those in jumpsuits trying to cross the node without getting killed or trampled. None of them were in a position to stop and help us find the infirmary.

Jun shouted over the din, "We can probably run through! We've still got the cardigans, and the invaders can't drain us, anyway."

"But we don't know where we're going," I shouted back, "and if we guess wrong, we'll have to cross again. And I don't trust my luck that far."

Jun grimaced, but didn't reply. I turned my attention back to the hub, wishing I had information that would help me guess accurately. A flock of invaders with short, stubby pinnae like hummingbird wings stripped of their feathers dove on a group of three Wardens in fatigues. The Wardens shot some of them, but the others dodged the missiles and fell on their victims, tearing at their faces. The screaming made me feel ill and horrified, but I couldn't do anything for them.

A giant crack echoed through the chamber, momentarily drowning out all the other sounds. A chunk of ceiling at least ten feet across detached and fell, crushing a Warden and six or seven invaders when it landed. My fingers went numb from fear as an amorphous shape, easily as big as a Volkswagen

Beetle, oozed through the hole it left. It was a deep, dried-blood red shading to near-black at its edges, and even though it had no visible face, its cautious movements and the way it shifted as if it were moving its head to look around told me it saw the room clearly.

Two of the Wardens noticed it and shouted, pointing. Then the room was full of the sounds of gunfire as every Warden opened up on the new threat. I cringed away from the percussive noise and put my hands over my ears. Forget the invaders; we'd be shot by our own people before we made it three steps.

Someone rushed past us from the hub. Jun had more presence of mind than I did and grabbed the woman's arm, bringing her to a halt. "Where's the infirmary?" Jun shouted.

"What the hell? Let go of me," the woman tech said.

"Infirmary," I said. "Where?"

"Green, of course." She wrenched away from Jun and continued her mad flight away from the carnage.

Jun and I peeked out again. The intelligent invader had oozed its way down to ground level. The gunfire continued without a pause. I couldn't immediately see the green door, what with the turmoil and the low red lighting, but Jun pointed, and there it was, about a third of the way around the hub from us.

"This is insanity," Jun said. "We're going to get killed."

"We can hug the wall and run," I said. "Wait for the Wardens to stop shooting—"

"They're not going to stop shooting! What do they call this, a target-rich environment?"

"When they kill that invader, they'll stop shooting so wildly," I said, hoping I was right. "Be ready to run."

The invader reared up like a giant ocean wave the color of

blood and pounced on one of its attackers, whose scream was horribly cut off. Bullet holes riddled its body, making it look moth-eaten. One of the Wardens shouted a warning and flung something at the invader, something the size and shape of a softball. It struck the ooze's side and sank in. Realization struck me, and I shouted, "Get down, Jun!" before flinging myself to the floor and covering my head with my arms.

An explosion rocked the hub, and even through my arms and my eyelids, pink light burned. The smell of burnt rubber filled the air strongly enough to make me cough. Dimly, I heard Jun coughing as well. I raised my head. Black smoke filled the hub, drifting upward as if the hole were sucking it out of the air. I couldn't see the invader and didn't see any other movement in the hub.

I pushed myself to my feet and helped Jun up. "We have to run," I said.

Jun nodded. We staggered through the door as if the blast had knocked us over instead of just nearly deafening us. All around us, Wardens were picking themselves up off the ground, and smaller invaders were shaking their limbs or heads or exoskeletons as if they'd been stunned by the blast as well.

There were too many fallen bodies, both human and monstrous, for us to be able to run. We moved as fast as we could, picking our way past obstacles. The smell of burnt flesh was starting to creep in past the smell of burnt rubber, and I gagged and made myself keep moving, hoping I wouldn't see anyone I knew among the dead.

A cry went up from the invaders, a mournful howl that made me think of wolves on a blasted heath, and the shooting began again. I ducked and covered my head with my arms, which would be no protection against a stray bullet, and sped up until I nearly tripped over a woman in bloodstained white fatigues. She opened her eyes, and I screamed in surprise and dropped to my knees beside her.

"Help," she whispered. I couldn't hear her, but the movement of her lips was unmistakable.

I got my hands under my arms and pulled. The woman grimaced, her lips pulling back from her teeth, and let out a hiss of pain. "Jun, help!" I called out.

Jun hurried to catch up to me. "I'll take her legs," she said.

Between us, we carried the woman to the green door and laid her down inside. It was the busiest of the doors, with people racing in both directions. "Somebody help us!" I shouted.

My cry for help was ignored. A couple of the hurrying people glanced our way, but no one stopped. I knelt beside the injured woman and wished I knew anything about first aid, or even how to tell how badly someone was hurt. Her eyes were closed, and she was breathing shallowly, but she'd looked at me a few seconds before and I didn't think she was unconscious.

"We can't leave her here," Jun said. "She'll—" She closed her lips hard on the word *die*.

I checked my phone again. Still no bars. Maybe that was why Lucia never answered her phone—she had to find somewhere in this stupid place that got reception. "We'll have to carry her."

"That could make her injuries worse."

"Do you have another idea?"

The woman wasn't huge, for which I was grateful, but she was heavy enough that even Jun and I working together had to stop often for rests. After the third rest, I leaned against the wall and wiped sweat out of my eyes. The stupid cardigan probably weighed ten pounds, but I didn't want to lose its protection. "There has to be a better way," I said. "We need—"

A cart zipped past us, headed for the hub. It looked like a golf cart with half a truck bed welded on. "We need that," I concluded. "How do we get one?"

Jun shook her head, then hopped up from where she'd been sitting crouched against the wall and stepped out into the corridor, spreading her arms wide. Another cart barreled down upon her, not looking like it meant to stop. Jun stood her ground. "Jun, don't!" I shouted.

The cart swerved to miss Jun. Jun sidestepped into its path. And with a squeal of tires, the cart came to a halt just inches from her. I gasped. I was sure it had actually run into her, or tried to—it had *bounced*, sort of, as if Jun were surrounded by a rubber barrier.

"What the hell?" the driver exclaimed. "Get out of the way!"

"This woman needs help," Jun said, as calmly as if she hadn't come close to being a grease spot on the concrete floor. "Can you carry her?"

"I got a full load," the man said. He looked at the injured woman and then back at Jun. "I'll come right back once I drop these people off."

The back of the cart held three people, two of them sitting, the third lying down. All of them were bloody, and one of them had a bandage wrapped around his head, covering one eye. "Thanks," I said, and the man drove off.

"I can't believe you did that," I said to Jun. "Did you know the force field would work like that?"

"No," Jun said. "But he was going to stop anyway. It was worth trying."

"I think you're insane."

"*I* think," Jun said with a smile, "you've done much crazier things than that."

I remembered some of the things I'd done since becoming the custodian of Abernathy's. "You're right."

We sat beside the injured woman and waited. It was only about five minutes before the man came back, but the woman's breathing grew increasingly shallow, and I wondered, by how pale she was, if she had internal bleeding. When the cart pulled up in front of us, I quickly helped load the woman into the back, then got in beside Jun. The driver was wasted in his current job; he should have gone out for NASCAR, with how fast he went and how he slipped past obstacles. No, maybe he wasn't wasted, if his driving would save this woman's life.

The walls speeding past us were painted a warm cream I'd never seen anywhere else in the Gunther Node. Wooden doors, each with a glass window filled with wire mesh in its upper half, lined the walls, reminding me of my old middle school. Unlike my school, most of the windows had curtains drawn across from the inside, but I could see into a few rooms and noticed beds and hospital monitors. It should have been comforting that there were empty rooms, like that meant there weren't too many badly injured, but all it meant to me was that too many people had died before making it this far.

The cart skidded to a halt outside a big open space, this one brightly lit with white lights instead of the red-tinged light we'd seen everywhere else. It was full of operating tables, all of them in use, but it didn't look like any operations were happening. Instead, magi in white scrubs surrounded each table, touching their occupants, while others held those occupants down as they bucked and fought and let out garbled screams. It was a scene out of some medieval torture chamber, and it unnerved me even as I knew the truth: magical healing could be more painful than the original injury, and these screaming people were grateful for it.

"Over here," the driver said. Jun and I helped him carry the injured woman out of the cart and across to an open door. Beyond was a room as large as the healing center, but much quieter, filled with chairs and cots occupied by the wounded. We found the woman an empty cot, and Jun helped her sit and sip some water as I talked to the bone magus in charge of triage.

The bone magus took the woman's hand, and she immediately went limp and unconscious. "Thanks for bringing her," he said. "She's taken some major internal injuries and needs immediate treatment."

"We're glad we found her in time," I said. "Um, doctor? Where's Lucia?"

He frowned. "In isolation. You can't see her."

"It's not that. We just need to know the room. It's…it's custodian business," I added, hoping that would overawe him sufficiently.

It did. His eyes widened. "Room 57. But you won't be allowed in."

"That's fine. Um…which way is that?"

The cart was gone when we returned. We followed his directions, running back the way we'd come to a side hall, still lined with those wooden, windowed doors. The lights here weren't as bright, as if the hall didn't see much use. Now that we weren't zipping along at a fraction of the speed of light, I could see numbers above each door. It seemed impractical for the Gunther Node, even as big as it was, to need this many hospital rooms. Then I remembered the attacks on the Holley and Krebbitz Nodes last year, and the battle going on right now. The hall might be deserted now, but that wouldn't last long.

"What's the point of finding Lucia if we can't get in to see her?" Jun asked as we ran.

"We just need to know that Nyla hasn't been there," I said. "Then we...I don't know. Stand guard?" It sounded stupider when I said it aloud, but I really was out of ideas.

"I want to prove I'm innocent," Jun said.

"We need Nyla to confess for that to happen. Or...I guess if you're in there with Lucia and she doesn't die, that's like proof, right?"

Jun stopped running. I took a few more steps and then returned to her side. "I can't get anywhere close to Lucia until she recovers or Nyla is caught. If anything happens to Lucia, I'll be blamed."

I glanced over my shoulder. There were a couple of people in the otherwise empty hallway about thirty feet away. They were looking in our direction. "I think that's her door," I said. "Wait here, and I'll find out."

The two Wardens, one in white fatigues, one in black, flanked the door numbered 57. They looked like a couple of chess pieces, though chess pieces armed with seriously scary guns and long steel knives. Both men gave me impassive stares. If they'd been more colorful, they could have been those guards outside Buckingham Palace, the ones who aren't allowed to react no matter what stupid things tourists do to get them to smile. The curtain hadn't been drawn across the window, but when I looked through, I couldn't see more than the foot of a hospital bed and the lumpy shape of someone's feet under the blanket.

I stopped in front of the guards and said, "Hi. I'm Helena Campbell. Custodian of Abernathy's? I want to see Lucia."

Neither of them moved or spoke, though I thought the Warden in white's eyes widened a little at my introduction. I'd hoped playing my custodian card would make a difference.

"It's okay if you won't let me in," I went on. "But I know who poisoned Lucia, and I want to make sure that person doesn't get past you. So I need you to tell me if anyone but Dave Henry has entered this room. Dave or the bone magi treating Lucia, I guess."

More silence, though now both of them had the look of people suppressing strong emotions—wide eyes, lips pinched shut. It pissed me off. "Look," I said angrily, "if Dave gave you your orders, fine. But I'm sure he didn't tell you to be stupid. I want to save Lucia's life. Just answer my question, and I'll leave."

The two guards looked at each other, then at me again. Finally, the Warden in black said, "No one's been inside since the bone magi brought Lucia here, Ms. Campbell."

I let out a relieved breath. "See? That wasn't so hard. Thank you."

"Who poisoned her?" the Warden in white said.

"I…I'm not allowed to say until the person is taken into custody," I improvised. I felt instinctively that I shouldn't spread the information around in case Nyla got wind of it and escaped. True, these men weren't likely to be in a position to reveal it, being stuck on guard duty, but I knew what Lucia would say if she found out I'd given it away. I hoped she would eventually be in a condition to yell at me again.

"We won't let anyone pass," the Warden in white said.

Movement at his hip caught my eye. Without anyone touching it, the steel knife slipped from its sheath and flashed upward. I stared at it, dumbfounded, as it flipped end over end and pressed against the Warden's neck. The man barely had time to let out a choked cry of astonishment before it slit his throat, sending a spray of arterial blood pulsing into the air.

I threw myself out of the way and landed heavily on my hip. The Warden sagged and collapsed, letting his gun fall from lifeless hands. The Warden in black brought his handgun up, then hesitated as if he realized how crazy it was that he was pointing his gun at a free-floating knife.

"Watch out!" I shrieked, pointing at the Warden's own knife, which had come halfway free of its sheath. The Warden clapped his free hand over it, shoving it back down, and the flying knife took advantage of his distraction to dart inside his guard and ram itself halfway to the hilt in his left eye. I screamed again and scrambled backward on hands and feet. "Jun! Run!"

"She's not running," a familiar voice said.

I scrabbled around to face the way I'd come and saw Nyla standing there, her hands on her hips and a satisfied smile on her lips. Jun, standing just behind her, was expressionless. I stared at Jun, willing her to grab Nyla, to do *something* to stop her. She didn't move. "Jun," I said, then couldn't think of anything else to say.

Nyla walked slowly toward me. "What an interesting complication you make," she said.

20

"I ought to kill you, too," Nyla said. "But I have a hard time killing people I know."

I ignored her. "How much of that story was true?" I asked Jun. "You met an intelligent invader, but you took its offer?"

"I told you it made a convincing argument," Jun said as Nyla half-turned to look at her. "Taking its deal made sense. But I'm not going to explain myself to you. I don't owe you anything."

"That's not entirely true," Nyla said. "We owe her for introducing us to this world. And putting us in a position where we can gain everything we ever wanted."

My chest felt tight with fear. "Nyla, what could you possibly want that only one of those treacherous, lying monsters could give you? Or claim to give you, since they have no reason to keep their word to humans. They only see us as walking repositories of magic, did you know that?"

Nyla turned back to me and took a few steps in my direction. "I know all about it," she said. "Know more than you, clearly. They only want a few humans, now and then, criminals and losers, people who won't be missed."

"They told me that too, but they lie. Why would they stop with just a few when there are so many of them starving for our magic?" I shook my hair out of my eyes where it had come loose from my ponytail. "They'll never stop until they've drained our world, and then they'll move on to the next one."

Nyla's smile was pitying. "You can't see the truth. It doesn't matter. They're winning, and anything you do to try to stop them is pointless. Jun and I accepted it—it's too bad you can't. Wouldn't you love to keep your husband safe? Keep all the Wardens safe? All you have to do is join us, and when the war is over, no more fighting, no more hunting. It's your heart's dream, isn't it?"

I shook my head. "Nyla, it's a trap, all of it. What did they promise you to get you to go along? Wealth?"

Nyla smiled more broadly. "They promised to take care of Mom."

"But I could do that!" I exclaimed. "Nyla, you don't have to bargain with them. If that's what you want, I can afford to get her the best care, or have a bone magus maybe even heal her—"

Nyla was shaking her head. "Not that kind of care," she said. "Do you have any idea what it's like to care for an invalid, day after night after day, never being able to do so much as get a damn haircut without making a production out of finding someone else to take over while you're gone? I'm *tired*, Helena, tired of living like a slave, and my new friends have promised to end that for me. Permanently. Just as soon as I wrap up this last little detail."

I got to my feet. "You'll have to get through me."

Nyla shrugged. "If that's what it takes."

An unseen force swept me off my feet and hurled me into the wall, knocking the wind out of me. I gasped, bending over, desperate for air, but the same force pressed me back, pushing me against the wall until I was spread-eagled and helpless. My head twisted painfully to one side, pressing one cheek against the wall that smelled of cold concrete.

Nyla walked up to me and patted my other cheek. "You stay there like a good girl, and we'll talk more when I'm done," she said.

I tried to speak, but my jaw was as immobile as the rest of me. This was so far beyond what I'd thought Nyla's talent was. She'd gotten more from the invaders than a promise that they'd kill her mother.

Nyla made her way around the fallen Wardens and the pools of blood to the door. She put her hand on the knob and cocked her head as if listening to distant music. "Complicated," she said, "but not beyond me." She rested her forehead against the wood and closed her eyes.

Jun passed in front of me. I glared at her, keeping my despair and embarrassment at having been fooled by her well hidden. I'd thought I was being so noble, and all I'd been was an idiot.

Jun stopped where I could see her, behind Nyla. She turned her head to face me.

And she winked.

I gaped at her, uncomprehending. Jun took a couple of casual steps away from Nyla and pulled a familiar white baton from beneath her cardigan. I hadn't realized she still had it. She twisted it, making it telescope out to a three-foot length, and said, "Nyla, what's that?"

"What?" Nyla said, turning.

Jun lunged and caught Nyla square at the base of her

throat, right where the cardigan fell open. Nyla's whole body jerked as if she'd been electrocuted. She landed in an awkward tangle of limbs in front of the door. The grip on my body disappeared, and I sagged and caught myself before I could join her.

Jun switched the baton to her left hand and offered me her right. "Sorry about that," she said. "She caught me by surprise, and I had to pretend I was her ally so she wouldn't kill me like she did those two."

"You were convincing." I rubbed my neck. "Is she dead?"

"I don't think so. It wasn't a head shot, at least not exactly." Jun knelt beside Nyla and felt for a pulse. "She's alive. I don't know if that's good or bad."

"The problem is, she's going to wake up eventually, and how are we supposed to keep a telekinetic captive? Especially one who's had her talent goosed to eleven by the invaders?"

We stared at each other. "We can't even lock ourselves in Lucia's room and wait for help," Jun said.

"And even if we had some way to tie her up, she'd just fling knives at us. Or figure out how to shoot a gun with her mind." I gathered up the Wardens' weapons and carried them far down the corridor, hoping out of sight would be out of the range of Nyla's talent.

When I returned, Jun held something small and crystalline in her fingers. "I wonder if this will still work?"

I took it. It was a glass earbud. "Is this Nyla's?"

"Yes, and I'm trying to overcome my revulsion at the idea of putting it in my ear after it's been in hers."

I grimaced. "I'll do it."

I wedged the thing into my ear and was relieved to feel the brief swelling sensation that said it was fitting itself to me.

When I was sure it was secure, I pressed my finger against it and said, "Malcolm?"

Nothing happened. I was about to repeat his name when a voice in my ear said, "*Helena?*"

"Oh, I'm so glad," I said. "Listen, Malcolm—"

"*Are you all right?*"

"Yes, but—"

"*I can't talk now. We were hit while I was taking the sports to a secure location. Nyla and Victor are both down, and Mike is badly wounded. We're trying to reach the infirmary—*"

"Malcolm, listen to me. Nyla is the traitor. She must have pretended to fall to get away from you. Jun and I caught her at Lucia's room, trying to finish what she started. I need someone to take Nyla into custody—she's powerful, Malcolm, the invaders altered her to be as strong a telekinetic as a stone magus."

Silence again. "Malcolm?"

"*Helena,*" Malcolm said. His voice was clear enough that I could tell he was suppressing a dozen exclamations. "*Helena, how did you stop her?*"

"I didn't. Jun did. I'm going to give Dave so much crap for not having her searched before taking her into custody. Look, we don't know how long Nyla will be unconscious, but we need help."

"*It kills me to admit I am in no position to join you. Contact Henry immediately. He'll know who to send.*"

"Be safe. I love you."

"*This will all be over soon. The Wardens are winning. I love you.*"

I shifted my hand and spoke again, before my aching heart could override me. "Dave? Dave Henry?"

Instantly the reply came, "*Who is this?*"

"It's Helena Campbell. Nyla Priest is the traitor who tried

to kill Lucia. Jun Li and I have her unconscious outside Lucia's hospital room and we need someone to take her into custody."

This time, the silence lasted so long I was afraid the communicator had broken. "Dave?"

"*Helena, what in the* hell *is going on?*"

"I just told you. I think I was very concise. Could you save your incredulity for later? We don't know when Nyla will wake up, and I don't know if it's good for her to be zapped repeatedly."

"*I don't understand half of that, but—Helena, stay put, and I'll send someone.*"

"And tell them not to arrest Jun. She's not a traitor."

"*I wish I had time to ask you how you managed to escape custody,*" Dave said. I removed my hand from the communicator without replying.

Jun stood over Nyla, her baton at the ready. "You said she was as strong as a…what kind of magus?"

"A stone magus. They're all powerful telekinetics. I saw one stop a speeding truck once. Well, it wasn't actually speeding, but it was a massive truck."

"So they'll have a way to contain her."

That hadn't occurred to me. "True. That's a relief. Although…" I looked down at the unconscious Nyla. "They'll try her for attempted murder, and their punishments aren't lenient. That makes me uncomfortable."

Jun didn't change her position at all. "I know. But it's not as if it's safe to let her roam free. Maybe she has trouble killing people she knows, but that might not last. Not to mention that there are billions of people she doesn't know and might not have any problem killing."

I heard footsteps, and the purr of a motorized cart, and turned to see a handful of people rushing down the hall toward us, followed by not one, but two of those carts, both traveling more sedately than the one that had brought us to the infirmary. "Be careful," I said when the people were within speaking distance. "She's a powerful telekinetic, and—"

"How powerful?" said a woman in teal scrubs who knelt beside Nyla, forcing Jun to take a step back.

"She killed those Wardens with their own knives. She's like a stone magus. And she's the one who poisoned Lucia."

The woman's face went grim. "Might be better if she never woke up. Better for her, at any rate."

"She has to face justice," I said, feeling cold at the realization that I'd just delivered Nyla into the hands of magi capable of killing with a touch. Blood clot to the brain, heart attack, disrupting the nervous system—and it would all look like a natural death. "Promise me she will."

The woman looked at me, and her expression softened. "Friend of yours?"

"I thought she was. I guess I was wrong."

"I promise no one will enact vigilante justice on her," the woman said. She stood and gestured to her companions, who lifted Nyla and deposited her, not very gently, into the back of the first cart. I thought about yelling at them, but realized I wouldn't have been very gentle myself and let it go.

The magi were gentler with the bodies of the fallen Wardens, putting them into the second cart. I ran back down the hall to retrieve their weapons and laid them atop their bodies. It felt like preparing someone for Viking funeral rites.

One of the Wardens, dressed in the black jumpsuit of a Gunther Node tech, unlocked Lucia's door and held it open for scrubs-suited magi to enter. I made as if to follow them, and the woman in teal scrubs who had climbed into the cart next to Nyla said, "You're not allowed in there."

Her peremptory tone irritated me. "Why not? We saved her life."

"Because you're not bone magi and will just get in the way of the healing."

"They're going to restore Lucia?"

The woman took Nyla's wrist as if checking for a pulse. "The fight's not going well. We need her in charge. And those bone magi are doing this instead of saving Warden lives. So stay out of the way."

I couldn't argue with that. "We'll wait out here."

"You should come back to the infirmary with us. There's nothing you can do here."

I wasn't about to tell her that the sight of Lucia's mottled, unconscious face had rattled me, nor that I superstitiously feared that some of these magi were corrupted by the invaders. It was irrational, but after the day I'd had—hell, it wasn't even a full day yet!—I felt inclined to give in to paranoia. "She'll need to know the truth about who poisoned her," I said.

The woman shrugged. "Fine. You're braver than me. She's going to be pissed off royally when she finds out what's been going on. You want to be the target of her fury, go ahead." She signaled the driver, who wheeled the cart around and drove back the way he'd come, followed by the other cart. The remaining Wardens grouped up on both sides of the door, like they thought numbers could make up for their fallen comrades.

I stood in the doorway and peered inside, ignoring the glares of the guards. There were enough bone magi in the room that all I could see of Lucia was the foot of her bed. Jun had retreated to the wall opposite the door. I joined her. "Malcolm said the Wardens were winning," I said.

"Maybe that was true where he was," Jun said. "This is a big place. The Wardens might not be able to hold all of it."

I nodded. I didn't like what the woman had said, about the bone magi being pulled off duty to take care of Lucia. I wasn't going to say Lucia's life was more valuable, fundamentally, than the nameless Wardens who might die because these magi weren't in the infirmary to save them, but there were things only Lucia could do that might save so many more lives. So didn't that make her more valuable in the long run?

The hall was perfectly silent, quiet enough that I could hear my pulse beating. The guards eyed us as if they weren't convinced we weren't a threat. I glared at them, but it didn't intimidate them. That was for the best. Lucia didn't need guards who could be overawed by anything.

Then I heard a voice croak, "Davies? Get in here!"

My heart beat faster. I rushed across the hall and into the room. It was crowded with six bone magi, the bed, and me, but I only cared that Lucia was sitting propped up against the elevated head of the bed. She looked way too pale, and her eyes were deep holes in her face, ringed with darkness, but they were alert and intelligent. "Lucia," I gasped.

"Save the exclamations and tell me what happened. I was poisoned?" Her voice sounded as raw as if she'd been screaming.

"By Nyla Priest. Only we thought it was Jun at first. Nyla made a bargain with the invaders—"

"All right, that's enough." Lucia sat up and winced, putting a hand to her abdomen.

"You should take it easy," one of the magi warned.

Lucia shot him a sardonic look, and the man subsided, looking like he'd just realized what a stupid thing he'd said.

"I feel like I vomited up my intestines," she said. "Let's

walk, and you can tell me the rest."

"Walk?" another of the magi said.

Lucia glared at him. "You want to carry me, Reintgen?"

Reintgen swallowed. "I'll call a cart."

Lucia put her hand to her ear and swore. "Who removed my communicator?"

Nobody looked willing to admit to having done it, or maybe none of them knew. Lucia snorted and swung her legs over the side of the bed. "Never mind. Davies, let's go."

Outside the room, Lucia eyed Jun skeptically. "You're sure it wasn't her?" she asked me.

"I'm sure. She zapped Nyla unconscious and saved your life."

"Which is exactly what I'd do if I were a Mercy operative who wanted access to the heart of the Gunther Node." Lucia smiled. It wasn't a pleasant expression. "But at some point paranoia has to give way to faith. Don't think I'm not watching you, Ms. Li."

"That's fair," Jun said, stepping up next to me. "I'd be suspicious of me, too."

Lucia shrugged. "Your communicator, Davies," she said, holding out her hand. I twisted it free of the nest of filaments and held it out to her. She scrubbed it on her shirt and popped it into her ear without a grimace of distaste. "Henry," she said. Then she smiled, an expression of tenderness that came and went so swiftly I almost doubted I'd seen it. "Report."

We walked down the hall in silence. I couldn't even hear the distant murmur of Dave's half of the conversation. Though it wasn't so much a conversation as Lucia listening intently to whatever he was saying. Her expression was one of unchanging grimness that frightened me. I didn't know if she was walking slower than her usual ground-eating stride because she was still injured, or because she was so intent on Dave's report, but I found myself speeding up and had to slow to keep pace with her.

Finally, Lucia said, "Meet me in Green 1. I want to see the tactical map. And get everyone clear of floor one and gas it. That's how they're getting in." A pause. "I know what you said about the hub, but that was a distraction. Floor one." She lowered her hand and increased her speed for about seven steps before pressing her hand to her stomach once again and coming to a halt. "I'm fine," she said irritably when I exclaimed. "It's already easier to walk."

She still looked far too pale, like someone on the brink of collapse, but I knew better than to suggest she rest. So I looked at the walls, which were still that pleasant cream color, and at Jun, who looked far calmer than I thought she should, and avoided staring at Lucia.

Eventually Lucia straightened and let out a deep breath. "So. Nyla," she said as she set off again. "How did she do it?"

"I don't know exactly," I said. "The bone magi who stopped the poison from killing you said it was encapsulated, so she could slip it under your skin and it would take a few minutes before releasing the poison. I guess that was to make it less obvious who'd done it."

"Clever." Lucia rubbed her stomach and made a pained face. "And it almost worked."

"I'm glad it didn't."

Lucia shot me an amused look. "Not as glad as I am, Davies."

It turned out Green 1 was, as I might have guessed, the big white room with all the operating tables. It was even busier than it had been before, with the waiting room overflowing into the corridor and men and women rushing through the doors carrying fallen Wardens. The noise was loud enough, after the silence of the side corridor, that it disoriented me, as if I'd stepped out of some hermetically sealed space into a shopping center on Black Friday.

Nobody stopped when Lucia entered the room, though I saw a couple of people do double-takes when they saw her. The bright lights made her look even paler, but she moved with assurance, crossing the open space swiftly enough I almost protested before coming to my senses. She grabbed one of the bone magi by the shoulder and said something I was too far away to hear, something that made the bone magus, who'd looked about to protest, shut her mouth and nod rapidly. They held a low-voiced conversation, during which the magus gestured at the room several times and Lucia listened intently.

"Helena," Dave said from behind me. "How did you get out?" He was addressing me, but all his attention was on Lucia.

"Um…we exploited a weakness in your security system," I said, not wanting to finger Jun right away, just in case Dave still suspected her and might think her extra-guilty for having broken out of detention.

"Fine, fine," Dave said absently. "Don't do it again." He crossed the room toward Lucia, who glanced once in his direction and then returned her attention to the bone magus. But it was a glance that said volumes I knew she would never say in public. It didn't matter that everyone knew she and Dave were lovers; Lucia never let personal get in the way of important, even when they were the same thing.

"So what do we do now?" Jun said, startling me out of my reverie. "It sounds like this is the safest place in the node, but I'm not really qualified to help the injured."

"I don't know. I helped the last time there was a battle, but this is far more serious." I stepped to one side to let a couple of Wardens supporting a third pass. The woman in the middle looked paler than Lucia and her entire left side was drenched in blood. The noise had gotten so loud it made the air hum, as if all those voices blended together into an eerie harmonic that echoed off the walls and ceiling and floor.

I looked at Jun. She was trembling, though her face was composed. "Are you all right?" I asked.

"I was about to ask you that. You're shaking," Jun replied.

"I'm not shaking," I said. I turned to survey the room and saw the trembling effect was everywhere. The hum was louder, and now I could clearly tell it wasn't coming from the Wardens, because everyone had stopped speaking and was looking around in confusion. Even the screams of pain were muted.

Then, far down the hallway, the red-tinted lights went out, as abruptly as if someone had draped a black curtain over that end of the hall. Another set of lights, closer than the first, winked out. Then more. The darkness advanced as if it were a creature drawing closer with every inexorable step.

And then I saw it. Its black, pointed head scraped the ceiling, its clawed, multi-jointed legs sent up sparks where they struck the concrete, and its dozen beady eyes like drops of blood were alarmingly intent on all of us. Tentacles waved where its mouth should be.

Someone screamed, a sound of fear rather than pain, and everyone who had been frozen in place erupted into action, pushing operating tables to more defensible positions, rushing the injured into the waiting room even though there was no space inside.

The invader had no features even remotely human, but it laughed. "*We win*," it said.

21

I retreated, not wanting to turn my back on the invader that, horribly, I recognized. It had torn its way out of the body of a man I'd known and liked, had stared at me through Abernathy's front window and made an incomprehensible threat, and had featured in my nightmares for months afterward.

I touched my side and found only the rough weave of the cardigan. I couldn't remember where I'd left my gun. It wouldn't have done me any good, since it was empty, but I felt unexpectedly afraid without it.

Beside me, Jun drew her baton and took a step forward. It looked like such a frail weapon I shouted, "Jun! Don't!"

Jun kept walking. "I don't think it sees me," she said in a normal voice that carried even over the din.

"But the baton can't possibly affect something its size!"

Jun shrugged. "I guess we'll find out."

I swore and ran after her. I had no idea what I would do, weaponless as I was, but I couldn't let Jun face the thing alone.

Behind me, Lucia shouted, "Get back here, Davies!" It

occurred to me Jun and I might be in the way of Wardens with guns. I glanced over my shoulder, but saw only the movement of Wardens carrying the injured to dubious safety, and Lucia, standing with her hands on her hips and looking furious. I waved her off and kept running until I caught up with Jun, twenty feet from the invader.

Who clearly saw me.

Its beady red eyes swiftly focused on my face, and it stopped moving, leaning back on its two pairs of hind legs like someone settling on a bar stool. *"Custodian,"* it said, its voice a creaky hiss. *"Changed your mind?"*

"That's never going to happen," I said, stopping where I was. Jun kept moving. The invader ignored her—or did it really not see her? She had the hood of her cardigan up as I did not.

"So you still foolishly believe your Wardens can win this war," it went on. *"You believe this even though we have penetrated your greatest stronghold and are poised to destroy everyone in it. Even though your own husband is among the fallen."*

"Malcolm's alive," I said. I resolutely didn't watch Jun, who was walking at a slower than normal pace as if she meant to pass to one side of the invader. "And you're bluffing."

"I never bluff. I don't need to. Without your leader, you cannot win."

That filled me with courage. So it didn't know everything. "You think so?" I said. "Good thing your assassin failed, then." I gestured behind me with my thumb, hoping Lucia was still there, watching this.

The invader's attention slipped from me to a point behind my head. It jerked in a movement that in a human would have been surprise. And Jun attacked.

It wasn't a perfect strike. Instead of hitting the invader on its pointed head, the baton caught the creature where its forelimb joined its chitinous black torso. The invader let out a screech and shook its injured limb. The baton, still wedged in the joint, flexed and then snapped, sending up a burst of blue sparks and making Jun cry out in pain and fling the broken half of the baton away. She shook her fingers as if they'd been burned.

Instantly the invader's head whipped around, darting back and forth like a snake scenting the air with its tongue. Jun went still, crouching on hands and knees. "Hey!" I shouted, waving to distract it. "That's just the beginning of what we can do. You ought to get out of here while you can." I was horribly aware that I had no weapons, and I might be immune to being drained of my magic, but it had razor-edged claws on all its eight legs, and any one of them might slice me to ribbons.

It rose up to its full height, which made it tower over me. "*I lied,*" it rasped. "*No more chances.*"

I screamed and stumbled backward as it brought two of its powerful forelimbs up to strike. A detached, numb part of my mind thought *Malcolm will never forgive me for dying this way,* but the rest of me was in a panic, terrifyingly aware that there was no way I could dodge these blows.

Something shoved me sideways, and I fell, landing too hard on one wrist, which sent a shock of pain through my arm. "No!" I screamed as the monstrous claws descended on Jun, who knelt where I'd stood.

As they struck her chest, there was a flash of pale violet light, and Jun sagged. I leaped to my feet and dove at the invader, hoping to distract it long enough for someone to get Jun to safety.

I slammed into it with my shoulder, and to my surprise, it wobbled and backed up a step. "I hate you and all your kind," I snarled. "This is *our* world, and you have no right to come here like thieves and then try to tell us it's all for our own good!" I slammed into it again.

It laughed again. The sound chilled me through my white-hot anger. *"We would have left you alive,"* it said. *"Your pain when we consume your magic is nothing to us. We don't take pleasure in it—for the most part. But I think I will enjoy seeing you scream and writhe, custodian."*

Its forelimbs wrapped around me, pinioning my arms. I thrashed and shouted, kicking it, but it held me tilted away from its body so my head was just below its eyes. It smelled of dank, musty attic rooms shut up for decades, of mushroom growth in dark cellars, and when its tentacles gaped wide, revealing rows of serrated teeth like a shark's, the smell redoubled. I screamed as those teeth closed over my shoulder.

Immediately a familiar lassitude swept over me, bubbling up into a laugh I couldn't contain. The teeth withdrew. I had a mental image of the teeth actually retracting into its mouth, like in *How to Train Your Dragon*, and I laughed again. "Toothless," I giggled.

The invader jerked, and its grip loosened. I bucked and writhed until it dropped me, and I landed like a cat on my hands and feet. That was *hilarious*, me as a cat. I'd be one of those long-haired Persians if I were a cat. I tried to purr and discovered my throat wasn't made for purring. "Damn," I said. "I'll have to be a voiceless cat." I giggled again at the thought.

"What are you doing?" the invader demanded.

I looked up at it. Something thin and bendy rolled beneath my hand, and I grabbed it. "You don't know everything, you bastard," I laughed, and stabbed the creature in the eye with the remains of Jun's baton.

It screamed and recoiled, screamed again, and then the air was full of shouting and gunfire. I shifted my position so I was on my back, crab-like, just like that stupid game they made us play in gym class that nobody liked. I sidled backward and watched as Wardens poured down the corridor from the hub, led by someone so familiar I wanted to cry.

Malcolm's knives intersected on one of the thing's hindlimbs, neatly severing it, and then the invader shook him off. Malcolm rolled with the blow, landing in a crouch with his knives at the ready. More Wardens surged past him, though it looked like most of them didn't want to fire for fear of hitting their friends and were resorting to their own knives.

The invader reared up to its full height and screamed again, this time in a voice that shook the walls and made everyone near it fall back several steps. Its body shimmered like it was passing through an oil slick, and then it flattened until it looked like a painting of itself. Malcolm leaped to his feet and ran at it, knives raised, but it folded in on itself and vanished just as his blades would have struck home.

Malcolm converted his run into another tumble and came to his feet near me. "Helena," he said, sheathing his knives. "Helena, are you all right?"

"Peachy keen," I giggled. "You're alive!"

"It bit you," Malcolm said, prodding at my shoulder. It didn't hurt, though there were a dozen tears in the wiry fabric. "You're bleeding."

"I can't believe it tore the cardigan," I said. "Mr. Wallach will be so mad." I'd never heard him yell, but he got disgusted with humanity's frailties on a regular basis. I pictured him lecturing that invader and giggled again.

Malcolm put his arms around me and held me close. "If I were not so relieved that it didn't kill you, I'd be able to laugh at how funny you are right now."

I nodded. It made the room dance as if I were drunk and

not just euphoric. Maybe the two were related. "How do you do somersaults with knives in your hands?" I wondered aloud. "You should slice yourself to ribbons."

"Long practice," Malcolm said with a smile.

His smile faded, and he stood, bringing me with him. I wobbled, but managed not to fall down. He wasn't looking at me anymore; his attention was fixed on a fallen shape, surrounded by magi in scrubs. "What…" I began.

Then I remembered. Jun.

I pulled free of Malcolm and found I couldn't walk properly. It felt like I was inside one of those inflatable bouncy houses they have at carnivals, where every step tried to launch me into the air. The image made me want to laugh, but the sight of Jun's body lying so still sobered me faster than a gallon of hot coffee. Then Malcolm was at my elbow, steadying me, and the two of us crossed the short distance to where she lay. It felt like a mile.

Jun's hood had slipped off her head, and her hair was disordered around her face, a windblown, healthy look so at odds with the stillness of her features I felt I was looking at a wax effigy rather than a living person. Blood stained her coat and the front of her shirt where the magi had torn open the cardigan—torn it more, since it looked like the invader's claws had shredded it over her heart, just like its teeth had torn mine.

The bone magi, as usual, looked like they were doing nothing, and I almost screamed at them to save her, to jump into action and bustle around like people in medical dramas did. I dug my fingers into Malcolm's arm, but he didn't protest. The bloodstain wasn't spreading. I couldn't tell if Jun was breathing or not. "Save her," I whispered, unable to help myself.

Malcolm put his arm around my shoulders. "Helena," he said, then seemed to run out of words.

"She probably thought her force field would protect her," I said. "It did, too, did something, anyway. I saw the light. But it wasn't enough. I know she didn't intend to d—" I choked on the final word.

The bone magi still crouched or knelt around Jun. There was still hope. I closed my eyes and prayed more fervently than ever before. I'd never been much for religion growing up—we weren't a churchgoing family—but the things I'd seen since becoming a Warden had inclined me more toward believing in God, or at least hoping He existed and cared about humanity. I never knew if I was doing prayer right, but I felt instinctively that God cared more about the intent of my heart than the form my prayers took.

When I opened my eyes, the bone magi had stood. They looked exhausted. Jun lay on the floor, still motionless. They'd straightened her limbs and adjusted the hood so her head wasn't canted to one side. I covered my mouth with one hand to hold in a cry. Malcolm's grip around my shoulders tightened. I tried to breathe around the knot of pain in my chest and couldn't manage it without making a lot of noise as my breath rasped in and out.

Lucia appeared beside me. She looked near collapse, looked the way I felt, but when she spoke, her voice was strong. "For someone who fought this knowledge," she said, "that woman died a Warden."

"She shouldn't have died at all," I cried out. "She thought she could survive where I couldn't. She thought—"

"She was tough and strong-willed, and she knew the limits of her talent," Lucia said. "And she thought yours was a life worth saving, or she wouldn't have done it."

"What are you saying?" Malcolm asked.

"Jun pushed me out of the way," I said. "It would have killed me, and it killed her instead. It——" I buried my face in Malcolm's shoulder and shook uncontrollably, my tears soaking his ruined fatigues.

Distantly, over the sound of my sobs, I heard Lucia say, "Find an empty room and let her rest. You too, Campbell. Don't think I don't know you're past your limit. When I get my hands on Tinsley, I'm going to rip him a new one for letting you talk him into illegally pumping you full of endorphins."

"I judged the need worth the risk," Malcolm said. I realized he was shaking and tried to pull away, but he held me too tightly.

"Well, when you collapse, I'd better not hear you complain. Now get out of here. I have work to do."

Malcolm steered me away from Green 1, down the hall. I looked over my shoulder once at Jun's motionless form just as they picked her up to carry her away. Guilt and horror and terrible sadness struck me, and I sobbed again, blinding myself with tears so I needed Malcolm's steadying arm to keep me from walking into the wall and staying there forever.

Eventually, I heard a door open, and Malcolm guided me to a chair. He helped me take off my boots and the ruined cardigan and lie down on the hospital bed, which was already raised at the head a little. "You're not bleeding much. It seems it only takes the slightest injury from an invader to make you euphoric." He laid a gentle hand on my shoulder, and I whimpered a little at the pain even that touch caused. Then a fizzing sensation like hydrogen peroxide on a wound bubbled up in several places around my shoulder, and I relaxed as the pain faded.

"That should do it," Malcolm said. He took off his own

boots and climbed up next to me, taking me in his arms and stroking my hair as I cried. I couldn't stop seeing Jun kneeling before the invader like some kind of sacrifice, the flash of violet light, then her body lying on the ground, still and lifeless. The images played out behind my eyelids over and over again like film on an endless reel until they jumbled together in my exhausted mind, and finally, I slept.

22

When I woke, the room was still well-lit, and I felt so disoriented I didn't know what day it was or what hour or even what year. It took seeing Malcolm asleep beside me to remind me where and when we were. All the events of the past twenty-four hours came trickling back, not in an orderly stream but in a disjointed flood, out of chronological order and confusing. Then I remembered that Jun was dead, and lay back on the pillow to stare at the ceiling. I felt too numb for more tears.

Malcolm stirred and opened his eyes. "You're awake," he said.

"So are you."

"I wish I weren't. I hurt everywhere, and I almost regret making Tinsley enhance me for that last assault."

I settled in more comfortably beside him. Those hospital beds were narrow. "What does that mean?"

"It means strengthening weakened muscles and building up my natural endorphins until I felt no pain."

"Lucia said it was illegal."

"Because too much of it can kill someone. But Tinsley is skilled, and I trust him. And it was worth the aftereffects." He shifted a little and let out a groan. "How do *you* feel?"

"Everything's sort of floating at a distance. I'm not in any physical pain, if that's what you mean."

"It's not." He rested his forehead against mine. "You lost a friend."

"We barely knew each other."

"That's sometimes all it takes for a friendship to form. You need to cherish that friendship, and try not to feel guilty at being alive when she isn't."

"But she's only dead because she saved me. How can I not feel guilty about that? It should have been me—would have been me if she hadn't been there, because nobody else was close enough to stop the invader." It turned out I wasn't too numb for tears, after all.

Malcolm kissed my forehead. "Love, when someone sacrifices for you, you have to have the humility to accept it. Otherwise you cheapen their gift. You're probably right that Jun thought she could survive that attack. But she was smart enough to know there was a chance she couldn't. And she did it anyway. That was her choice. Don't make that choice have been in vain."

I nodded. "I understand. I feel guilty anyway."

"That's grief, not guilt. And that's natural."

I snuggled in closer. "You sound like you know this from experience."

"I do. Twice. Once in Afghanistan, once in Indonesia. Both times someone saved my life at the cost of his own. Once it was by accident. The other time…it was very much like what happened with Jun. And I felt guilty for a long time afterward, too. So understanding doesn't mean you stop feeling sorrow and anger and guilt over having lived."

"She didn't deserve to die."

"Most people don't."

"What about the ones who do? Who decides that?"

"I don't know. I prefer not to take on that responsibility."

I remembered shooting Santiago. It had nearly gone out of my head, what with everything else that had happened, but now I relived the moment my first shot had gone home, how stunned and incredulous he'd looked, as if he couldn't believe I'd dared shoot him. "Malcolm," I said quietly, "I killed someone."

He tensed. "What?"

"Rafael Santiago. He threw you off the platform, and I shot him to keep him from killing me too. I mean, you didn't die—you know what I mean."

"You shot him?"

"Many, many times. I was so angry and afraid, and my heart was broken because I thought you were dead, so I just kept firing until the gun was empty. I didn't need to shoot him so many times—"

"Helena, don't think like that."

I tilted my head so I could see his face. "Like what?"

"Like you did something wrong in protecting yourself. Even if you shot him in anger, or retribution."

"But did he deserve to die?"

"Does it matter?" He rested his cheek, slightly scratchy with beard growth, against mine. "In a way, this is the same as Jun dying to save your life, except that Santiago only chose that sacrifice in the sense that he put you in the position to either kill him or let him kill you. You're alive now because he isn't. I won't tell you to take pleasure in having killed him, but you can be glad to be alive, even at that cost."

"I worry because I *don't* feel guilty at killing him. Doesn't that make me a bad person?"

"Love, only you could think like that. That you have that worry at all means you are the opposite of a bad person."

Unexpected peace touched my heart. "Thank you."

"I love you, Helena. I don't think I could bear it if you were gone."

"I feel the same. Malcolm, when I thought you were dead...it was like everything was happening at a distance, like it wasn't real and nothing would ever be all right again."

Malcolm kissed me, a real kiss that made me ache for more. "I wish I could promise that will never happen again."

"I know. I wish I could say it will get easier to watch you go on the hunt, now that my worst fear has come true. Not that I will ever stand in your way."

"Of course." Malcolm hugged me, then sat up, groaning like an old man. "I feel as if I've been beaten with a lead-lined hose."

"That seems awfully specific. *Have* you ever been beaten with a lead-lined hose?"

"Yes. You don't want to know the details."

I sat up and shuddered. "I don't. What do we do now?"

Malcolm managed to stand after only two tries. "We talk to Lucia. I assume, if I was wrong and we weren't pushing the invaders back, we would not have slept undisturbed. But the node is locked down if there's an invasion, to prevent invaders from using the node as a gateway into the Portland area, so if the attack is still ongoing, we will not be able to leave."

The numb feeling had returned. I considered his words,

the possibility that it wasn't over yet, and felt nothing but tiredness. "Then let's find Lucia."

Malcolm made me stand back when he opened the door and peeked out, but I heard nothing. He opened the door fully and beckoned to me. The hall looked like the one where they'd put Lucia, but the room numbers were a different sequence, so I guessed the infirmary was as bland as any hospital ward. Everything was totally silent, with only the sound of my boots disrupting the quiet. Malcolm moved as silently as he ever did, so if I closed my eyes, I could imagine myself alone in the hall. I did that for a couple of steps and it filled me with horror. I didn't want to be alone.

Ahead, I saw a side hall, and from it came the faint sounds of conversation. I hurried faster and then had to slow my pace so Malcolm could keep up. I didn't like the look of him; his face was gray and pinched with pain, and he walked with a slight limp. I took his hand, partly for comfort and partly so I'd have a little warning if he decided to collapse.

The side hall led to the main corridor, the wide one that led to Green 1 and the heart of the infirmary. It was louder there, but there were no screams of pain, and the conversations the Wardens were carrying on didn't have the frantic, tense edge they'd had when I was here earlier.

Malcolm immediately eased himself into a chair and leaned forward with his elbows on his knees. "I'm just a little dizzy," he said when I exclaimed over him. "It will pass. See if anyone knows where Lucia went."

Nobody was too busy, this time, to stop and answer my questions, though all the bone magi knew was that the battle was over, the invaders thoroughly killed or repulsed, and Lucia was somewhere else in the node. I thanked them and returned to Malcolm's side. He looked better, but not by much. I made an executive decision and commandeered a cart, since there were a bunch of them just sitting around. Malcolm didn't protest, which frightened me a little; if he'd stopped pretending he was better than he was, his condition might be more serious than I thought.

The cart drove like the golf cart it resembled, though the handling was better. I wouldn't speed in it, but I could see how that Warden who'd taken Jun and me to the infirmary had made it perform to NASCAR standards. Malcolm held on to the frame in silence, and I kept checking on him to make sure he wouldn't faint and topple out of the cart. But the grayness in his face had subsided, and he looked well enough.

When we reached the central hub, I stopped the cart and got out to gawk. A couple of Wardens, probably stone magi, had lifted the big chunk of concrete magically into place, where its edges glowed with purple light. It was three stories up, and the glow made it hard to see anything, but it looked like it was rippling like a pond when someone throws a rock into it. The floor had been swept clean of grit and debris, the fallen Wardens were gone, and the invaders were either collected or disintegrated. I'd been told that invader bodies didn't last long once they were dead, but I guessed the Wardens didn't want to leave monsters lying around even if they'd disintegrate fast.

Other than the few Wardens involved in mending the ceiling, the place was empty. I'd never seen it so quiet. I took a few steps toward the Wardens, then decided not to interrupt them. Instead, I returned to Malcolm and said, "I think we should check Lucia's office first. Can you walk that far?"

"I'm not on my deathbed, love." Malcolm climbed down from the cart more easily than I'd feared and took my hand.

"Though I hope the attack truly is over, because I am not in a condition to defend either of us."

The long, snaking corridor to Lucia's office felt longer this time, but at least there were people there. Wardens passed us going in both directions, some of them carrying tablets or pieces of paper. Some of them nodded at us, but no one stopped to talk. It was a relief to see everyone moving with such assurance without being panicked. It told me the battle really was over.

I knocked on Lucia's door and received a muffled command to enter. Lucia was alone with her laptop open on the desk in front of her. She glanced up at us, then went on typing. "Glad to see you're not dead," she said to Malcolm.

"Likewise," Malcolm said.

Lucia looked much better than Malcolm did, though her eyes were still deeply shadowed and her skin paler than usual. "Were there any side effects from the poison?" I asked.

"I still feel like I've been punched in the gut, and my appetite is gone, but nothing metabolic or permanent." Lucia shut the laptop and regarded us closely. "And everything else around here is returning to normal. Far too many Wardens died to get us to this point, but the reports I'm getting from around the world say the Mercy have been destroyed."

"Really destroyed?" I asked.

"Or as near enough as makes no difference. There are probably a few members still on the run, but none of them are in a position to hurt the Wardens again."

"But how can you know that? If they were hidden, doesn't that mean they might not have bases you don't know about, or something?"

Lucia smiled. "All those auguries went to good use, Davies. We struck at the places the oracle indicated, and the nodes that didn't go on the attack examined the pattern of Mercy activity that resulted. They're behaving like a bunch of headless chickens now, scattered and acting randomly where before their behavior was orderly and directed. We won't stop watching for them, but...we've won the battle. In case you needed a reminder that your sports made the difference."

I blushed. "I wasn't fishing for compliments."

"And I don't give them for the asking. Good work."

"I am more concerned," Malcolm said, "with how the invaders were able to breach this node's protections so completely."

Lucia's smile disappeared. "Those bastards," she said, her Italian accent growing stronger, "planted mines on our fallen dead. Magical bombs," she said in the face of my obvious confusion. "We brought the bodies back with no idea we were carrying the seeds of our own destruction. The mines went off, dropping the wards, and the invaders were ready for the wards to fall." She clenched one fist. "Those Mercy operatives should be glad they died in battle."

"Did they all die?" I asked.

"I'm not interested in tribunals. Though it seems there's one I've been spared. Nyla Priest is dead."

I gasped. "They promised they wouldn't enact vigilante justice!"

Lucia eyed me suspiciously. "What are you talking about?"

"Um...nothing?" I felt horribly torn between gratitude that I wouldn't be indirectly responsible for Nyla's execution and anger at the magi who'd killed her.

"Well, nobody took justice into their own hands. She was killed by one of the intelligent invaders, or so the survivors said. They claim she didn't try to defend herself when they attacked, like she was looking for death. In any case, she's no longer our problem."

"She was one of us for a while. Doesn't that make her our problem?" I said.

"Davies," Lucia sighed, "she was a traitor. She was going to get the same justice all our traitors faced. Be grateful she took the easy way out."

I really doubted death at the claws or tentacles of an invader qualified as the easy way. "I think we should take care of her mother."

"Excuse me?"

I leaned forward, bracing myself on the desk. "Nyla was her mother's only caretaker. I think we need to have a bone magus see if they can heal her. Otherwise, who knows what will happen to her?"

Lucia arched an eyebrow. "I'm guessing the Campbell fortune is what will happen to her."

I blushed again. "Maybe. So what? We should still do it."

"You are going to be the death of me someday," Lucia said. "Though it sounds like you were the life of me earlier, so...fine. I'll see to it."

"Thank you."

"I don't suppose you know what happened to my team?" Malcolm said.

"And the rest of the sports," I added, feeling bad about not having asked this question earlier. Malcolm had said Victor had gone down; did that mean he'd died, too? My little team was shrinking fast, and I felt like crying again.

"Let's see," Lucia said. She pulled a sleek red tablet with a cracked screen out of her desk drawer and began tapping. "Conti is in recovery from his healing. Judy Rasmussen insisted on staying with him. I don't suppose either of you know anything about that?" She gave us both a narrow-eyed look and grunted when neither of us spoke. "Whatever. Tinsley and Canales are with him, or were half an hour ago. Victor Crowson is in the infirmary too, as is Kapoor. It looks like they saved Kapoor's arm. I don't know about the rest of your merry band, but I'm sure they're close to the others."

"Where did Viv go?"

More tapping. "She and Washburn were in Blue 19, helping with the cleanup. I think Haley didn't want to leave before seeing you again, but nobody knew where you went, so she volunteered. Like I need more of you helpful types hanging around."

"You like us, you know it," I said with a smile.

Lucia's eyebrow went up again. "I'll never admit it. Now, get out of here. Collect your comrades and go home. I don't want to see you again until Campbell is capable of standing unsupported."

I realized Malcolm was leaning on the desk himself, but in his case, he looked like he needed it. I put his arm around my shoulder and helped him stand. "Thanks, Lucia."

"Don't thank me for doing my job. Go on, get."

We left the office and slowly walked back to where we'd left the cart. "I guess we should have stayed in the infirmary, after all," I said.

Malcolm settled in beside me and leaned his forehead against the frame. "I'm ready for it all to be over," he confessed.

"Isn't it?" I asked. I started the cart and wheeled it around.

"Love," Malcolm said, "in war, it's never entirely over."

23

The sun had shone indirectly through the northwest-facing glass back wall of my living room all that Sunday, and now, as it was setting, the warmth made the room feel like spring. The ice storm of three days ago was nothing but a memory, though when I thought about that drive I'd made to the Gunther Node, it was a memory not distant enough. "Thanks for coming one last time," I said.

"We have been through war together," Ines said. "It is right that we say goodbye." She perched on the chair next to my love seat and looked as bright and untroubled by her memories as she had the night we'd all met.

"Maybe not goodbye forever," Victor said. "I'm thinking about moving to Portland."

I sat up. "You didn't mention that!"

Victor shrugged. "I've learned a lot about myself these past few days. I don't like conflict, and that hasn't changed. But I never knew I was the kind of guy who could go into danger to protect others. Not like I thought I was a coward, but…I don't know."

"You thought you were made for watching from the sidelines," Acosta said.

"Yeah. That's it. When we were fighting those invaders, I realized I could use my talent for something more than winning at craps. It felt good, being part of something bigger than me."

"But you don't have to move here to do that," I protested, though I wasn't sure why I was trying to talk him out of it.

"No, but I like the people here, and there's nothing much keeping me in Atlantic City. Plus, Lucia said she might have work for me at the Gunther Node, or there might be a job at Campbell Security. So…I haven't decided for sure yet, but it looks like I will."

I refrained from cheering. "That would be great."

"I have family in Phoenix," Ines said, "and I would miss them if I left. But we will stay in touch, and I will come if needed. Though I hope I can be needed where I live."

"I will see you often," Mangesh told her. "There is a ward restoration project I have been asked to participate in in Tucson."

Ines smiled. "I will enjoy that."

Acosta cleared his throat. "What happened to Nyla's body?"

Suddenly the room didn't feel so warm anymore. "They harvested her magic and made it look like she had a stroke," I said. "They didn't want to make it suicide, in case that affected her life insurance payout…her mother will need that money to get back on her feet, now that she's no longer an invalid." I hated thinking about Nyla's fate. It was so cold and unemotional a way to dispose of someone, I didn't care that she'd been a traitor. But as the Wardens persisted in telling me, the Long War was cold and hard, and cold and hard things sometimes had to be done.

"And you are going to Jun's funeral in two days," Mangesh said. "I wish I could attend, but I am required elsewhere."

"It's all right. It would look strange if all of us went, since it's not like any of Jun's friends or coworkers know about us." I'd decided I was going no matter how strange it looked.

"We will think of her always," Ines said, taking my hand.

"Nobody ever did tell us what her talent was," Victor said.

I squeezed Ines's hand back. "It doesn't matter now, does it?" I said. "Her real talent was being a Warden, at the end."

Victor looked like he wanted to protest, but just shook his head and said nothing.

I saw everyone to the door, where the Ford Explorer from Campbell Security waited to take Victor and Ines to the airport. Acosta and Mangesh nodded farewell, and then I shut the door and leaned against it. Going to the funeral was the last thing I could do for the woman who'd saved my life.

I'd thought I would have to fight the Board about it, what with me wanting to close Abernathy's for a day mid-week after I'd essentially deserted my post on Friday, but Ariadne Duwelt had agreed, with nothing more than a quiet expression of sympathy. Maybe I was wrong about the Board's inflexibility, at least when it really mattered.

I went upstairs to check on Malcolm, who was asleep again. He'd slept most of the time since we'd come home from the node two days ago, waking only to eat and relieve himself. I hoped he would recover soon, because I was lonely without him. Viv had texted a couple of times but was otherwise busy at the node, which surprised me. I wouldn't have thought she felt any need to help with the cleanup. Judy had been unusually quiet at work yesterday, and I'd been preoccupied with Malcolm's condition enough I hadn't been very talkative myself. I'd kept meaning to ask her about Mike, but the timing had never been right. Maybe tomorrow.

I went back downstairs and fixed myself a bowl of soup for dinner. I didn't feel up to anything more complicated. I ate in front of the television, not really paying attention to the show, washed my bowl and spoon, and trudged back upstairs. Maybe I could find a book to read, or a movie to watch. At the moment, everything felt like too much work.

Malcolm was sitting up when I entered the bedroom. My heart felt instantly lighter. "You look better!"

"I feel better," Malcolm said. "Come sit with me."

I sat on his side of the bed and squeaked when he gathered me into his arms and pulled me down to lie beside him. "You're not just better, you're actively frisky," I teased.

"I still feel weak enough that this is all the frisky I'm good for," Malcolm said. "Unfortunately. But I want to hold you, and talk to you—I feel as if I've slept for days."

"You have. Two days, anyway. How much longer?" I said. "I feel no shame at being impatient."

"I'll be back to normal by tomorrow."

He kissed me, and I put my arms around his neck and returned his kiss. Desire rushed through me, a need to feel his body against mine and let our love settle my ghosts. I slipped my hands beneath the T-shirt he wore to sleep in. He smiled against my mouth. "I did say I'm not—"

"Shh," I said. "Let me do the work."

THE CHAPEL JUN's family had chosen for the funeral was much different than the funeral home I remembered from my grandfather's funeral. That had been dark and somber, with lots of heavy wood paneling that had, embarrassingly, been the same color as my grandfather's casket, which had made him in his open casket appear to be floating if you sat at the right distance. This was like a tiny cathedral, complete with stained glass windows, surrounded by a garden that would be beautiful in summer, with all those flowers blooming. Inside, the walls were painted a dark cream above maple paneling, and the carpet was a muted rose that made the chapel feel comfortable rather than mournful.

Malcolm and I sat near the back of the chapel, on pews that were the least comfortable thing about it. I didn't know anything about Episcopalians and hadn't known what to expect. But it had been a lovely service, sad mainly because so few people attended. It made my heart ache for Jun, who hadn't wanted to push people away. Even her family was small, just her father and her sister.

I spotted a handful of people who might have been Jun's coworkers, but nobody who was likely a boyfriend or girlfriend. My inappropriate guilt surged, and I tried to ignore it. Worse was the sadness I felt that I would never get the chance to truly be Jun's friend, because despite the differences in our age and lifestyles, she had been someone I wanted to know better. And that would never happen because of damned invaders and the damned Long War.

"You're doing it again, Helena," Malcolm whispered.

We stood respectfully as they brought the casket past. "Doing what?" I asked.

"Crushing my hand. Let go."

I released him instantly and felt him take my hand again. "Sorry."

"I meant let go of your pain. Remember Jun as she was, not as your regrets make her."

He was right. "I keep trying," I whispered, "but it hurts."

He squeezed my hand gently. "It will pass."

We waited for everyone else to exit before following them out into the bright sunlight. The last few days had felt like the sky was apologizing for the ice storm tantrum it had thrown, and once more the weather felt like spring. The hearse waited outside while everyone milled around, apparently unwilling to just blithely head to their cars even though the funeral procession to the cemetery wouldn't begin without them.

"Excuse me," someone said, and I turned to find myself face to face with Jun's father.

"Oh!" I exclaimed. "Mr. Li. I'm so sorry for your loss."

"Thank you." Mr. Li examined us. "I don't know you. I thought I knew all of Jun's friends."

"Jun was a business colleague of mine," Malcolm said smoothly. "We did business online, and she and my wife became good friends. Long-distance friends. We felt we should pay our respects."

"That's very kind of you." Mr. Li shook hands with each of us. "We're having a small luncheon after the burial. I would be pleased to have you join us."

"Thank you. We'd be happy to," Malcolm said.

When Mr. Li had left, I said, "Malcolm, I don't think I can bear any more social stuff."

"You can," Malcolm said, "and I think it will do you good to hear stories of Jun's life."

He was right. After the burial, we followed the cars to Jun's father's house, which was a modest rambler much like my own parents' house. Cold cuts and cheeses and vegetables had been laid out as if someone had known no one would have much of an appetite. I filled my plate with carrots and broccoli, but couldn't do more than nibble. Instead, I wandered through the house, wondering what it had been like when Jun was a child.

"…would have been regional champion again this year," said a middle-aged man to his two companions, a couple of women dressed in somber business suits. "It was always the most interesting thing about her, the fencing."

"It's so strange to think of her having an undiagnosed heart condition," the thinner of the two women said. "She seemed so healthy. You'd expect someone that athletic not to be struck down so young."

I remembered Jun's perfect lunge, taking that tentacled invader in the back of its head, and said without thinking, "She was really good."

All three turned to look at me. "Did you see her fence?" the plump woman asked.

"I did. She won every, um, match I saw her fight."

"I wish she'd been less distant…I hope this doesn't sound like speaking ill of the dead, because I don't mean it as a criticism," the thin woman said. "I just wish I'd known her better. She was really nice when you got to know her."

"That's how I felt," I said. "But she didn't mean to be standoffish. It was just who she was."

"I'm sorry, have we met?" the thin woman said. "You're not one of the Heritek employees."

"Jun and my husband did business together, and that's how I got to know her," I lied.

"Oh," the plump woman said, like that made any sense. "It's nice that Jun had friends outside the company."

"I just hope they figure out a solution for Cyrus and Xerxes," the man said. "Jun would hate for them to go to the pound."

"Cyrus and Xerxes?" I asked.

"Jun's cats," the plump woman said. "She loved those hairballs. But her father and her sister are allergic, and I don't know anyone else who wants to take them on. It's not like they're purebreds."

"Jun was opposed to cat breeding," the thin woman said. "She always said there were plenty of mongrels in the world who needed good homes without anyone paying a thousand dollars for the privilege. So they're not purebred Persians. But they are beautiful. I'd take them, but my dogs wouldn't stand for it."

I felt something warm growing in my chest. "So they need a home?"

"Yes, but they'll probably have to go to the animal shelter, and no doubt split up. Jun would be heartbroken," the man said. "The cats have been together since they were kittens, and separating them—"

"That would be awful," I agreed. "Would you excuse me?"

I crossed the room to where Mr. Li stood, chatting with a couple of men his own age. I set my plate down on the nearest table and said, "Mr. Li? Could I talk to you about Jun's cats?"

"YOU DID NOT," Viv said. "You don't even like cats."

"I do so, if they're smart cats," I retorted. "And Persians are very smart. Plus, these are like brothers. It would be cruel to separate them."

"I think you've let your inappropriate guilt take the wheel."

"Well, I don't. Malcolm's going back on Friday to bring them home. It turns out it's not that hard to import pets from Canada, but they needed time to get the documentation together." I leaned against Abernathy's counter. "And Xerxes and Cyrus are very sweet."

"Xerxes and Cyrus. Jun was a history nerd."

"There are far more obscure Persian names she could have used. Or contemporary ones. Xerxes and Cyrus were emperors, isn't that interesting?"

"Unless it means those cats took on the personalities of their namesakes, and you're going to end up feeding them chopped liver by hand and fanning them with ostrich plumes." Viv unwound her scarf and folded it around her hands.

"Just wait until you meet them. You'll change your tune." I took the scarf from Viv and wound it around my own neck. I felt more cheerful than I had in days. Why adopting Jun's cats had made me feel at peace with myself and with her, I didn't know, but I was looking forward to sharing our home with my new furry friends. Malcolm had sighed when I told him my plan, but he'd been smiling, too, so I figured it was all right.

"Helena?" Judy said from within the stacks. "You need to look at this."

I let Viv retrieve her scarf and turned to face Judy as she emerged. She had Mr. Briggs's diary open in front of her and extended it to me as she approached. "Start with November twelfth," she said.

"Did something bad happen?" I asked as I took the little book from her.

"Just read it." Judy's face was paler than usual, and her eyes looked enormous. Frightened, I did as she insisted.

The text was written in dark black ink that almost showed

through to the other side of the page, casting a shadow on the words. Mr. Briggs hadn't used days of the week, just the date, and he only put the year on the first entry of that year, so the place Judy wanted me to start just read *November 12.*

I read aloud: *"Ten customers today. Made $86 in 1%s. Ross came back again wanting the same thing as before, though I told him there was no way I would falsify an augury for friendship. If he persists, I'll have to threaten to reveal his secret to the Ambrosite Archmagus. No idea how much he'd pay to prevent that."* I lowered the book. "So he did write down that he was a blackmailer!"

"That's not the important part. Keep reading," Judy said.

I shrugged. *"My need for an assistant is becoming urgent. I can't take on the Rasmussen girl; she's too smart and too nosy not to realize what I'm doing. But I can't choose some other Warden, or William Rasmussen will pitch a fit. I need advice. Mother said there was a way around the proscription against the custodian of Abernathy's asking for an augury for himself, and tonight I'll do that."*

"Wow, Briggs sure didn't think much of you," Viv said to Judy. She irritably waved that aside.

"November 13: It worked. I'd almost think the oracle was a living creature if I didn't know that was a stupid idea. Every augury today has had a newspaper clipping from The Oregonian *inside the front cover, none of them complete stories. It's the initial letters, the drop capitals, that are important, I'm sure of it. Only six auguries today, and not enough clippings to spell a complete word or words. More tomorrow.*

"November 14: The mail-in auguries contained clippings as well as the walk-in ones. The later clippings are want ads for employment, as if I weren't smart enough to figure out how to lure this person here. The clippings with the initials say her name is Helena Davies—"

I sucked in a breath. The book fell from my hands and hit the floor with a crack.

"See?" Judy said. She looked as dumbfounded as I felt.

"But," I said, "Mr. Briggs didn't…all he said was that I was quiet and knew how to type."

"Of course he wouldn't come out and say he'd seen your name in a bunch of newspaper clippings produced by an oracular bookstore," Viv said. "Helena, stop freaking out."

"I have to go," I said, and rushed into the silence of the oracle.

I ran through the narrow aisles until I came to the heart of the oracle, a place where four massive bookcases faced each other like ancient monoliths on a windswept moor. "Why did you tell him my name?" I demanded. "You knew who I was before I entered this store. Why me?"

The oracle said nothing, but its attention was fully on me. "*Why me?*" I shouted. My voice echoed back to me as if I were deep within a stony canyon: *memememeeee.* "What made you choose me out of all the people in the world to do…I don't even know what you wanted, except that it wasn't to be doomed Mr. Briggs' assistant. Has everything I've done as custodian been planned by you? Do I have a destiny, after all?"

Still nothing. I waited, breathing heavily, my heart filled with a strange blend of anger and fear. Finally, I thought, **Not alone, Helena.**

"I don't believe that," I said. "You didn't pluck me out of my old life just so you could have a friend. You can see the future. So what future did you see that required me to be a part of it?"

I felt an enormous pressure build within my skull, bearing down on me like a giant thumb pushing me into the ground. With a great effort, I made myself stand against it. "You can't…make me…become…your body…whenever…you feel like it," I said through gritted teeth. "Just talk to me. Tell me what you want."

The pressure eased. As if someone had flipped a switch, golden light filled the air, lining the bookcases with gold and turning the words printed or imprinted on the books' spines into dancing golden letters. I stared at the beautiful display openmouthed. Books drifted off the shelves and spun in midair, trailing sparks of light. They floated past me in a complex waltz, settled on other shelves until the configuration was entirely new. Then the oracle said, through my thoughts, **There will be an end.**

"An end? Of what?"

An end of me.

Stunned, I said, "What are you talking about? You mean something will try to destroy you?"

An end. I will end.

"You can't end. You're the oracle!" I gasped as the pressure built again, not quite as powerful as before. "We can stop this. We strengthen the wards, we set up alarms against anyone who tries to get in—or do you need to be moved again to somewhere safer? It will be hard, but we can do it."

An ending comes. I will end.

The thoughts that ran through me felt inexorable, like an oncoming train. I wiped tears from my eyes. "You can't give up!" I shouted. "I won't let this happen!"

No. I will end. Helena will end.

I froze. "What did you say?"

The pressure vanished. The golden light dimmed and then disappeared. The oracle's presence shrank almost to nothing, so that if I hadn't been so familiar with my charge, I might have thought it was gone entirely.

"Hey! Answer me!" I shouted. "What do you mean, Helena will end?"

The oracle didn't answer. I backed up until I ran into one of the bookcases, then slid down it to sit at its base, clutching my knees to my chest. *Helena will end.* The oracle was sometimes vague, but I had never known it to be wrong while it was in its right mind. And I had no reason to believe it was wrong now. I tried to think of other ways to interpret its words and came up empty. The oracle believed that it, and I, were going to die.

I wiped more tears from my eyes and then slammed my fist against the bookcase behind me. No. This was stupid. I was acting like the oracle's prediction was fated to come true. There were plenty of times the oracle's auguries hadn't come to pass, sometimes because their recipient figured them out too slowly, sometimes because people made an effort to stop them coming true. Whatever the oracle saw in our future, it could be changed. I refused to believe otherwise.

I stood and dusted myself off before returning to Viv and Judy at the front counter. They both looked so concerned when I emerged I decided not to tell them what the oracle had said. Soon, I'd share everything with them, but for today, I needed a normal life. "It wouldn't tell me why it chose me," I said, perfectly truthfully.

"Didn't it say anything?" Viv said.

"Nothing conclusive." That was closer to a lie. I added, "I'll keep asking. Someday, it will give me an answer. On its own schedule, of course."

"It's unsettling," Judy said. "Like maybe you had a destiny after all. Maybe you're the only one who can become the oracle. Or maybe you're the only one it's willing to talk to."

"It could be anything," I agreed. "Though it does make me wonder what would have happened if Mr. Briggs hadn't been murdered. He couldn't have kept the secret of the magical world from me forever."

"You might have quit when you learned about it," Viv said. "And you wouldn't have found Malcolm, and I wouldn't have met Jeremiah, and we three wouldn't be friends."

"And if Helena hadn't married Malcolm, I wouldn't have met Mike," Judy said, blushing, "and we wouldn't be going out tonight."

Viv shrieked and hugged Judy, who turned even redder. "Oh! Does your father know?"

"He does not," Judy said, "but he will soon. When Mike nearly died during the attack, I realized I was stupid to let my fears get in the way of what might be a wonderful relationship. We still have a lot to work out, Mike and I, but we're going to talk tonight, and..." She let her words trail off and shrugged.

"I'm so glad," I said, hugging Judy, not as exuberantly as Viv had. She hugged me back.

"And Malcolm's well again," I added, "and I have new pets, and the sports are all Wardens—this is turning out to be a good day. I almost don't mind that it's another hour before closing."

"Tomorrow, girls' night out," Viv declared.

"It's a date," Judy said.

I nodded, and bent to pick up Mr. Briggs's diary. The spine had cracked when it hit the floor, and now it naturally fell open to the fateful entry on November fourteenth. As Viv and Judy started talking about where we would go tomorrow, I read over the words again—*her name is Helena Davies*—and my cheerful mood evaporated. The oracle had chosen me for some purpose it wouldn't share. It knew my name before I'd ever walked into the store. And it had a destiny for me:

Helena will end.

The story of The Last Oracle will conclude in *The Book of Destiny*

THE AUGURIES, AND MOVIES
REFERENCED

Edith Wharton, *The House of Mirth*
Sun Tzu, *The Art of War*
Ellen Raskin, *The Westing Game*
Scott Adams, *It's Obvious You Won't Survive By Your Wits Alone*
Helen Fielding, *Bridget Jones' Diary*
Daphne du Maurier, *Rebecca*
Wilanne Schneider Belden, *Mind-Call*
Kate Elliott, *Poisoned Blade*
John R. Lott, Jr., *More Guns, Less Crime*
Zack Emerson, *Stand Down*
Sharon Shinn, *Dark Moon Defender*
Lois Duncan, *A Gift of Magic*
Rumer Godden, *In This House of Brede*
Kristin Cashore, *Jane, Unlimited*

Charlie's Angels (2000)
His Girl Friday
Austenland

ABOUT THE AUTHOR

In addition to The Last Oracle series, Melissa McShane is the author of The Extraordinaries series, beginning with BURNING BRIGHT, the Crown of Tremontane series, beginning with SERVANT OF THE CROWN, as well as COMPANY OF STRANGERS and many others.

After a childhood spent roaming the United States, she settled in Utah with her husband, four children and a niece, four very needy cats, and a library that continues to grow out of control. She wrote reviews and critical essays for many years before turning to fiction, which is much more fun than anyone ought to be allowed to have.

You can visit her at her website www. melissamcshanewrites.com for more information on other books.

For information on new releases, fun extras, and more, sign up for Melissa's newsletter: http://eepurl.com/brannP

THE LAST ORACLE

The Book of Secrets

The Book of Peril

The Book of Mayhem

The Book of Lies

The Book of Betrayal

The Book of Havoc

The Book of Harmony

The Book of War

The Book of Destiny (forthcoming)

COMPANY OF STRANGERS

Company of Strangers

Stone of Inheritance

Mortal Rites

Shifting Loyalties

Sands of Memory

Call of Wizardry

THE CONVERGENCE TRILOGY

The Summoned Mage

The Wandering Mage

The Unconquered Mage

THE BOOKS OF DALANINE

The Smoke-Scented Girl

The God-Touched Man

Emissary

Warts and All: A Fairy Tale Collection

The View from Castle Always

Made in the USA
Coppell, TX
01 August 2020